THE VATICAN JOB

By
R.T. Braun

ISBN: 978-1-4251-8018-8 (soft cover)
ISBN: 978-1-4269-0049-5 (eBook)

 www.trafford.com

North America & international
toll-free: 1 888 232 4444 (USA & Canada)
phone: 250 383 6864 ♦ fax: 250 383 6804 ♦ email: info@trafford.com

The United Kingdom & Europe
phone: +44 (0)1865 487 395 ♦ local rate: 0845 230 9601
facsimile: +44 (0)1865 481 507 ♦ email: info.uk@trafford.com

10 9 8 7 6 5 4 3 2 1

This novel is dedicated to Toni, my relentless editor, typist, and friend. And to my friends and family who supported me and continued to believe. I also want to thank my Coach of Coaches, Action, and MM29 whom helped me realize, "Better to be heard and face being unpopular than remain silent and unnoticed thinking of what could have been."

Chapter 1

New Orleans.   March 1996.

During dinner Mieko heard the murders' engine die outside from across the street. He peered through the kitchen's rusty screen door into the spring night; attempting to pick out shadows and noises.

The neighbor's clapboard house had no lights on and the streetlamp two houses up the road had been shot out a month ago during Mardi gras.

The smell of gasoline hit his teenage nose from the open metal cans next to his family's doorway. Mieko and his father siphon gas from unsuspecting outsiders. Pay for nothing when it can be taken for free. That was their law. One of many laws that he was forced to memorize when he was eight years old.

Mieko put his ear up to the rusty screen. He heard crickets and a transformer humming from up the street. The family drinking glasses sweated. It was hot out. Everything sweated.

Mieko returned to the kitchen table.

Father pulled a .38 revolver from behind his back and laid the gun down next to his plate. He continued eating, his eyes never leaving his supper.

Momma passed father the steaming cheese and pork *prujaumani* in a squat ceramic bowl that they'd stolen at the flea market a month earlier. She had offered Mieko some earlier but he had ignored her. She

1

had presented him in the same way to the outsider. Casually. *Here, do you want him? I know you do.*

He felt dirty. She had rubbed baby oil all over him that day before her fake trip.

Father was forbidden to know. If he found out, Mieko could no longer be his son. Honor demanded that his father kill him.

Momma fingered the thin gold chains and amulet around her neck. She stared at the dripping sink. She had to wait for father to finish eating before she could go and wash dishes. Her favorite television show had already started.

Mieko hoped that she'd miss the whole damn thing. He sat very still and watched his father eat the *prujaumani* on his plate.

Father was a short round man with a large bald spot and parsley sprigs for hair. He loved gold wristwatches. He wore three of them on his left wrist. He disarmed the outsiders with his quaint little smile and unimposing height. They usually mistook the whole family for being Mexicans or Arabs.

Father started snorting as he closed in on finishing his meal. He sounded like a hog with reverse sniffles.

Mieko sipped on a dripping glass of water to choke his giggling.

Momma reached to pet Mieko's hand. He jerked it away, focusing on his father. On his birthday his father would get him a bride. In six months it would all be arranged. Romani tradition.

Momma walked in everyone's shadows. She moved and rested with the awkward grace of a dancing giraffe. She was always complimenting father. It was her way of gaining control over him.

She was sneaky like the rest of the family but twice as cruel. Mieko blamed her father, his grandfather, for what she did to them. He had given mother to father when she was only thirteen. Grandma wasn't there to protest the early marriage because she was doing time in Gainesville prison for murdering a city councilman. She had put too much dope in the rob-and-roll Mickey she had given him and he had stopped breathing. Permanently.

Grandfather was glad to be rid of both of them. He took the cash that they had all earned and moved back to the old country.

"*Prathatti*," Mieko said. "*Dosh-sayiet apok vu?*"

Father waved his hand granting permission.

Mieko got up from the table with his empty plate, donated it to the soap-water sink, and left his parents for the room that he shared with his teenage sister, Tienya.

The hallway that led to their room had dozens of unpacked moving boxes stacked on top of one another. They were all pushed up against the same wall. The boxes contained the year's take; carpets, plates, watches, jewelry, clothes, and computer equipment. Mieko walked down the hallway sideways to reach his room.

There was no sense in unpacking the boxes because after Uncle Sasha's rental car scam they would all be on the move again.

Uncle Sasha was a real bastard. Mieko's four cousins, their older kids, and Tienya, were all put to work in the scam. They would ride in used cars, claim that these vehicles were new (with the assistance of a little bogus paperwork and switched VIN tags) and Sasha would ram into them from behind in a rental car.

The rental car companies would have their cars insured. They would pay the "victim" that Uncle hit a bunch of money for new cars that weren't new and for injuries that no one had. The problem was Uncle Sasha's passion for realism. He demanded that everyone be in the car that he slammed into. This insured that the witnesses would back the claims that were made when viewed by the authorities as legitimate. He hit the cars way too hard and enjoyed the crashes for the rush that they gave him.

Mieko slid into his room from the hallway and leaped onto his magazine filled bed. He had a thing for motorcycles. If there was a picture of a motorcycle in a rag at the local Wal-Mart then chances were that either he or Tienya had lifted it.

Mieko's only complaints about his sister were her smelly perfumes which changed every day and her stuffed animal collection that littered both sides of their room. She had way too many of the fluffy creatures, especially teddy bears. She was supposed to have been given away to another Romani family but Momma fought it. She reasoned that it was far cheaper to have Mieko and Tienya wedding at the same time. Father would never go against that type of logic.

A series of metal fracturing noises came from the kitchen.

The screen door opened for a moment and then shut.

Seconds later a chair over-turned followed by a loud thud.

Momma yelled out. "*Vitromne!*"

She doesn't mean the cops, Mieko reasoned. *The neighbors?* He remembered stealing the tires off of the neighbor's Astor van three days before. It had been raining out and he was pretty sure that no one had seen him.

Another chair fell in the kitchen followed by a bowl dropping, silverware sliding, breaking glasses, and a flurry of varied footsteps.

Momma grunted as she fought with someone.

"Her feet," a calm raspy voice said. "Grab *the feet*."

Mieko squeezed his knife's handle. His knuckles turned white.

Heavy footsteps pounded down the hall past Mieko's room door. The unseen stranger scraped the hallway with his arm along the way.

They must be checking rooms.

The steps started back from Mieko's parent's bedroom towards him in his. He hid against the panel wall behind his bedroom door.

Just as he reached his would-be hiding spot, the door flew open inward. Mieko carefully lowered the sharp edge of his knife downward. He planned to stab up hard if he was suddenly discovered.

Mieko tried to smother his breathing. His breaths kept racing despite his attempts to muffle them.

An exposed fluorescent lamp lit the bedroom from the ceiling. It burned into the room giving off way too much light. Mieko felt like the light cast a direct spotlight on him even with the shelter of the door shade that the back of the door offered him. From a crack between the door and wall he saw a huge man creep in.

The stranger wore an oily dark green mechanic's jumpsuit with a hood, shiny white latex gloves, and a red-and-white checkered carnival mask. He used a gray pistol with a black rolling-pin-style silencer to lift up Mieko's bed covers. He lowered one of his mammoth knees to the floor and crouched down to peer under the bed.

Mieko slid out from behind the door and out into the hallway. His hand throbbed from squeezing his knife handle too hard.

"*Dov'e e cosa?!*" A gruff voice said in the kitchen.

"I don't understand," Momma said.

"*Dov'e?!*"

"Speak English," Momma pleaded.

Mieko crept down the hall sideways so the he wouldn't scrape up against the boxes. He used the point of his knife to push open his

4

parents' bedroom door and glanced over his shoulder to make sure that he was undetected. He wished that they had a telephone to call the cops but they were always moving so they never bothered to get one.

Momma's bed quilt lay crumpled on the floor. Her bed's mattress was pushed off of its iron bed frame.

Mieko soft-stepped over to his parent's French dresser cabinet. He carefully slid out the bottom drawer. Father's guns greeted him. They were always kept loaded with the safeties off. Mieko and his sister were forbidden to touch them unless they were target shooting with Father.

Mieko picked through the drawer's fourteen guns and grabbed the biggest two.

"She doesn't speak Italian, dumb ass," the raspy voice said from the kitchen. *"Non parla l'italiano. Io saro tradurre dall'inglese in italiano, va bene?*

"Si."

"What do you want from me?" She *knew*. She was just buying time.

Mieko thought about the ceramic serving dish and the priest…

If Father is dead then there is no point in saving her, he thought. *She'll use me for leverage with the outsiders. I should have heard threats from Father if he's still alive.*

Mieko headed for the bedroom window and then stopped. The window was directly in front of him. He could easily slide open the glass and be gone.

She's your mother. Mieko wedged one gun between his back and pants. The cold weapon rubbed against his skin causing him to experience a heavy shiver.

He took the other gun and held it with both hands. A laser sight was mounted on the underside of the gun close to the trigger guard. A thin red laser beam shot outward from the laser sight as Mieko feathered the trigger.

"Look bitch," the raspy voice said. "We just want the fuckin' tape. Just give it up an' we're gone from your life."

"I know of no….tape."

"Racconta bugia!"

"Fuck yeah, she's lying," the raspy voice agreed with his partner. Two strong flesh-on-flesh slaps echoed out of the kitchen.

Someone drew from deep within their throat and nose, then spat.

"You gypsy whore!" A hot slap followed. "Where's the tape, lady?!"

"I don't know."

"What d'ya just say:" The stranger belted her one across the mouth. "Did you just say…?" He slapped her again. "…that you don't know…" A loud double-smack rang out followed by a whimper. "…where my fuckin' tape is?"

Momma remained quiet. An awkward pause followed until some pots and pans began to be rubbed together and thrown to the floor.

Mieko's heart pounded rapidly. He made his way back down the hallway. The red laser beam swept across the cardboard boxes and rested on his partially open room door.

The gun gained weight with every step he took until it felt like a hundred pounds. His skinny arms were shaking miserably. The weapon's beam bobbed up and down. He steadied himself as best he could and eased himself into his bedroom. The red beam found the back of killer's hood.

You could use your knife, Mieko thought. *Cut his throat like on Bobby Phillips pit-bull. It'd make no noise. But what if you miss? What then?*

The image of the man shooting him in the head raced into his mind. Mieko decided to stick with using Father's gun.

The killer had already trashed Mieko's side of the bedroom. The killer was in the process of raiding Tienya's dresser. He had laid his gun down on his left side next to a pile of her clothes. Two of the four drawers had been pulled out and placed upside-down on Mieko's freshly shredded bed. The man was meticulous. An experienced professional.

Mieko led his laser beam off of the big man's head and over his shoulder. The beam's bright tiny red dot rested on a spot on the speckled pea-green dresser for the killer to see.

The man's head twisted slightly. He recognized the electric dot and all of its implications.

Mieko moved the dot back onto the man's head. "Shhh," Mieko said softly.

The masked man froze in place. His right hand was stuck in the lower third drawer while his left hand rested on the glitter varnished dresser-top.

Mieko used his foot to swing the door shut behind him. The faint "click" of the door terrified him. *Did they hear it?*

More pots and pans rumbled from the kitchen.

Go for his gun. He knows that you're just a kid. He'll make a move. He's got no choice.

"*Bolle la sua mono,*" the gruff voice said.

"Yeah," the raspy voice replied to his Italian friend.

"But she'll scream her fuckin' head off." Duct-tape being peeled from its tape roll interrupted him. "Oh shit, sorry. Uhh….*Si, ma gridera a squarciagola.*"

Mieko's left foot swept the killer's gun away from him. The deadly tool skipped across the shaggy rug floor until it stopped under Mieko's trashed bed.

The man in the mask remained shocked still.

"Get up mister."

He didn't move.

"*Get up.*" Mieko put his gun's muzzle up against the back of the man's head. He pushed the cold steel directly into the thick black strap that held the carnival mask onto the man's face. He pulled one of his hands from the gun, let it tremble, and then grabbed a hold of killer's dark green jumpsuit, tugging upward.

The man took the hint and rose up slowly. Carefully,

Mieko backed away. The killer's height was awesome. He pointed his shaking gun toward the man's neck, then to the nape of his back, and then back toward his head again.

The room felt like the house's heater had been turned on in the middle of summer. Sweat poured out from under Mieko's armpits. He kept swallowing until no spit was left.

"Can you feel the water heatin' up?" Raspy voice asked Momma from the kitchen. "It takes about three minutes ta boil. I'm guessin' in two you'll be ready to sing. Look at your hand! It's already turnin' dark pink."

"I have children," she said in a tortured octave. "Please…"

"Where's the tape?"

The house went silent. More duct-tape was then unrolled.

"Fine, lady. Be that way." Drawers were being yanked open and pawed through. "Hey. You got any pliers around here?" A drawer slammed shut.

"No."

"Oh." The sound of a metallic object tapping on the reverse side of a pan sounded. "Fuck it then. I'll use this two-prong pork fork." He stuck her in her rump with it.

She shrieked at the top of her lungs. "*Please...*"

"You stupid cow." He stuck her and she screamed again.

"Your ass is gonna be pretty sore in the mornin' if you keep stone walling me. You're a tough old broad though. I'll give ya that."

"*Dov'e Lorenzo?*" The gruff voice asked him.

"Good question." A few cautious footsteps led out of the kitchen toward the mouth of the hallway. "*Lorenzo? Come bene la recerca Fa progressi? Hai il nastro?*

Mieko focused on the man in his bedroom. The killer stared out through the checker red-white mask straight into the wall over Mieko's shoulder. Turning the man around had been quite difficult.

Mieko put his off-hand's pointing finger up to his lips indicating silence was expected of his prisoner. Both of them remained quiet together. The electric red dot bounced between the killer's eyes making the fiend blink excessively. The tactic kept him honest.

"*Lorenzo?*"

"Please...my hand." Momma distracted. "The water is *almost* boiling now!"

"So where's the tape?"

She wouldn't answer.

Raspy voice hurled the pork fork into the kitchen's linoleum floor. "It's over, lady. You fucked the wrong people."

A hush fell over the house with the exception of Momma's groaning.

The hallway floor creaked softly from what might have been an errant step. Mieko's breathing was racing out loud. He couldn't be sure. If there had been a noise, he figured that it was only five feet away in the hallway. The air in his room turned thick. His ears burned with heat as he tried to use them.

"These guys are from Catania, Sicily, lady. They don't play. When the order comes down and they send in the heavies from the old country… you really fucked up." A brutal slap rang out over her groaning and then Raspy voice grunted. "Fuck! You cut my hand on your teeth."

"Plaw-ese." Momma sputtered in tortured high-pitched English. "My 'and…its…the 'ater is 'oiling!'"

"Honestly. I got better things to do on a Saturday night than torture you but if you keep this cowboy shit up…well, I'm gonna have ta get your fuckin' kids. I don't want ta hurt no kids lady."

She didn't reply. She was too busy screaming and using her bound feet to kick nearby pots and dishes. Her agony sounded like that of a freight train speeding full steam off the edge of a cliff.

"Surely your kids mean more ta you then some petty shakedown money, right?"

More moaning.

"You're one sick bitch, lady. Just remember. It was *you* that forced my hand. *You*."

The door knob to Mieko's room turned slowly. A light scraping noise hit their ears.

The unarmed killer that faced Mieko slowly began inching backward. He was preparing to dive out of the way when his friend appeared.

A primal calling surged throughout Mieko's lithe body. His father was murdered, his mother tortured, and the bad men probably had plans in store for him. He squeezed his gun's trigger twice. The gun kicked in his hand, nearly slamming back into the top of his face. The gun's report ripped at his eardrums causing a dismal continuous ringing to stay in his ears. He didn't have time to register whether or not he'd killed the man in front of him.

He spun around in a semi-circle preparing to fire again. He faced a bullet that came screaming through his bedroom door. The tumbling metal slug hit him hard in the belly, directly above his navel.

Mieko slumped to the floor on his knees. The smell of spent gun powder bit into his nostrils. He kept gasping for air like a goldfish out of water. Sharp stabbing pains spiked outward from his bullet wound.

Mieko looked up from the growing red spot that radiated out from his belly wound. The coward had shot him by randomly firing through the hallway wall and closed bedroom door. Half a dozen bullet holes went in a line from the door to the far end of the wall. The hallway killer's silencer covered the sound of the multiple shots.

As Mieko tried to shake off the effects of shock, the killer fired a second volley.

One bullet whizzed by Mieko's right ear. Another sailed in and blasted into his left front shoulder, directly above the arm pit. Tiny bone fragments ripped into the surrounding tissue from the force of deadly invader.

Mieko's gun fell from his hand. He picked it back up with his right hand and fired back into the wall wildly. He kept squeezing the trigger even though no more bullets fired and he fell to the floor backwards. His head landed on the dead killer that he'd shot earlier. A good portion of the man's skull was missing. Little crimson specks were everywhere.

Momma's screams reached a crescendo. She made sounds that ceased to be human. Mieko realized that he was screaming too. There was so much God damned screaming!

Mieko felt cold. His body's shaking took on an urgent tone. The clicking noises that his ringing ears heard were that of his clattering teeth. Moving felt impossible to him. He felt as if someone laid him down with four fifty-pound sandbags.

"Lorenzo? Roberto?" Raspy voice called out.

Quiet followed.

"Gimme *the tape* whoever you are," the Raspy voice shouted over Momma's agony. "Give it and I'll let this bitch go."

Mieko kept gasping for air.

"All right?"

"It's …in…the…car!" Warm tears streaked down Mieko's face. "Pop the hood on the old Buick. It's wrapped in electrical tape near the battery!"

"What about Roberto and Lorenzo?"

"*Ho ferite!*" Roberto grunted from the hallway floor.

"Let my momma go!"

"*Per Lorenzo dobbiamo vendetta a loro,*" Roberto called out.

He fired his gun through the wall in Mieko's room again. Bullets sprayed out everywhere. White stuffing clumps from Tienya's teddy bears snowed in the air. Some of the fibers floated into pools of blood next to mangled piles of pulp, flesh, and bone. He was dizzy and the room kept spinning while the ringing in his ears got louder and louder. A strange tingling sensation erupted from the undersides of his tongue; it was a sign that he needed to vomit.

Momma had stopped screaming. "Leave us," she said from the kitchen.

"This wouldn't have happened if you'd cooperated."

"Abbiamo ordini assassinare tutti Lorro," Roberto said. He stood up from the floor, pushed against the hallway boxes, and shuffled into the kitchen. *"Questro a dare un messaggio."*

"No!"Raspy voice protested. "No kids!"

"Si! Si! Abbiamo ordini," the voice responded fanatically.

A loud shot retorted.

A body slumped to the floor causing a spoon to slide hard against a metal pot.

"Lady, go help your kid."

Momma spent several minutes ripping duct-tape from her legs and arm.

"There's no copies, *right?"*

Silence.

"If there are, and you're fuckin' lyin' ta me, I'm gonna come back." A pot got slammed hard into a counter top. "And I'm gonna hurt ya, understand?"

"Yes."

"Get the fuck outta here." He left out through the kitchen screen door. "You didn't see me lady. It was just these two fellas. You don't know why they attacked you. Say that they must have mistaken you with the crack house up the street. The newspapers will make up the rest."

Momma was sobbing. She bolted down the hallway past Mieko's room and entered hers. Several items were tossed around until Mieko heard the distinct sound of a revolver being cocked. She raced back down the hallway ignoring her dying son's call to her for help.

A pan scrapped across the linoleum floor. A series of same-caliber gunshots barked out. Momma got off six shots.

A single .38 revolver answered back through the screen door. Dishes smashed from the weight of Momma's falling body.

The house came to rest.

"Ya crazy bitch," Raspy voice spat at the house.

Mieko listened as the man dragged his foot. One of the family gasoline cans sloshed about. The echo of pouring liquid haunted the kitchen followed by the dragging noises of Raspy voice's foot. The gas can was thrown to the ground.

Mieko's room began to get dark in front of him. He craned his neck to view the dead assassin that he'd killed earlier. He vomited onto the man and then he looked away. He couldn't muster the strength to move as the fire began from the kitchen. He smelled smoke. Sirens blared in the distance.

Good response time, Mieko thought. *They hardly ever respond to calls in this neighborhood.*

Black smoke wafted through the holes in the wall and slithered out from under the door.

Carnival music echoed in the back of Mieko's mind as he lay on the carpet bleeding to death. Children were laughing. He smelled cotton candy. His father, mother, and sister were there. He was at the Iowa state fair which happened two years ago in the summer. It was the only time that they'd been like an outsider family. No cons. No scams. They rode rides and enjoyed one another's company.

Tienya threw white plastic rings over glass bottle-necks. She won a bright pink panda bear with a metal heart symbol attached to its plastic ribbon collar.

Mieko's eyes focused on the blood-soaked bear that lay on the carpet next to him. He let out a long slow sigh as he lost control of his bladder. His chest stopped moving. His open glassy eyes stared at the bear. He never blinked again.

Chapter 2

Venice, Island of Pegveillia. July 2004

The illegal art auction was being held in an old abandoned sanatorium on the forgotten island of Pegveillia. A heavy summer storm was rolling in. Lightning struck in the distance illuminating the island's empty structure's gaping square eyes. A torrent of overgrown vines and weeds wrestled back and forth in the beginning onslaught of heavy rain. The dark blue-green waters of the lagoon were getting choppy and the smell of ozone was fresh in the air.

Clayton Keasley arrived around midnight. He came alone in his jet stern drive Polaris EX2100 speedboat. Brass fire urns lit the way from the overgrown boat landing up to the reception hall. His former aristocratic nose was hit hard by the smell of cheap lamp oil and the perfume of various women.

Clayton reached for the inside pocket of his waist-length leather jacket.

A grinning mulatto stood in front of a long red curtain that blocked the reception hall entrance. Electric light spilled out from beneath the fine fabric's crimson folds. The light showcased Clayton's black Vans sneakers. They added mystique to his Miu Miu whicker-yellow-white wool tweed three button suit, white cotton shirt, and black silk tie.

He was very careful with the suit. His employer had leased it for him so that he would look convincing for his assignment.

The mulatto seemed a little too impressed with himself. He showed his over-confidence in his gold teeth smile.

A lightning streak shot over them, followed by a loud crack of thunder.

Clayton produced a silver-and-green alligator hologram card from his jacket. The mulatto snatched it from him and examined the card's symbol intensely.

"You're late, *Monsieur*." the mulatto said with a thick French accent.

"And?"

"And nothing, *Monsieur*."

The rain poured down steadily. It bounced off of the vines and leaves that were latched onto the building.

The mulatto frisked Clayton for weapons. "Enjoy the auction." His dreadlocks lunged at Clayton as he leaned over to pull back the curtain. "All sales final. No cell phone use without house's permission and no cell phones with cameras."

Clayton was glad to step inside. His short springy blond hair was darkened from the rain water that had soaked through it. Tiny beads of water rolled off of his leather jacket onto the dusty floor.

The auction room was very raw. Dark green vines grew up the ruined plaster walls to the concrete ceiling. A large oriental rug had been tossed out to add a touch of class. Rows of armless black wood chairs and an auction podium were set on top of it.

Two dozen auction guests fidgeted in their seats. The people appeared to be a cross between United Nations delegates without the translator headphones and spoiled actors who were dressed for the Academy Awards show.

A hostess approached Clayton with a silver tray holding champagne glasses. She was a native Italian model; one of three who worked the room. They all wore the same transparent one-piece gray-and-silver glitter dresses and nothing else.

Clayton tried to keep his brown eyes focused on the champagne hostess' face but he quickly found himself checking out the rest of her. The outside storm was inviting cold ocean wind to blow into the crowded auction room. He inquired about getting an auction paddle.

The hostess motioned for one of her model friends. The girl came over with a stack of stick-and-circle bidding paddles. She handed Clayton a paddle with the number eighteen printed on it and asked him for his bidding name.

"Uhh...do either of you like seafood?" Clayton asked.

The paddle girl extended her middle finger and walked off.

The champagne girl laughed at him. She was drunk.

You've got to come up with a better come-on line then that, he thought. *They're probably the only ones you'll be able to get close enough to that can help you get in with your guy. Better play it safe. There's not much time.*

Thunder rumbled from outside. Clayton found a chair in the back row.

A young red haired woman in her mid-twenties sat to Clayton's right. She had a fifty-year-old boyfriend with her who eyed Clayton jealously. She had a circular paddle in her lap with the number seven on it.

"My father," she said after catching Clayton examining them.

"Sorry for staring. It's just..."

"I'm too old to be with *daddy?*" She winked. "Well, I love art and only *daddy* here can afford these prices. I'm worth it though." She turned to her man. "Right *dad?*"

The gentlemen snickered.

Clayton offered his hand to her. "I'm Clayton Keasley. And you are?"

"Discrete with *our* identity at a private auction," he answered for her. He ripped the paddle from her. She fumbled with her empty hands and wouldn't speak anymore.

The woman's reaction reminded Clayton of his second ex-wife, Laura. When they had been together, Laura would start berating him with all that was wrong with him. She would remind him of his old drug problem and she'd poisoned their daughter against him.

The divorce led to his relapse, the near death of his daughter Kathreen, and then there was the incident with the gun at the hotel in Gattlingburg.

A blinding white flash blasted through the red curtain covered window holes followed by thunder.

Always remember, he told himself. *There's a reason.*

15

Clayton rubbed a lump that protruded out from under his tie. He had his lucky bullet made into a necklace.

"Ladies and gentleman," the drunken champagne hostess spoke into the podium microphone in sing-song English. "Your host...Renauld."

A short wiry man with salt-and-pepper hair walked into the room accompanied by the mulatto thug. The man was dressed in a tan three-piece suit with a light blue necktie and handkerchief. He squeezed the mulatto's thick shoulder and patted him on the stomach.

"That's the Frenchman," the red haired woman whispered next to Clayton. "They say he's *connected*. That's who supplies his paintings."

"Oh." *Great,* Clayton thought. *Anybody could be his supplier. I'm so screwed.*

A shy woman in her twenties walked in the Frenchman's shadow. She had long black hair that complimented her exotic olive skin and light green eyes that promised to keep secrets. She followed Renauld up to the podium. He had a peculiar wind-up toy walk to him. He was very artificial.

The mulatto retrieved the first painting which was covered in a thick velvet blanket.

Green eyes carried a notebook and fountain pen. She clasped the notebook in front of her, trying not to make eye contact with anyone. The auctioneer women leered at her. Green eyes presence drew all of the men's eyes in the room.

"Before we begin," Renauld's French accent was slightly better than the mulatto's. "I wish to remind everyone that the art for sale here is from a *private* collection. The owner wishes to remain...anonymous. I am just a middle man. I make no claims as to these art works origins. It is buyer beware." He made eye contact with the obvious high-rollers. They were a fickle bunch. Some were known to run to the authorities if they didn't like their purchases. "If you go public then it is *you* who shall take all of the risk and liability of such a careless action." Renauld wore his hair short, greasy, and slicked back with a slimy gel that made him stink of ripe strawberries. "The first painting up for bid is called, *La Orgia.*"

The mulatto yanked off the velvet covering on the first painting.

A large faded canvas depicted a graphic Roman orgy taking place inside of a stone columned bathhouse. An ornate gold leaf picture frame hinted of its material worth.

The room was silent as everyone started. They were transfixed.

The painting was a work of unapologetic, hard core, Renaissance era porn. It was a sea of withering, rigid, and flaccid body parts. A regular sexual delicatessen. Each frozen face revealed a different state of enjoyment. Nothing was taboo.

"We shall start the bidding at $100,000 U.S. Dollars."

Bright light flashed from behind the curtains on the left side of the room again. The rain began to hiss in steady protest.

Everyone's paddles shot up at the same time. The quality of the painting's depiction of human form and function guaranteed that it was painted by a Renaissance master. No mimicry of the style could ever come close. One only had to look to *know*. The painting was both authentic and incredible.

The bids took off like the space shuttle. It was fiscal gravity in reverse. The higher the bids went; the least resistance there was to go higher.

Clayton had to return to earth. His last offer was six-hundred-thousand dollars. His employer had only authorized five, but he had to fake being a player to get close to the auctioneer.

Renauld slammed his miniature gavel. "Sold to number nine for four *million* dollars."

Green eyes wrote furiously in her notebook.

Renauld stared at his guests like they were chattel. A strange twinkle shimmered behind his beady eyes. The auctioneers were mesmerized and his for the taking.

The rain was coming down harder and the wind caused the room to cool considerably. Several of the auctioneer ladies sent the models to fetch their coats and yet no one departed. Not with the promise of more paintings for sale.

The mulatto hauled up the next painting and held it up high for all to see.

A middle-aged Roman noble woman lay nude on her bed. She was being groped by her young male slaves. One slave with curly black hair and a rope tied around his neck engaged in congress with her from behind. The bed sheets were torn to shreds.

"If these are authentic, then these paintings are priceless," the red haired woman whispered into Clayton's ear.

"I've seen provocative art before."

"Modern art," she said. "This is different. These pieces show that they were painting more than just angles back then. Only nobility or clergy could afford to commission works like this."

"That's why they're fakes," her man interjected for her. He looked hard at Clayton. "None of these should go for over two-hundred-thousand."

"La Carne," Renauld announced. "Starting bid at $150,000 US Dollars."

Paddles waved into the air as the wind blew in heavily. It smelled of almonds and colognes.

A disheveled fat man from the third row launched out of his chair with his legs spaced out awkwardly. He wore a white one-piece Arab Kutra shirt and a red-white Arad head covering. He tossed his headdress to the ground as he reached under his robe for his crotch area. Several of the women turned their heads to look away.

"Pardon me, sir…" Renauld began.

The man grabbed a long slim object out from under his robe. It appeared to be an old fashioned straight-razor. He spun around to face Renauld. His hand flicked the speckled blue handle once causing a sharp metal square to swing out and lock into place.

The color from Renauld's face fled quickly as he recognized the man.

Green eyes trembled and took a step backward closer to Renauld.

The Arab made a demand in guttural French.

The red head translated out loud for the benefit of her company. "Uh…Are you going to pay what you owe, he says. His French is terrible. Oh gosh, it's more like Louisiana Creole than true French."

Renauld motioned for the Mulatto to do something. The gold teeth thug started to put the painting on the ground but he felt uncertain on how to rest it.

The fat Arab rushed out of his row of chairs and ran up on Renauld at the podium. The razor's shiny metal blade captured the room's light and flashed it wildly into the spectators' faces.

Renauld snatched Green eyes from her place and maneuvered her directly between him and the Arab. He gave her a shove.

Green Eyes tried to regain her balance from the sudden hook-and-lunge. Her high-heeled leather boots made her wobble in place.

The fat man seized her. He wrapped his arm around her throat, razor next to her jugular vein.

"I *cut* her," he threatened. "Or you pay me now."

Renauld turned to the mulatto. The man was still worried about where to lay the painting down. It was worth at least $150,000 USD and he wasn't about to toss it to the floor over the boss's assistant girl.

Clayton casually stood up from his chair and moved back toward the rear of the room.

The rain was coming down extremely hard. Thousands of water droplets drilled into the old sanatorium rooftop creating a cacophony of splattering noises. Bright flashes of white light lightening flickered outside along with the loud rattles of thunder.

The three Italian models clustered together. Each was drinking the champagne that they were supposed to be offering.

Clayton passed the three women and traveled to the far right corner of the room. There was a tall red curtain blowing inward. He half-hid between the curtain folds as he advanced to the next curtain in front of him. The last fabric of sanctuary was one of three and was only two feet away from the Arab.

The crazy man tightened his grip on the straight razor that he held tight against Green Eyes throat. His attention was focused solely on Renauld. One of the gentlemen in the front row could have easily taken him but no one bothered. The girl was just hired-help and the patrons wanted to get one with the auction.

"You pay?" The Arab said in poor English.

Green Eyes gagged as her assailant's thick arm tightened around her throat.

"Go ahead, Monsieur." Renauld's mouth twisted into a sick smile. "Cut the bitch."

Clayton moved along towards the attacker using the blowing curtains as camouflage. His sneakers scraped across the cement floor as he made wide rapid steps. His Zoloft anti-depressant pills rattled in the container in his pocket. He wondered if the noise tipped his hand.

The attacker's head cocked slightly. He'd heard something close to him.

Clayton lunged for the man's razor holding hand and bit the Arab's neck as hard as he could. A fold of fat filled his mouth.

The fat man wailed out in pain. His grip on the girl's throat lessened and Clayton successfully pulled it away.

Hot copper blood drenched Clayton's mouth. The man's sweat stuck on Clayton's chin and cheek. His heart pounded as he spit out the soiled blood from his mouth and sprayed it onto the fat man's face. The frothy crimson fluid landed in gooey clumps.

The attacker was furious. He wrestled the razor from Clayton's grasp and brought the deadly blade in a dangerous arc upward.

Clayton danced backwards. The razor missed his chest and chin by inches.

Green Eyes fell to the floor and scurried away.

Renauld exited the room through one of the windows and returned with a double-barrel shotgun that was wrapped in a wet plastic bag.

Several of the auctioneers began to flee. Chairs overturned and people began to shuffle toward the back of the room. A razor they could deal with but the gun made them all nervous.

The mulatto leaped onto the fat man. He wrapped his legs around the fat man's waist and latched his hands around the man's bloody thick neck.

The open razor lay on the floor.

Renauld ran up on the Arab and put the shotgun next to the man's temple. "We'll have none of this, *Monsieur*."

The attacker stopped struggling and allowed the mulatto to unattach himself. The mulatto took the gun from Renauld and led the attacker outside at gun point.

Clayton got up from the floor and brushed himself off.

The rain had died down to a silent drizzle. The curtains teased in and out from the remaining winds.

Renauld reached out and shook Clayton's hand. "*Monsieur*, you saved my auction."

Only half of the auctioneers remained. Most of them were the people who sat in the back rows.

Renauld tried to be charming. "I'd offer you one of my paintings but I'm a poor man. I have creditors, debts, you know… With your wealth I'm sure you've seen this before. The desperate trying to victimize the legitimate, no?"

Clayton nodded. *Jackass.*

"I believe that Tonya is in your debt now, no?"

Tonya blushed. She continued hugging her own waist.

"She's *yours.*" Renauld brightened at his own genius. "She tires me. Always sulking, you know?"

"I believe that you told him to cut her," Clayton mumbled under his breath. He had to restrain himself. His job required that he befriend this man.

"Pardon?"

"Nothing."

"As an assistant she has no formal schooling," he explained. "I put her through University painting classes. She was dumped on me by her Uncle. I believe that you just met him."

"Your offer's nice but…"

He shoved her toward him. "I insist!"

Her boots made her stumble to the floor. Clayton helped her back to her feet. She looked away from him.

"Are you okay?" Clayton asked her.

She winced and then nodded politely.

What the hell are you going to do with as assistant girl, Clayton thought. *Have her get you close to the Frenchman, that's what.*

"You see? She's already warming up to you," He ran his hand through his slicked-back hair.

Tonya locked eyes with her former employer. Her eyes began to water slightly as she silently begged for a reprieve. Renauld would have none of it.

"She will help me with the rest of my auction. After, she will leave with you, yes?"

"Fine."

"Very good." Renauld's cell phone chimed the acid rock tune 'Sunshine of Your Life.' He pressed the receive button. "Ello?"

A minute passed as he listened. "Yes, yes. Very good," he said into his phone. "Not until three. I don't want him coming back here again."

Long pause. Renauld maneuvered away from Clayton and lowered his voice. "Tell him she's no longer with me." He peered over his shoulder. "He forced her on me. Not vice versa. I'm not going to pay for it! Tell him...hell; tell him that *he* owes me if anything."

Two minutes later Renauld ended his call and restarted the auction. Tonya rejoined Renauld's side. She never once looked at Clayton. She didn't want to. He owned her now and she hated him for it.

Chapter 3

New York City. December 1996

Anthony "Big Tony" Bassano entered the sleek architectural steel-and-glass offices of UBT Dutch Bank.

The Bank had their Christmas decorations displayed throughout their offices. Plain white light-bulb Christmas lights were strung along the main teller room ceiling. Canned radio music was piped in through the whole building. They were playing the parody song, '*Grandma Got Ran Over By a Reindeer.*' It was snowing heavily outside and the bank was toasty warm.

Big Tony was wearing a green-and-white football jacket, blue jeans, and banana yellow Chuck Taylor Converse basketball shoes. He was a thirty-eight year old ex-con on a mission.

Everyone in the plush carpeted lobby stared at him as he limped toward the bank manager's desk. The modern antique desk was in the back next to a reflective brass paneled elevator.

A middle-aged woman with light brown hair that was wrapped into a ponytail sat behind the manager's desk. She shook Big Tony's hand firmly and then she straightened the American flag pin on her red-and-black checkered power suit. Her eyes traveled over his shoulder to see if the security guard was watching them.

"Can I help you, sir?"

"I fuckin' hope so," Big Tony said in a calm *raspy voice*. "I'm supposed ta be makin' a phone call overseas. The letter said ta show up here at three o'clock and see the bank manager, Miss Crane. Is that you?"

She leaned back in her special ergonomic leather chair. She raised the end of her gold fountain pen up to her mouth where she bit softly.

Her boss had told her to assist a wealthy gentleman place a call to a private number. No name was given. She was pretty sure that the area code "06" meant Rome. Her caller was scheduled to arrive at three o'clock. Her digital desk clock read 3:05.

Big Tony snatched a dish of plastic-wrapped lemon candies off her desktop and poured the whole bowl into his jacket pocket. Deep creases flexed across his sloping brow as he used his thug-like powers to stare right through her.

No way is this my wealthy gentleman, she thought. *There must be some sort of mistake.*

"Excuse me!" She said in a shrill voice. Her blood pressure shot up in response to the plunder of her candies. She rose up out of her chair and tugged down on her suit-shirt to pull out the wrinkles. "You'll have to leave, sir." She pointed toward the entrance door that had big cardboard candy canes on either side. "There are payphones down the street at Grand Central Station."

"Lady, did I fuckin' ask you for a pay phone?" His hand pointed to her in the shape of a gun.

She picked up her telephone. "I think you need to leave sir. I'm calling security."

Big Tony leaned over her desk. His pit bull face snarled without making a sound.

She could smell the wild onions in his breath. He'd eaten at Artrellio's, a greasy spoon in Soho.

The security guard started casually drifting toward them. He unlatched the leather safety clasp that holstered his sidearm.

"I have a very important call ta make." Big Tony leaned back. *"You* have the phone number so Grand Central Station isn't going to cut it. *Capisce?"*

She put the phone receiver back down. *This guy couldn't have known about the number unless he was the caller,* she thought. *You better clean this mess up.*

"Is there a problem, Miss Crane?" The security guard asked in a strained polite voice. He watched Big Tony the whole time.

People in the bank stared at the three of them. The brief encounter had turned into a scene.

Miss Crane blushed. Her fingers found her American flag pin and tugged on it softly. She waved off the guard. Her company smile returned. "It was just a simple misunderstanding," she said. She reached into her desk and retrieved gold metal key that had a silver metal bead chain with a thick magnetic strip card attached to it. "If you would please follow me, sir."

Big Tony took notice of the guard and mouthed the word "what." He took a threatening step toward the man.

The bank manager grabbed Big Tony by the arm and led him over to the elevator. She inserted her gold key into a key receptacle that was mounted next to the shiny brass doors. The elevator's doors rolled open allowing her and Big Tony to board it. They turned to face the bank guard.

"What? Are you a faggot or somethin'?" Big Tony grinned.

The insult slapped the man. He started to respond as the brass doors closed between them. The fancy little room began to descend.

"That fuckin' guy…"

She coughed into her hand. "He's really very nice. I'm sorry about earlier. I didn't know that you were my three o'clock appointment. I was told you would be a wealthy client."

The inference didn't bother him. "Forget about it." He dug around in his jacket pocket. Candy wrappers crinkled. "Do ya want a lemon drop?"

"No." *Unbelievable!*

The elevator played a canned rendition of Mozart's 5th Symphony through the speakers that were mounted in the ceiling. The small cubicle smelled of Lysol disinfectant and lemon drops.

Big Tony tossed three empty wrappers down onto the simulated marble floor. He craned his neck to ogle her posterior. His mouth made terrible smacking noises as he batted the lemon balls around in his mouth.

Miss Crane bolted out of the elevator the second that the bell dinged and the doors opened.   Big Tony trailed after her.

They were in an underground subsection of the bank building. There were no windows, just plain oak doors with chrome numbers mounted over them.

Miss Crane led him to a black steel door at the end of the short hallway.   The words "Private" were stenciled in the center of it in white paint.   She retrieved the plastic magnetic strip card and ran it through a slim electronic scanner that was mounted next to the door.

A lock clicked inside of the door.   Miss Crane pushed the door inward as overhead lights flickered on automatically.

The room was very cold.   In the center of the modest rectangular chamber was an ornate conference room table, which was made out of stained cherry wood.   Four leather chairs flanked it.   Two fax machines, a laptop computer, and a triangular conference phone, lay onto the polished tabletop.   All four walls were purposely unfinished with wires snaking in uniform coils behind a transparent coating.   The coils covered all of the room's walls and ceiling.

"What's with the walls?"

"The wires have a continuous electric current running through them to prevent electronic eavesdropping."

"Oh."

"The phone is PGP3 secure."   She hurried over to the dinning room table.   Her hand modeled the top of the pyramid-shaped conference phone.   "A green light means that the line is secure.   Red indicates a suspected breach.   Your call will go through our corporation's private fiber optic network.   We've never had a red light."

"Fuckin' Feds probably still listen though.   They've got their hands in everything."

"I suppose."   She read off of a manila card and dialed its number into the conference phone.

An electronic chirping echoed from the phone's rings over the product's tiny speakers.   There was a loud click.

"Un attimo un minuto, per favore," a faint female voice instructed. More clicking and chirping ensued followed by a second dialing.

"That's weird. We've been redialed to another location." She saw that the green LED light was still shining. "It's still secure though."

Big Tony limped over to a table chair and sat down. The chair creaked in protest.

"Cia il mio figlo, io La parla sono aspetto." A scratchy male Italian voice said. He sounded very ancient.

"I'll leave you now," Miss Crane whispered. She hurried out of the room and turned to close the door. "I'll be out in the hall if you need me."

Big Tony gave a friendly wave as he popped another lemon candy into his mouth.

"Lei e li?" The old man asked.

"You'll have to speak English," Big Tony commanded. "You speak Italian way too fast for me. I speak *slow*. I learned the language in prison."

"Very well, my son. Where's Lorenzo?"

"Dead."

"Roberto?"

"He's fuckin' dead too."

There was a long pause.

Big Tony waited patiently. He thought he could hear church bells ringing through the telephone line.

"What happened to the people that they were sent to ...eh, *convince?*"

"You've got one dead kid, his old man, and his mother. The daughter wasn't home." He put his feet up on the table. "The mother was a straight gangster. She tried to kill me."

"Destino ha destinato cosi."

"Yeah," he sighed. "Whatever you said. All I know is that Lorenzo is one bloodthirsty son-of-a-bitch. It didn't have ta go down like it did."

"You were there, my son?"

"Fuck yeah! I got clipped in the leg." Even though the man couldn't see him, Big Tony undid his pant's button and let them fall to his ankles. An envelope-size bandage lay poorly affixed to his left upper thigh. A blood spot showed through the bandage. "It's not too bad though. I got the bullet taken out three months ago. Cost me ten grand in dude's basement. He had a bunch of fuckin' cats. A veterinarian or some shit. One of the furry fuckers jumped up onto my chest during surgery. It was an orange tabby or some shit."

"You're a *family* man then."

"Family man?"

"Si. Like Lorenzo and Roberto."

It took a minute for Big Tony to catch on.

"Oh no. I'm not in *a family*. I work for Crazy Paul Lastanzi."

"No names!" the oldster barked.

"Yeah... sorry." He pulled his pants back up. "The bank says this phone's safe though."

"Nothing is safe in this world, child. Why did your employer place you on... the task we'd sent them him if you're not... family?"

"Because I'm fuckin' *loyal!*" Big Tony took the man's question as an insult. "I met him in Marion. The federal pen. I was doing time for six counts of credit card fraud. They ran the sentences wild. That's one right after the other. Crazy Pa... my *employer* helped me with the law in there. He's a regular fuckin' Perry Mason. We got my shit run concurrent and I got out."

"Yes, but he has family."

"Sure. All four of them ratted him out to avoid federal drug charges. Mandatory Minimum sentencing. His whole crew turned out ta be snitches. That's why I was assigned ta take it. 'Cause I ain't a fuckin' rat. He trusts me. I'm his eyes and ears out here for the next two decades. Don't you keep tabs on your own people?"

"He is an associate of an associate."

"So you say. What's this call all about?"

"Are you Catholic, my son?"

"My dad was." Big Tony started playing with an empty lemon candy wrapper on the table. "He died in prison. I was fourteen."

"Fate willed it."

"Naw." He squeezed the empty wrapper. "That was my mother's fault. She fucked around with her boss at the restaurant she worked at. Dad found out and beat her close to death. The neighbor's called the cops which is rare in our part of Hoboken, so you can imagine the screaming."

"I share your burden."

Big Tony put four lemon drops in his mouth. The bittersweet taste soothed him. "She's all fucked up. Her nose... she still asks people if it looks okay. That shit was over ten years ago." He sniffed. "So what, are you a priest or somethin'?"

Silence.

"Well then, if there's nothin' else..."

"What about the tape, my son? Did you recover *the tape?*"

"No." Big Tony's eyes burned into the phone. The green LED light went dark. The red light glowed steadily.

"What happened to it?" The voice was becoming agitated.

"I saw the dead woman clutch the tape in her hand as the house fire burned down on top of her."

"Good, good." Loud church bells rang. "It was God's will."

"So do you have a message for Crazy Pa... my employer? Cause I got this hooker, Gloria. She's on his approved vistin' list and she can tell him next time she sees him behind the glass."

"That will not be necessary. You have served us well."

"So, okay then, when are you guy's gonna wire me some cash for my leg and stuff? I risked my..."

Click-clunk!

A familiar dial tone sounded. "Hello?!"

No answer.

Big Tony hurled the pyramid phone across the room. "Fuck!" He reached behind his back up underneath his football jacket. He retrieved a VHS tape. It was in a box that had black electrical tape wrapped around it. He slid the tape into his outer jacket pocket and limped out of the phone room into the hallway.

The bank manager leaned against the wall rubbing her temples in an attempt to relieve her migraine headache.

"Hey!"

She glanced up toward him.

"Do you guys have safety deposit boxes that nobody would know about but you and me?"

"Sure."

"How much to rent one for a couple years?"

"Depends on the size."

"I need a deposit box that could hold something about the size of a tape."

"A cassette tape?"

"No." He smiled. "VHS."

Chapter 4

The Vatican. February 2004.

A *conclave* had assembled in this Sistine Chapel eighteen days after Pope John Paul the Second died. The somber men who pondered their vote for the future leader of the Roman Catholic Church prayed to the Almighty for holy guidance. The history of God stared downward from directly above them. Each frescoed panel depicted a miraculous scene from the Holy Bible in freshly restored color.

God was shown doing amazing things. He divided light from darkness, created the Sun and Moon, and made Adam and Eve. In small triangles interspaced between Prophets and Sibyls, were painted representations of the ancestors of Jesus Christ.

It was ten o'clock in the morning on the second day of *conclave*. The cardinals had voted several times with no success. They began to make a second vote for the morning round. Politics had come into play and one name was quickly making a move. Cardinal Augustus Ravasini.

Cardinal Ravasini was a plain but graceful man. He wore a modest black cassock and a red skullcap, which balanced, precariously on his thick white hair. He was 65, born in Lazio, and he walked with a funny little shuffle that was the legacy of a horse-cart racing misadventure that occurred in his childhood. His broken leg had never healed properly.

Ravasini was too modest to know that his name was in play. He had been successful understudy of Pope John Paul the Second. He learned early on that it was best to see everything, listen to all that was said, and say as little as possible. This behavior made most man view him as an ally even if he wasn't. They all assumed that he was conservative like his mentor.

The Pontiff had sent Ravasini on many special and sensitive missions. He was ordered to America to deal with the pedophile priest problems, the lawsuits, and reorganization of the American Archdiocese. There seemed to be a rebellion brewing and the Pope had wanted it stopped. Women wished to be ordained, gays wanted to be married, aborted fetus tissue was being used to heal people, and many wanted the ban lifted on contraception. It all seemed to come from America. The rest of the world watched and waited on the side.

Ravasini proceeded with caution. He always tried to represent several of the different majorities' interests: the people, the churches, and the priests'.

The Sacred College of Cardinals scribbled down their preference for the new Holy Father on the blank ballots that had been distributed.

Most of the men sat while a few clergy walked around in pairs whispering. No one wished to be seen openly lobbying for themselves. Such behavior would instantly kick them out of consideration.

Each serious contender had their own advocates who took it upon themselves to speak strongly in support of their friend. One man had to receive two-thirds of the Sacred College's vote, plus one, to be elected Pope.

Ravasini wrote down his friend's name on the ballot. Cardinal Scaramella.

The Church was quietly fighting a civil war within itself. Scandals kept popping up every four or five years. Every time a new scandal came one ideological side suppressed the other side's call for change.

A dark shadow fell on the Church in the post-inquisition era. In 1929, the Vatican entered into an agreement with Benito Mussolini. He gave them sovereignty and millions of dollars in return for their quiet acceptance of fascism. The Institute of Religious Works, the IOR or Vatican Bank, was born and the great money laundry machine began.

At first, wealthy Italians entrusted their money to the IOR to keep it away from the Germans. Then they used the IOR to avoid Italian banking laws and taxes.

The Church was charging the public interest on the loans it made. They began to branch out into corporate investments and ownership. The Vatican was implicated in smuggling Nazis out of Europe as it began to fall to the Allies and relocated them in South America. This included the Nazi intelligence chief Reinhard Gehlen. In return, certain stolen art treasures made their way into the Church's hands as payment.

Pope John Paul the First was shocked to learn that the IOR had allowed millions of dollars of the Faithfull's money to disappear into Roberto Salvi's *Banco Ambrussiano*.

Just like running water, the Church's money went into Salvi's outside private bank, through it, and then out into an ocean of dummy corporations, which happened to be operated by international dope men and organized crime families.

Salvi died. He hung himself before he could provide adequate answers to the Italian authorities or mother Church when it was announced that there would be an investigation.

Ravasini was a Bishop back then. He worked as an executive secretary for Cardinal Lucius Ferroli.

Ferroli was indirectly charged with the task of operating the IOR. Bogus letters of credit baring the Vatican's official seal had been written to keep *Banco Ambrussiano* afloat. Ferroli admitted to His Holiness at the start of the investigation that the Church owned eight phantom companies that Salvi used to channel the money through. He conceded that Salvi had several clergy on the inside helping him.

The next revelation signaled the beginning of the Church's civil war. A majority of the players in the bank scandal inside the Vatican and in Rome were active members of the P2 Masonic Lodge.

Freemasonry was banned by Papal Bull in the 18th century. The ban was openly known to still be in affect. The pope's law states that *any* Catholic who becomes a member or participates in this secret society is to be immediately excommunicated. Dozens of Bishops and Cardinals were discovered as being members of this Lodge yet repercussions never followed. The P2 group orchestrated manipulation of the IOR through its brothers in both the Church and Italian government.

Before Pope John Paul could take action he died in his sleep. He had been Pope for thirty-three days. Accountability for those guilty in the scandal died with him. No autopsy was performed and the Faithfull's money was never recovered. The new old guard had established itself and the worst part was that a majority of the clergy involved was being controlled by non-Catholic outsiders.

Cardinal Ferroli knew where the Church's financial bodies were buried. No one dared challenge him or his authority. He was 71 years old, short, balding, and his teeth were rotting. He could have easily been elected Pope but he openly preferred to run the IOR. He had commitments to keep and an agenda to push.

Ferroli paced over to Cardinal Ravasini.

"Augustus," Ferroli said. A foul stench emitted from his mouth that was his signature bad breath. "You've been hiding from me."

Ravasini forced a polite smile.

"Who have you chosen?" Ferroli asked. "That's, if you don't mind me asking."

"There are many who are worthy than others. Yes?"

"We're all equal in God's eyes." Ravasini was careful.

"So true." Ferroli glanced around to see if they would be overheard. He saw no one in range. "I'll show you my vote, Augustus. I believe many will be following my choice."

Ferroli carried a lot of weight within the Sacred College. The man was an institution. He had turned the IOR into a multi-billion dollar juggernaut. The IOR owned controlling shares of several multinational corporations throughout the world.

"I don't think I should see your vote," Ravasini whispered apologetically. "This is highly irregular. We shouldn't discuss the vote in this way."

Ferroli ignored him. He held up his ballot for Ravasini to see. In shaky black letter scrawl it read, "Augustus Ravasini." He lowered the ballot and patted Ravasini on the shoulder. "You deserve it. You are a natural leader and we'll need your youth if we are to survive."

"I'm 65."

"You have the divine spark." He tipped Ravasini's head back with a push from his shaking thumbs. "It is there. You'll see. *You* can inspire the faithful and they desperately need inspiring, my friend."

"That is your only reason?"

"No. I still remember your sacrifice in the IOR's time of need. You're loyal."

"I didn't know about the P2s," he said under his breath. "They're cancer, Cardinal. I don't understand how you could be with them."

"There are things that you don't know, Augustus. There are circles working within circles to bring about a new order of things. You can't expect the Church to be dealt out. Not over some basic 18th century ideological differences." Ferroli moved closer to him. "Government boundaries will soon cease to exist. The world will be united through consolidation of privatized natural resources and global commerce. There will be *one* central political and governmental authority. Mother Church can become *thee* new secular authority. All others will be absorbed or dissolved. *Ordo ab Chao.*" Order from Chaos.

"It'll never happen, Cardinal. The world is too divided. They're just using you."

"Tell that to me in the next twenty years, Augustus. You will be a part of it or you will be dead."

Ravasini's eyes widened considerably.

"Not by me," Ferroli promised. "Men who stand in the way of destiny always meet the unfortunate."

"I'll have no part in it."

"I see. But, I can count on receiving an audience with you at any time though?"

"Of course."

"Despite my... *associations?*"

"Yes." He played it safe again. His first challenge, if elected Pope, would be the destruction of the P2 associated clergy and the dissolution and reorganization of the IOR. The thought terrified him. His dream and nightmare were occurring at the same time. "I remember those who help, even despite our *differences.*"

"You see. We've chosen well." Ferroli walked away.

Ravasini let out a deep breath that he'd been holding.

Another hour passed as each Cardinal approached an alter to pledge his integrity of purpose in deciding their vote. They voted in order of seniority. After declaring their intent, they placed their folded ballot in a receptacle that was covered by a large ceramic plate.

35

After all of the ballots were turned in, three tellers began the process of reading each ballot. The final teller standing in the line would take the ballot handed to him and read it out loud for all of the college to hear. The teller's voice began to stumble as the same name kept being read by him. Cardinal Ravasini.

Ravasini's mouth hung open slightly. He face went flush. All of the Cardinal's in the room focused their collective gaze on him. His heart kept pounding as the already warm chapel became scorching hot to him.

Smiles erupted around the chapel's inhabitants. Everyone seemed pleased by their choice.

The traditionalists felt that Ravasini would hold the *status quo*, if not install a stricter code of morals later in the future. Ferroli assured them that Ravasini wouldn't attempt to carry out further reforms like those of the Second Council, held by Pope John Paul the First.

Ravasini had been to the United States often. He had been the Pope's *nuncio* to the Council on Foreign Relations, the Trilateral Commission, and the board of the U.S. Federal Reserve. He always wondered why the American public perceived the Federal Reserve as a public institution instead of being a private corporation run by private banks, which it really was.

Ferroli and the P2 Lodge hoped to bring the Church back into hegemonic power with the nation-states before these countries shed their national sovereignty and joined the new one world government. They wanted the Church to be re-established as the world moral authority. The big three wanted an organization to keep the coming impoverished masses in line. They hoped the Church would push the idea of: *Don't attempt to stop or change the coming new government.* Accept the new rule, ignore the creeping insufferable conditions, and wait for the Savior to come out of the clouds to save you.

The levers of fear and ignorance were being used to drive the masses forward into the desired ends. Many "new" global threats were deliberately manufactured to push the end game onto the people. A final terror was coming; its use was to terrify the populations into begging their "democratic" governments save them from the terror, no matter what the personal cost. The death of national sovereignty would be the price. It never occurred to people that terror was created by the people whose job it was to protect them initially.

The progressives felt that Ravasini was the best chance at representing their interests. He was young and intelligent. The faithful could identify with him and he could lead the Church into the new dawn. He appeared conservative but they felt that outside forces and a crisis might force him into carrying out much needed reform. He was known not to belong to the P2 group and they felt he would most likely resist the outside influences being continuously thrust on the Church by ambitious world architects.

The progressives wanted a spiritual Renaissance where man and woman *both*, experienced a true spiritual awakening and rise in consciousness. They liked the idea of striving to create new social models which empower the poor and underprivileged. The young could dare to hope for a better world again. Not a world led by commercialism, self-interest, and greed.

Invisible lines had been drawn by both sides in the chapel. Each side believed that they had won a major victory in the election of Augustus Ravasini to the Holy Office of Pope.

A 70-year-old Cardinal with a copy of the *conclave* rules prepared to address the Sacred College. Ravasini stepped forward to stand next to the man.

"The required majority vote has been reached," the 70-year-old dean said. The chapel was silent. The Michelangelo frescoes watched them form above. "Do you, Cardinal Augustus Ravasini, accept the results of our election of you to the Holy Office of Supreme Pontiff?"

Ravasini bowed his head forward in humility. "Yes. I accept the Holy Office."

"What name shall you choose, Your Holiness?"

Ravasini's mind froze. He was now *infallible* when he spoke for the Church on matters concerning faith and morals. He could take the name of another Pope as almost every other pontiff had done in the past or he could start a new name.

There was so much pain in the world. So many people felt lost, broken, and abandoned. The Church had fallen too. Much needed to be rebuilt. The Church had fallen too. Much needed to be rebuilt. The Church had to be *redeemed*.

Ravasini lifted his head and addressed the Dean of Cardinals.

"Il Redentore," he answered. The Redeemer.

The Dean noticed the astonished faces cross the room. He cleared his throat. *"Il Redentore,"* he announced a second time to the Cardinals. The name echoed through the hollowed chapel ceiling.

The Cardinals were stunned. He was expected to have chosen the name of John Paul the Third. His choice was a radical departure. No one moved and several mouths hung open. An ancient Cardinal started coughing violently in the back of the room.

Il Redentore walked over to Cardinal Ferroli. He held out his right hand in his first show of power. The other Cardinals had to see the power-broker of the secret groups demonstrating first allegiance.

Ferroli sunk to one knee and kissed the ruby ring that was on *Il Redentore's* finger.

The gesture broke the spell on the men in the chapel. All of the Cardinals swarmed around the new Pope to pay their respects. Forty minutes later white smoke billowed out from the chimney on top of the Papal Palace rooftop.

The crowd waiting outside in Saint Peter's square began to cheer. *Il Redentore* would shortly deliver his first blessings to the faithful in Rome and throughout the world.

Chapter 5

Venice, Island of Pegveillia. July, 2004.

The cool ocean air blew into the sleepy auction room. The storm had passed. Puddles were everywhere, giving the false impression that the large island was sinking. It was 4:30 in the morning. Renauld had made ten million dollars. He was bitter that it wasn't more. The auction had gone on longer than expected.

Clayton sat in a chair watching the Italian models. Each one of the women sat in a former auctioneers chair that they'd repositioned into a disheveled semi-circle. They were drunk and behaving badly. All of the guests had gone.

The tall model with the sexy space between her front teeth had taken it upon herself to make a pyramid of empty champagne glasses on a chair seat. The current glass structure that she had erected continuously wavered. Several failed attempts lay shuttered on the oriental carpet. She kept laughing at her own jokes. Her hair stuck to the front of her face.

Green Eyes remained at Renauld's side. She waited for him to release her as if she were a kept bird of prey. Renauld kept toying with his computer. He had to be sure that his money was in order.

Clayton moved his chair close to a model that was sleeping. He nudged her in the ribs softly. "Where does Renauld live?"

"*Non so,*" She murmured and didn't open her eyes.

Renauld raised his head from his computer to look at Clayton.

Oh shit, Clayton thought. *He heard me.* "Just waiting to go," he covered. "No hurry."

Renauld snorted. He waved Tonya away from him with the flick of the back of his wrist. She sauntered over to Clayton in robotic fashion and turned to Renauld for further instruction.

"Just go," he said with his condescending accent. "You're *his* problem now. I no longer wish to deal with you."

"Goodbye then." She studied his reaction.

"Yes, yes." He was back to pushing computer buttons. "And take the relics we didn't sell back to our flat sometime today. I have to do some banking." He ran his hand through his slicked-back hair and drooled over his accounts.

Tonya clasped Clayton's hand and tugged him along like a little child. She led him out into the early morning darkness. In her free arm she carried a strange metal box with the words, "Relics of Saint Sebastian," written in Italian on it. The mulatto was nowhere to be found. They traveled down the over-grown trail that Clayton had followed earlier to reach the place.

The island was deathly quiet and everything was still.

The brass fire urns were extinguished, making their journey even more difficult.

Tonya's perfume was strong. It tickled Clayton's nose between the scents of wet cement and fresh greenery. She was wearing an orange silk dress with Lotus-petal designs sewed into it, spiked heel brown leather boots, and a gold amulet around her neck that appeared part melted.

"Do you know where we're going?" He asked.

"To the boat launch."

"You've been on this island before?"

"Many times."

"Renauld too?"

"Yes."

"Where does he live?"

She released her grasp of his hand. "You ask too many questions."

"Sorry," he lied. "People say that I talk too much. It's in my nature."

Tonya's green eyes adjusted to the early morning darkness. A tiny sliver of moon light beat through a school of trailing storm clouds. She made out the lone silhouette of Clayton's speedboat.

They discovered that the Polaris EX2100's weather tarp had been taken off and thrown in a large wad up in the front of the craft.

They didn't notice the passenger who hid under it. Water had soaked through everything.

The image of the disgruntled auctioneer woman's boyfriend-father came to him as the probable culprit.

"How petty," Clayton said out loud. "What an asshole."

Tonya boarded the boat and felt along the interior. "At least he didn't slash the carpet or leather."

A faint white light appeared through a thicket of trees and bushes over Tonya' shoulder. It moved in a steady line from right to left.

Clayton jumped aboard and got behind his boat's driver's seat. He fished around in his suit coat pocket for his keys and sat up, examining his butt.

"What's wrong?"

He hit the steering wheel hard with his fists. The wet seat had soaked through his designer suit pants. "I'm wet."

Tonya focused her attention on an approaching moving light in the distance out in the water.

Clayton put his key in the ignition and turned it on. Red, green, and white running lights came on along with tiny lights that were concealed on the inside of the boat's interior.

A large cabin cruiser pulled out from around the thicket and idled in front of the boat launch. Clayton pulled their boat out in reverse and started heading toward the foreign ship.

"We don't have to back out," Tonya volunteered. "We can drive forward. The launch goes in a square U."

"I'm curious who it is."

"I don't know," she lied. It was Renauld's boat and encountering it wasn't part of the plan.

A young woman with short blond hair and a Venice University t-shirt greeted them as both boats pulled up along side of one another. The woman was driving alone.

"The auction's over," Tonya said.

"I know." She talked like an American. "I'm not here for that."

"Well then what are you here for then?"

"None of your business." The blonde winked. "Just do as you're told."

Clayton began to enjoy himself as he sensed a cat fight brewing. "You're not gonna take that from her are you?"

Tonya ignored him. She stood on the edge of her seat attempting to peer inside Renauld's boat. She half-expected to see him crouched over close to the boat's floor hiding from her. "Nice boat. Looks a lot like a friend of mine's. Is she yours?"

The blonde gunned her boat's engine and glided past them into the Pegeveillia boat launch.

Tonya sat back down in her seat and softly bit the sideways part of the middle of her index finger. She held it in her mouth thinking.

"Where to?" Clayton prompted.

"Cannaregio."

"That's where you live?" He revved the boat up two-thirds of its full power.

"No. But it is where we're going."

"Why?"

"To get a decent hotel room." She didn't look at him.

The fine salt water mist splattered into Clayton's face awakening him. Caked blood had dried on his rented tweed suit. It was the Arab's blood from the man's neck wound.

Clayton stole a glance at his pretty passenger. The wind picked up her straight black hair and caressed it backward. She stared out into the black lagoon. The sounds of choppy waves breaking across the ship's bow disturbed her.

A large green channel buoy emerged out of the darkness. The oblong steel cylinder was on the front left side of them, bobbing five feet out of the water line. Their boats raced passed it. The fiberglass hull came within inches of colliding into the monstrous steel obstruction.

"Watch what you're doing," she hissed. "You're in the cargo shipping lane."

Clayton tried to gain a better view of what was ahead of them. The congested clutter of Venice loomed in the horizon. The city's light offered a surrealistic beacon as they traversed the cold and windy void.

The city amazed him. Water abounded everywhere and for no apparent reason the city suddenly appears. The dreamy buildings seemed unreal yet they were built with brick and mortar.

"Do you have a preference for which hotel we go to?" She asked matter-of-factly.

"We haven't even been properly introduced. What's your hurry with a hotel?"

"I just want to get it over with, okay?"

"Get what over with?"

"Paying off my obligation to you. It's Renauld's *way*." She shivered from a blast of cold air.

"You don't *owe* me anything." He rubbed the bullet necklace under his shirt. "I would have mixed it up with the Arab guy no matter who was at stake. I'm living on extended time."

"Whatever."

"It's true. I have a debt that I'll never be able to pay."

The thought of his sister screaming form the trunk of his parents care hit him. *Clayton*, she'd cried. *Let me out! Let me go!* He'd told her to fuck off. He had to get a fix. He'd been jonesing for over a week. Forced residency during drug rehab. His parent's idea.

There was a crack house on the South side. The dealer's name was Kilo. He was the only black guy Clayton knew who liked to listen to heavy metal music.

Clayton figured that by keeping Kathreen in the trunk that the treatment center wouldn't come after him. He never made it to the crack house. A street light pole got them.

"What's your name anyway?"

"Clayton Keasley." It was his real name. VanAucken said that it would work great for him undercover. His real life past was sordid enough to give him high credit on the street as a bonifide scoundrel.

"Well, Clayton Keasley, the hotel offer is still open." She moved over to him, mindful of the bouncing floor which sank and rose with each hit of the wave. She leaned against his side and kissed his cheek as her right hand teased her hair. "We don't need a room if you don't want one."

He punched the speedboat's throttle forward. The engine groaned in protest. The craft darted ahead faster; the interior floor rose and sank a lot harder. The move made it extremely difficult for her to continue coming on to him.

The city of Venice was a lot closer. The early morning light highlighted unique features of various Venetian and Gothic-style architecture.

Tonya lurched back into her seat.

"Who was the Arab guy that attacked you?" Clayton half-shouted. The breaking waves and roaring engine made so each difficult.

"He's Romani. *Not* Arab."

"Oh. Whatever the hell that is..."

"He's also my Uncle."

"I thought you were Italian."

"Nope. Romani." She grinned. Her teeth were exceptionally white but offered a slightly crooked smile, "You'd call us gypsies in America."

The passenger under the boat's weather tarp peered through a canvas fold at them. Rage was quietly building.

Clayton slowed the boat slightly. "I thought gypsies live in horse drawn wagons and play the violin."

"That's Hollywood's version. I guess we used to live like that. Now we travel in trucks and cars. Our families travel around with one another. There's arranged marriages, gatherings, and shard *schaurathu*."

"Schaur..."

"Scams, cons, things of that nature. We do them to live."

Clayton started laughing.

"What?" Her faced lightened. She stomped her foot.

"*Gypsies?!* Come on. I know you are with Renauld and you run some games with him but you don't strike me as the con artist type."

"I've shoplifted since I've learned to walk. I've been a fake slip-and-fall victim, car accident victim, and food poisoning victim over and over again. We take insurance settlement money as if the corporations are paying us rent. The roofing scams pulled on little old ladies...nine out of ten times it was a Romani scam. We take through deception, rarely by force."

"Except for your Uncle."

"He's different. He's crazy."

"Liar!" Uncle Sasha dove out from under the weather tarp in the front of the boat. He brandished a light wood rowing paddle in his hand and he swung the handle-end at Clayton.

Clayton ducked to the floor. The handle-end hit the empty seat.

Uncle Sasha grabbed for the windshield to regain his balance.

The boat drove erratically. The two and three story Venice buildings were almost on top of them. Lines of rotting wood mooring poles stood quietly out of the water. They were used by *gondolas* and motorboats to pull in-between and tie-off to; parking spaces for boats.

Tonya dove into the driver's seat. She grabbed the thin chrome steering-wheel and turned it hard right.

Her uncle lunged at Clayton again. He swung the long end of the paddle in a cutting arc. Clayton turned sideways allowing the fat paddle to hit him across his back and ribs.

The wild turn of the boat caused Sasha to fall into the passenger seat. Clayton crawled up to the man and punched him hard in the jaw. Sasha grabbed one far end on each side of the paddle that lay next to him. He used the passenger chair to launch himself directly onto Clayton where the paddle quickly found itself held across Clayton's neck. Sasha attempted to use the wooden instrument as a primitive garrote.

The boat hit a stack of poles that were lashed together for strength. The craft dipped sideways. Darkened lagoon water poured in and a large crack-and-pop erupted.

They were all thrown into the left side of the craft where the water gushed in. The engine died.

They hadn't capsized but the boat was swamped. Tonya stayed in the flooded boat while Clayton and her Uncle had been thrown into the canal. Both men used all of their strength to stay afloat as the weight of their clothes began to try and drown them. The box of bones Tonya had brought on board floated past Clayton's face as he tread water to stay afloat.

The old cement sidewalk of the *Fondamenta di San Giobbe* was not too far away from them. A pair of early-bird tourists gawked at them from the sidewalk. The female tourist began snapping pictures of them with her instant camera.

Clayton shouted at Tonya's Uncle. "What the hell is your problem?! We could've been killed!"

"I am owed money." His breathing was labored as he dog-paddled. "I gave the Frenchman my niece years ago in return for a percentage. He reneged and now he won't pay for the liberties he has taken nor compensate me for our previous deal!" He had forgotten that Tonya was there.

"You sold me?!" She screamed.

The tourist loved watching the private show unfold in front of her camera.

Tonya tried to restart the boat. Her body was shaking. She wanted to run her Uncle over like he'd done to her as a kid.

Clayton was oblivious. "I don't get it. Why come after me then?"

"Because you took away my collateral!" He started swimming toward Clayton who was closer to the sidewalk than he was.

"Tonya's your niece for Christ's sake!"

"Her parents *owed* me." Sasha spat out water that hit his face. "Especially her mother. I did things for her that could have gotten me killed. That stupid bitch lost our only leverage. We could have retired."

"*You* killed Momma?!" Tonya shrieked.

"No, no! It was *the tape.* She should have been more careful." He gasped with every stroke he took. His clothes weighed a ton.

A police boat siren announced its presence off in the distance. The fierce electronic wail was getting louder.

"We can't stick around," Clayton snapped. He pushed the floating box of bones with the end of his nose as he swam. Something suddenly reminded him that Venice used the canals also as a sewer. He swam toward the sidewalk with the tourists and spoke between swimming strokes to the Uncle. He hoped to reason with the man before another fight broke out. "I have...a...proposition for you."

Sasha remained mute. The salt water from the lagoon burned into the open bite wound that Clayton had inflicted upon him.

"Uhh...Clayton," Tonya shouted. "The boat's sinking!"

Bubbles danced around the remains of the boat's edges.

Tonya's waist was underwater all the way up to her belly-button. The tourist's camera hurt her eyes because the photographer kept using the bright flash over and over.

Clayton surrendered to the whole disaster. "Fuck it, Tonya. Just swim over here sweetie."

The police siren was getting very near to them.

Clayton helped pulled Sasha out of the water as Tonya began her swim.

"Look," Clayton reasoned. "We *both* want the Frenchman. The only way is through Tonya. She hates you but she can be led to trust me. We can help each other."

"What do I get out of it?"

"Whatever you can get out of him. I don't care. I just need to learn where the paintings are coming form."

Sasha already knew but didn't volunteer anything. "Fine."

"Good. Leave us alone and take my information how to contact me. Call my voice mail in an hour and leave me a phone number to call you back on."

"Very well."

"One more thing." Clayton waved his hand to encourage Tonya to hurry swimming. She tried to swim with dignity but the bottom of her dress had risen up to her stomach to accommodate her moving legs. "Say goodbye to Tonya. This will be the last time that you'll ever see her again. That's apart of my deal."

The Uncle remained still. Water continued to roll off of him.

"Do you agree?"

Sasha got up from the sidewalk that he'd been sitting on and left without saying a word.

Clayton watched him walk away. He turned his attention toward Tonya by helping her up out of the canal. He tried to ignore her naked bottom as she pulled her dress back down to cover herself.

The speedboat disappeared beneath the unlit lagoon water leaving a gasoline and floatation cushion wake.

"It's over Tonya. He should be gone from your life now."

He hugged her. Minutes later a police boat cruised by using it's searchlight on the water to look for something. They both held their breath as the police drove directly over their sunken speedboat. They wondered how deep their fiberglass craft had already sunk. Was it deep enough to avoid the cop's propeller?

The searchlight shined on them and stayed frozen.

Clayton grabbed Tonya and started kissing her. The light left them and the boat patrolled onward. As the police left their sight he released her. "Where to?"

"*San Polo*. The place overlooks the lovely *Ruga Vecchia San Giovanni*."

"It'll walk you there."

She glanced at the canal. Pieces of broken mooring pole floated close by along with a boat cushion. She kissed him on the cheek. Water still dripped from her hair. "I think I've had enough excitement of the night. I'm going to go soak in a tub and get into some dry clothes."

"Can I see you tomorrow?"

"Sure," she called out over her shoulder. Her silk dress clung to her body casting strange and exotic wrinkles. "My building is to the left of *Calle D Madonna* where it ends into *Ruga Vecchia San Giovanni*. It's four stories, eggshell white, and has a cracked window front door. You can't miss it. Third floor, Apartment 9B." She tugged on her dress snap the water out. "Come in the afternoon."

"It's a date."

Chapter 6

Yonkers, New York. January 2004.

Yurgi Svoboccen was a 43-year-old Russian gangster. Originally from Odessa, Ukraine, he snuck into the United States during the Cold War and claimed that he was persecuted by the Soviet government for being a dissident. He was granted political asylum shortly after. His new citizenship was the United States loss and Russia's gain. The man was a one person crime wave and he held allegiance to no one.

Yurgi's older brother Zandor sent word from Vladivostok to one of the Miami *Troika's* to sponsor his younger brother. The local mobsters passed the hat around and Yurgi found himself with a nice war chest of starting money. He set up shop with his sponsors in Brighton Beach; married a retail catalogue model named Talli, and started his own crime family.

Brighton Beach was like a fish tank exhibit at *Sea World*. A lot of sharks swam around in one confined space and all they knew how to do was act natural and feed. If the handler forgot to feed them then the likelihood of one shark attacking the others dramatically increased. After all, there was only so much food to go around and as predators they could each sense it.

Yurgi got smart. He moved his crew and coke-head wife to New York. He planned to compete with what was left of the Italians.

The FBI was brutal and Italians had gotten soft. The Feds threatened the Italian guys with massive amounts of time in prison verses the promise of little or no jail time if they rolled on the bosses. It was a no-brainer. Drugs had destroyed them and the labor unions had lost most of their power to strike and bargain because big business shipped most of the jobs off to Mexico and India. There was little left for those who were unimaginative.

The Russian mob was different. They remained all but invisible. Many of Yurgi's soldiers were ex-intelligence; KGB. They were trained in counter-espionage and thwarting surveillance. Yurgi's crew had discipline. The weak link in his chain was Talli. She almost destroyed him twice.

It was ten thirty at night when Big Tony showed up at Yurgi's legitimate business. Yurgi's miniature golf course was across the street from a deserted strip mall. Bright white floodlights, which the average mid-westerner puts up outside of their homes to light up their patio, lay mounted on top of vertical railroad beams that were sunk into the ground. They illuminated the artificial green turf that made up each theme hole.

Big Tony limped along as he approached the place from the barren asphalt parking lot. Snow and slush piles were pushed up into the waist-high chain link fence that separated the lot from the courses. Big Tony could see his breath pour from his mouth as he helped himself over the fence.

Yurgi was at the fifth hole. He stood in a peculiar position; his legs were together while his arms were spread out. He was attempting to knock his neon-orange golf ball over a narrow bridge that had a water trap on either side of it.

Two Ukrainian hookers held putters. They leaned against one another for warmth several feet behind him.

"*Dross vu-e Toe-varish*," Big Tony said phonetically.

"It is good to see you too my friend," Yurgi said with his moderate Russian accent. He was dressed in a red fleece jogging suit with white stripes running down both sides. He'd been alerted to Big Tony's car when it tripped an invisible laser beam in the parking lot. "You remember our language lessons in prisons."

"Yeah…but only Italian stuck." Big Tony approached him with a slight limp and then embraced him in a bear hug.

"Time has been good to you," Yurgi said. "You neglect me. It took two years after I am out for you to visit…no?"

"I've been runnin' for Crazy Paul."

Yurgi seemed amused. "Lastanzi. Old School. From B-House?"

"Yeah." Big Tony checked out the hookers. Each wore spandex tiger-strip pants and fake fur coats that ended above their belly-buttons. "Paul needed someone he could trust."

"Not *family*, eh?" Yurgi laughed like a weasel. "I told this man, he cannot do traditional. Today, we must adapt. Like computer commercial, *da?*"

"*Da.*" He winked. "So Yurg, you're lookin' good. How ya been?"

Yurgi leered at the hookers. "That piece-of-shit bitch-slut-whore Talli left me."

"Shit. Sorry."

"Dat bitch-slut-whore was fuck-ing Sal Goldenberg. Fuck-ing lawyer-to-da-stars. Big financial orgy. She fucked him." His hand tightened on his golf club. "And *he* fucked me!"

The two Russian hookers started drifting away slowly.

"Dat bitch-slut-whore lives with him in L.A. now. They have big new house and sports cars. I must pay her fuck-ing five thousand dollars every month!" He hit the turf with the end of his golf club several times. "They call dis shit justice! Fuck-ing allitory…allegory…ali…"

"Alimony?"

"Yes. Yes. Dis is what I am saying. The courts are the real gangsters, I tell you!" Yurgi whacked his golf ball. The tiny orange sphere bobbled along the thing grass runway and rolled hard to the left, falling into the clear water trap. "Shit!"

One of the hookers giggled and instantly regretted it.

Yurgi pointed the end of his club at her and then swung it to point toward the water. "Get my ball…*bitch.*"

The tall blond hooker scurried over to the water pool and stared at its reflective water, hesitating.

"Use your fuck-ing hand," Yurgi commanded. A mist began to roll off of Yurgi's head and joined his winter breath. "Or I push your face in to get better look."

She started fishing for the ball. Her fur coat and spandex took the water poorly. She was reduced to the image of a beaten French-poodle.

"You like?" Yurgi displayed his jogging suit to Big Tony in a fake model pose.

He shrugged.

"Dis is Nike-Tiger Woods shit, I tell you. Quality one." He pinched the material and held it toward his visitor. "I got ten of them. Same color and everything. Like scientist, Einstein. I don't fuck-ing bother to think of what to wear for day. I just wear 'dis shit."

"It's tight, Yurg."

"Oh fuck yeah jack." Yurgi amused himself with his prison-language spoof. Prison ruined Yurgi. "I clown dis shit to all my bitches." His weasel laugh rang out again. He squinted. "Ya know-what-I'm-sayin'?" He laughed harder.

Big Tony laughed along politely. He began to have reservations about making his proposal. He focused his attention on the deserted shopping mall across the street. His eye caught what seemed to be a small flame flicker from the mall's roof top level.

"So," Yurgi grunted. "What brings you to me, eh? Employment. You wish to work for me?"

"Nah." Big Ton sat down on a nearby bench. "I need to know something' about you."

"Da?"

Big Tony hesitated. "Hum…is you religious?"

Yurgi took a moment to think it through. No one he respected had ever asked him a question like that before. The golf course floodlights gave everything a washed out appearance. Two dark shades covered up the expression in Yurgi's eyes. I have religion. Yes."

"What I mean is…do you believe that priests are closer to God than you or me are?"

"Nyet. They are hustlers."

"So they're not sacred people to you?"

"Nyet." His eyebrow rose. "Why?"

"Cause I got one doing' some sick shit on video," Big Tony whispered. He used his fat knuckles as a screen to deflect his voice to Yurgi and not the hookers. "He freaked and now I can link him to the murder of his victim and the victim's family."

Yurgi lowered his head saying nothing. He shoved his hands in his jogging suit-top's pockets as his breath rolled out and drifted off into the night.

"Well, what d'ya think?"

"You are son of bitch." Yurgi's head rose. "You're shaking down priest!" A grimace formed from Yurgi's mouth. "You won't get much, Tony. He's a priest. The church will cry its poor, but not so poor they need to sell their gold crucifixes and gold leaf robes, eh?"

"This guy paid the family that got killed *two hundred thousand dollars* in six months before he had 'em killed." Big Tony leaned forward and thrust out two fingers. "The priest paid out two lump sum payments. Only two. In cash."

Yurgi's eyes became electric. The lightning bolt of quick cash struck him. Here was the chance to pay off Goldenberg and whack Talli. No more payments. No more calls. The bitch would finally be gone.

"Two hundred K, in six months, Yurg. That's not plate collection money that we're talkin' about here. That's bank." He produced a video tape that was stored in a box which was wrapped in black electrical tape. "I've done research on this guy the priest. He's a fuckin' Cardinal!"

"We are talking Catholic Church?"

"He lives and works in the Vatican itself. They used to move him around from church to church until they finally brought him home. He couldn't keep his dick in his pants. The sick bastard."

"You think he has more money? Maybe the two hundred thousand was his life savings."

"Doesn't matter." He leaned back into the wood bench gloating. "His name is Cardinal Francis D'Anglese. He's 58 years old and in charge of the Vatican's *art restoration and administration.*"

"Holy shit."

"Exactly." Big Tony shot Yurgi with a hand-gun gesture. "I'm guessin' he hawked a piece of art anonymously ta get the two hundred K."

"And he can do this again, *da?*"

"*Da.* Especially with the fuckin' tape danglin' in front of him. The family he killed were gypsies. As soon as he knew about the tape the first time, he tried to shake them by fleein' ta Rome. The gypsies found him somehow so he hired hit men."

"Fuck-ing Stalin killed all of your gypsies."

The soggy hooker came over from the water trap still dripping. Her simulated-fur coat was drenched. She handed Yurgi his orange golf ball.

Yurgi reached around her side and grabbed her ass. He spoke to her in Russian and told her and her girlfriend to get lost.

The two women traversed the miniature golf course brick walkway and headed toward the heated office trailer.

"There's a problem."

"Which is why you come to me."

"Yeah. The video tape was supposed ta be destroyed. Crazy Paul ordered me to escort the heavies from *Catania* to the gypsy house in New Orleans. They were supposed ta lean on the gypsy bitch and retrieve the tape. Somehow it all got fucked up."

"Lastanzi knows you have tape?"

"Hell no." His eyes widened. "I told him and some priest. Well, Gloria told Paul through the glass at Marion eight years ago. I told the priest on the bank phone. They think it's destroyed but actually I've sat on it ever since."

"Lastanzi has no reach anymore, Tony. You don't need my protection."

"This ain't about that, Yurg." He started coughing. The cold night air was affecting his lungs. He coughed up a large chunk of phlegm and blood.

Yurgi turned pale and patted him on the back as Big Tony tried to regain his breath.

"It's all right...I'm okay."

"If you say so." Yurgi tucked his own hands back into his pockets. "Why did you wait so long with the tape?"

"Loyalty."

"Lastanzi rat on you?"

"No."

"What then?"

"He treats me like I'm his bitch," he said softly. "Tony do this! Tony do that! Take the message to so-and-so. Take the return message to Gloria. I'm dealin' with that whore so often it's like we're married."

"This is reason?"

"Naw." He stared at the blood splotches on the brick between his feet. "I've got lung cancer. The oncologist wants ta get aggressive. Cut the shit out and radiate me." He rested his hand on Yurgi's shoulder staring at the ground.

"Sounds painful."

"It just buys time. Lung cancer is ninety-nine percent fatal. I just want to live large before I go out, ya know? Runnin' errands for Big Paul ain't cuttin' it no more."

Yurgi didn't respond. He patted Big Tony's hand and then pushed it off of his red jogging suit shoulder.

"It was the fuckin' chain-smoking in Marion. They say smokin' is all about givin' your hands somethin' ta do. I shoulda chewed on a toothpick instead."

"How long do you have to live?"

"A year. Maybe two." He put his hand on Yurgi's shoulder again... "When I told Crazy Paul he blinked twice and then asked me if I'd give some messages to Gloria!"

Yurgi shed Tony's hand for a second time. "You must be angry."

"Yeah. Like you over Talli."

The words stung Yurgi hard. Talli's sick laugh echoed in his mind. Yurgi kicked over a garbage can.

"You should whack her, Yurg. Her and the douche-bag lawyer."

"Her lawyer thought of this already. Before I knew she was fuck-ing him, she puts on sexy teddie, gets me drunk, and tells me she wants to be screwed by gangster. I tell her gangster stories as we did the dirty. She humped my brains out, I tell you. I told her lots of shit. Some true, some false. She acted all turned on!"

"So what, they found some witnesses from your stories?"

"*Nyet.* She recorded it. Every word as if a confession."

"Damn."

"Yes, damn." Yurgi ran his hands over his bald head. It was steaming in the cold night air... "I gave dat bitch everything and she took it all!"

"I supposed that if anything happens to either one of them the tape goes to the Feds."

"Yes, is true."

"I guess you feel for the priest then, hunh?"

He nodded yes, feeling the irony. "It is bad having axe hanging over you that can fall at any time."

"So you're out."

"*Nyet!* I am in! I tell you." He stuck his hand down his jogging pants and used his thumb to push outward to simulate an exaggerated erection. He gyrated his hips in a wide circle. "We fuck him good."

"Him and Crazy Paul."

"*Da!*"

"There's a problem though, Yurg. The priest. He's in Rome."

Chapter 7

Venice, San Marco. July, 2004

The *Piazza San Marco* was famous for its onion-domed Bascilica, vast Open Square, and bold, procrastinating pigeons. The heart of the 13th century Venice was here with the tan brick Campanile bell tower which overlooked the plaza and Doges' Palace.

The mid afternoon was humid and warm. The sun faded in and out between gray cloudy shades.

Clayton sat in an outside café chair near the golden yellow *Torre dell'Orologio* mechanical clock tower. Tourists and native Venetians milled about enjoying the day. Clayton rubbed the thick lump on the upper right side of his forehead. He still couldn't believe that his head had hit the speedboat windshield frame so hard, from the night before. He refocused his attention and searched the plaza for his contact.

A tall man dressed in jeans and a white muscle-shirt sat down in a wire-frame chair next to him. He carried a large flat suitcase with him.

"Keasley?" The stranger asked in a United Kingdom, English accent.

"Yes."

"Van Aucken sent me." The man produced a pack of Italian brand cigarettes. "Your ex-wife Laura wants you to contact her. She wants to renegotiate child custody and alimony payments. She knows that you're working for the company and she's threatened Mr. Van Aucken with disclosure to your mother; a major share holder."

"Obviously."

"Things have gotten out of control. Van Aucken has a board meeting soon and needs answers quickly."

"He could've said all of this on the phone."

"Here." The stranger lit his cigarette with a cheap yellow lighter, took a drag off of the cigarette, and handed it to Clayton.

Clayton held the smoke awkwardly between his thumb and forefinger.

The stranger moved slow and deliberately. He unzipped his black suit case and allowed the canvas flap to fall to the ground. A bronze engraving peeked out at them. The stranger pulled the rectangular engraving out of the case and put it in Clayton's lap. He made sure the front of the piece faced toward the Correr museum.

Two middle-aged Italian men lingered beneath a row of plaza columns. They trained their long lens cameras on Clayton and the engraving and frantically began snapping pictures at the sight of the engraving. One of the men cursed as several pigeons flew into his shot.

"It's an Albrecht Durer," the stranger said. "15th century art. The Nazi's stole it from a Jewish family in Czechoslovakia in 1939. The owner was named Ben Katzenburgh. He was arrested by the SS and sent to Buchenwald."

Clayton put the engraving face-down in his lap.

"We bought the company which initially insured it." The stranger took his cigarette back. "It surfaced in Lyon, France. Ironically our new customer bought the piece and wanted our head corporation to insure it. The initial company's policy was opened by a Nazi General and admits that the company insured the piece after it was confiscated by the SS."

"Damn."

"Yes. An obvious conflict of interest. Katzenburgh was survived by a wife and child. She's dead now. The kid grew up to become an attorney from Harvard Law School and he immigrated to Israel to become a full fledged Israeli."

"A dangerous combination."

"Yes indeed." The man put the cigarette on the ground and stomped it out; virtually unsmoked.

That's odd, Clayton thought. *Maybe he's trying to quit.*

"Van Aucken wants you to sell this piece to Renauld the Frenchman."

Clayton tried to hand the engraving back to the man. He wouldn't touch it.

"The Frenchman will know it is hot. You will gain a credible reputation with him. We'll be able to trace back the source of Renauld's rare art supplier."

"What about the authorities?"

"What about them? They don't know what's going on, nor should they. Everything's been taken care of. You work for Blackburn & Gosset. As our acting agent we will shield you from all liability and prosecution."

"That's a big promise."

"Van Aucken gives you his personal word. We're an international conglomerate, old boy. Boundaries cease to exist for companies like us. We have arrangements with almost everyone who is anyone. This is Italy. There can be…arrangements."

Fuck it, Clayton thought. *Van Aucken took a risk by hiring me and it's not like I have a lot to live for anyway. I wonder what Tonya is doing. Probably still drying out from the night's boat wreck.* The image of her wet, form-clinging dress slipped into his mind. He had wanted to grab her and hold her and tell her everything would turn out right. He wished someone would do that for him.

"Van Aucken will send you some forgeries to sell. Renauld will find you the customers and we'll give you different account numbers to park the funds in." He stood. The two cameramen in the distance appeared as if they'd caught his cigarette-stomp signal. "Just play the part, Clayton. We need you to establish trust with Renauld."

"Is this VanAucken's plan or yours?"

"He'll call you." The stranger put his hand out; palm facing upward. "I spent my last Euro on a water taxi. Can you help me out?"

Clayton handed the man an orange-and-white 50 Euro note.

The two cameramen burned through a second roll of film. One man with a camera spoke to the other. "I'm glad we've got him taking the money," he said in his native Italian. "Should we go and arrest him now?"

"No," his senior replied. "We're in the evidence building phase. Our source told us about the meeting to verify her story. Besides, no one would believe that the American bought a stolen engraving for 50 Euro."

"So what now?"

"We wait. The woman promised us more. She just says that she needs more time."

The engraving courier took the Euro not and shoved it in his pocket.

"Hey," Clayton said to him. "What did VanAucken say about the symbol?"

"Sorry?"

"I received a box from my boat crash last night. I took a photo of the symbol on the side of the box with my cell phone camera and sent the image to VanAucken's secretary. There were two old-world keys crossed. One key was white and the other gold. There was a shield between the key tops, and a red rope that ties the two keys together and loops through the key ends. There was a Latin inscription above it too, but I don't speak Latin."

The stranger hesitated. If he bolted then Clayton would become suspicious.

"Well?"

"Sell it," the stranger said. "Dump the cash into one of the accounts we gave you."

"What is it?"

"The bones of Saint Sebastion."

"What did the Latin text say?"

"Secret and Sacred." The stranger began to walk away. He glanced at his wristwatch to indicate the he was late for another appointment.

Clayton watched the man melt into a crowd of tourists. A pigeon approached and pecked the ground near his feet.

Clayton sat with the engraving resting heavy on his lap. The front side was facing the ground. He began to contemplate his next move as he spaced-out.

His sister Kathreen was screaming from the inside of his parent's car trunk. *"Let me out, Clayton!"* She screamed from the back of his mind.

Stupid bitch, he remembered himself thinking. *It'll only be until I can get high.*

The two cameramen snapped a few more pictures of their target. The American's mouth was practically open. He stared out into nothing with a stolen engraving on his lap. He had the look of a haunted man.

Chapter 8

Rome. April, 2004

Cardinal Francis D'Anglese appeared lost in his civilian clothing that he had borrowed from a parishioner. He was a heavy man with a mammoth fifty pound belly, pig jowls for a face, and upside down street-cone legs that tapered off the closer that they came to his ankles. He was 52 years old and never addressed the problem of his continuously disheveled gray hair.

D'Anglese followed and received permission to leave Vatican City from the new Pope, *Il Redentore*. He had lied to His Holiness by claiming that he needed to visit a local church in Rome to administer the faith. He was filling in for a friend. The real reason for his scheduled departure had yet to fully impact him.

D'Anglese was certain of only one thing. Cardinal Ferroli's men had botched the job they'd been given years ago because the tape had finally come back to bite him.

He was pretty sure that his new blackmailers were gypsies but he wanted to be sure. This time he was going to handle the problem himself.

The letter he had received a week ago told him to come to the Columbus Hotel. The beautiful Columbus had been renovated from a former monastery near Saint Peter's square into a warm commercial facility. The time for the meeting was set for noon. Room twenty-three.

The sky was overcast and promising rain.

Before D'Anglese entered the hotel he patted the steel bulge that he'd tucked into the front of his pants under his t-shirt. He was carrying a Glock 9 millimeter semi-automatic handgun. He was proud that he had acquired it without the help of his mentor, Cardinal Ferroli.

D'Anglese tried to keep a low profile when he entered the hotel. If he had to kill these people he didn't wish to be seen by any would-be witnesses. After slow and casual walking he arrived at room twenty-three.

He began to wonder if he had what it took to shoot a person even if they were a gypsy. Before he could bring himself to knock, the hotel room door swung open.

A short thin man who was wearing a red fleece jogging suit met him. "You speak the English?" Yurgi Svobbocen asked. "Because I speak no Italian, yes?"

D'Anglese felt ill. This man wasn't a gypsy. His accent made him Russian.

"Well? I wait for answer."

"I speak English," D'Anglese said. His voice was light, brisk, and effeminate. "Do invite me in."

Yurgi grabbed the priest's sausage arm and yanked him inside. The door slammed shut. Yurgi slipped on the courtesy security chain, activated the regular door lock, and propped a chair up under the door knob just to make sure.

D'Anglese wattled into the large bedroom with twin queen-sized beds. He noticed a stocky gentleman who wore a green-and-white football jacket. The man sat on the second bed leering at him.

"I profess that I do not understand why you have summoned me here gentlemen," D'Anglese said. Sweat rolled down his chubby face. "I do not know of any "tape" or anything else mentioned in your letter."

"Yet you come anyway," Yurgi teased.

"Sit down," Big Tony commanded. He brandished a television remote control in his hand like it was a hand grenade. A video camera sat on top of the modest television.

"Not until…"

Yurgi threw his fist hard into the priest by delivering a kidney shot into D'Anglese's back. The strike sent waves of fat blubbering.

D'Anglese fell to his knees gasping and groaning.

"Watch the tape," Big Tony instructed.

The television went from snow-static to black screen. Faded video bars briefly danced across the screen.

D'Anglese propped himself up from the floor. His eyes burned deep into the television. Hot spikes of heat shot up and down his spine.

A living room appeared that looked faintly familiar to him. A gypsy woman came into view. She stared straight into the camera. "I don't trust our babysitter, Misses Jameson. If she hits Mieko while we're away, we'll have proof this time."

She left the room and then came back in. She activated the family television in the video's background. She set it on the Cable News Network.

"She's usin' the TV news show to establish time and date," Big Tony explained.

A string of Russian phrases crackled out from under a pillow on the hotel bed closest to where Yurgi was standing. He pulled the radio out from under the pillow and responded in Russian while pressing in the radio's communication handle. "Is all clear," Yurgi said. "My guys say no unusual activity. Streets outside of hotel are crowded today. They'll keep me updated."

On the television screen a telephone rang off-camera.

"Hello?" the gypsy woman said. She waited a few minutes in silence. "Oh, I'm sorry Miss Jameson. That's terrible. Yes. Of course I understand." Long pause. "Well, we'll just find someone else to watch Mieko then. Call me when you know more. All right. Goodbye."

"That's good game," Big Tony said appreciatively. He fast forwarded the tape and looked at D'Anglese. "That's how she reeled you in, isn't it? She set it up like it was an abusive babysitter sting and then she left the camera on by a fake mistake."

D'Anglese crouched on the floor. He leaned against the bed mattress to use it as a backrest. His hands were folded directly over his semi-automatic handgun.

"We don't need ta hear the second phone call cause *you* received that one."

D'Anglese wanted to vomit. He knew what was coming. He'd relived it in his mind all the time. The memory was like a favorite painting. He enjoyed looking at it often.

"It must have seemed like a miracle. The perfect situation."

Yurgi giggled.

"She told ya the boy was retarded for Christ's sake! Fuckin' *retarded*!" Big Tony shook his head. "You couldn't get there quick enough, could ya? Did your fat ass run or did ya drive?"

D'Anglese watched the TV screen in fascination.

Big Tony slowed the video to normal speed.

A noticeably younger and slimmer D'Anglese entered the home wearing his priestly vestments. He brought his Holy Bible.

"I asked you a fuckin' question shit bag!" Big Tony kicked D'Anglese in the neck. "Did ya *run or drive?!*"

"I drove," D'Anglese scowled. "Please, stop."

"Is that what the boy said *father?*"

D'Anglese began to pinch the skin between his thumb and finger.

A young teen gypsy boy lay on the floor in front of the camera watching the news channel.

Young D'Anglese was grinning at the sight of the lad. He was shiny. Like he'd been oiled.

"I shouldn't be gone for more than two hours," she said. "No one should be coming by between now and then, so he shouldn't pose too much trouble. If he misbehaves you have my permission to spank him."

"Go with God."

"Thank you again, Father. I don't know what I would've done if you hadn't been able to help me."

"Really, it's not a problem." Young D'Anglese's knuckles were white from his continuous iron grip on the Bible. "Go now and have fun."

Mieko turned to his mother. He made a desperate appeal in Romani for her to reconsider. She spit out a harsh retort, smiled to the priest, and left abruptly.

"You're a sick fuck!" Big Tony belted D'Anglese across the face.

The fat cleric began to reach under his t-shirt for the gun but thought better of it.

"The gypsy knows," Yurgi said. "I cannot believe she makes him go along with dis shit. She is sick, twisted bitch."

"Like Talli and Goldenburg."

"Yes, yes. Like them."

The video played on.

D'Anglese sat up noticeably. His senses heightened. He leaned forward to get a better view of his younger self take off his white collar. His thick fingers began to fumble with his black shirt buttons.

Big Tony caught Yurgi's attention. Yurgi followed his lead and watched D'Anglese's face. The man was enthralled. He was projecting himself back in time to that exact moment. A bead of spit hung off of his lower lip as he salivated.

The TV screen went black.

Big Tony rested the remote control on the bed.

D'Anglese's anger at the interruption made him forget himself. *"Excuse me!"*

"Yeah, sure." Big Tony started kicking the fat man repeatedly. *"Excuse you!"* He kicked him in the head. *"Excuse you!"* He kicked him in the fat ass. *"Excuse you!* You sick perverted mother fucker! And you're the keeper of the word of God?!!"

Yurgi maneuvered behind his friend. He pulled and pushed him away from the cowering D'Anglese. "Tony! Tony! Tony!" He shouted. "Don't kill golden goose eggs, yes?!"

Big Tony spat on the quivering creature in front of him. Red welts were forming on D'Anglese's face.

"He wasn't retarded," Big Tony said. "I had to kill him cause of you!"

"I am *so sorry,*" D'Anglese sobbed. *"Please..."*

"You pay," Yurgi said. "You fuck-ing pay us *one-million US dollars.* Next year you pay additional five hundred thousand. Each year after, you pay us two hundred thousand."

D'Anglese drew out his gun and shoved it in Big Tony's face. His whole body trembled in terror. "I won't be paying anything to the likes of *you.*" He pulled the trigger.

The gun failed to fire. He'd left the safety feature on.

"Put gun away," Yurgi commanded. "We have *copies*. We have *associates*. People know of dis meeting. You shoot gun and all is over for you."

"I am a simple priest." His gun carrying hand began to waver. "I don't have that type of money."

Big Tony limped past the priest and reached for a stack of brochures that lay on the table that the television rested on. He handed D'Anglese one of the brochures and took the man's gun.

"That brochure says you guys have one of the most important art collections in the world. Paintin's and sculptures that are worth millions of dollars each."

"You're not suggesting..."

"Fuck yes he is *suggesting*," Yurgi said. "I own you now, bitch." Yurgi's weasel laugh hurt all of their ears.

"*We* own you now," Big Tony corrected. He eyed his partner and then snatched the brochure from D'Anglese. "You're the Vatican's art restoration guy. You paid the gypsies before, so now you can pay us. How you steal and hawk the paintin's an' shit is your business."

Yurgi slapped D'Anglese open-handed. "Just have our fucking money, fat boy!"

"Yeah. In *six* months." Big Tony seemed pleased. "We're flyin' back to the United States right after this meetin'. I fuckin' *hate* ta fly and so does Yurg. All the 9-11 shit has the Feds sniffin' up everyone's asses. We have to fly to Mexico and do all sorts of shit just to get around."

D'Anglese folded his arms and pouted. "Six months is impossible."

"It's possible."

"I won't pay." D'Anglese was still in denial. "It's an embarrassing *indiscretion*...surely. But not worth the type of money you're asking for."

Big Tony shoved a pile of faded yellow newspaper clippings into the priest's hands. "These are from New Orleans in '96. The year you had the teen from the tape and his family killed."

D'Anglese began to waddle toward the barricaded door. "You can't prove that I had anything to do with that."

"I got the tape," Big Tony called out. He threw it hard into the priest's back. "The shit on there is enough for motive. You're not safe from extradition on a murder. Catholic priest or not, you'll go to prison. Trust me, when I say you won't like what they do to sick fuckers like you in there. Hell *can* be on Earth, *Father.*"

"The Church won't believe these lies! I have standing."

"Your goons didn't kill the whole family, Father. There was a girl and her Uncle. I wonder how long the Church will protect you if those two get a copy of the tape and file a multi-million dollar lawsuit. I can see the headlines in the newspapers now: Holy Hit men Kill Pedophiles Victim and Family!" he snorted. "I wonder how bad the Church will squeal when an anonymous caller supplies the papers with a copy of the tape along with names and places."

D'Anglese halted. Reality finally caught up with him. Wiggle room had suddenly ceased to exist. "Very well then. I will have your money in six months."

"You better," Big Tony threatened. "I hate flyin'. If I come back to this shithole country...I will hurt you."

"I understand."

"Oh yeah. And ya better not try an' send any of your Italian friends on us either. We already thought about that shit an' if a crew shows up ta shake us down for the tape or ta kill us; you won't like the fuckin' results." Big Tony tossed D'Anglese's gun back to him.

"Remember," Yurgi said. "*We* own you now, bitch." He started laughing. "Now get the fuck out."

Chapter 9

Venice, Island of Torcello. July, 2004.

Uncle Sasha tied his modest rowboat to a mooring pole in the twenty-five foot wide canal that was directly in front of Renauld's house.

The island of Torcello was a strange place for Renauld to live on. It was a sleepy kind of island with crumbling rural buildings and long forgotten canals. Tall spear-like trees grew everywhere along with low hanging trees that boasted hypnotic orange-gray leaves.

Sasha had followed Renauld to his home twice before. He had learned to use the old world Byzantine church of *Santa Fosca* to mark the way. The church's long square bell tower loomed above the spear-trees off in the distance.

Sasha's wristwatch informed him that it was slightly past ten-thirty. It would be lunch time soon and his stomach was already complaining.

Thoughts of the early morning auction and boat fight clung to him. His niece was working the American and the fool had already fallen for her charm.

Sasha had taught her to be a seductress as a teen. He felt that she owed him.

Sasha surveyed the Frenchman's home. The two-story white plaster rectangular structure was in heavy disrepair. A hedge-row of spear-trees flanked both sides of the house. A granular pebble sidewalk swept by in front of the home separating it from the narrow canal.

He watched the ground floor stain-glass windows for movement as he approached the house from the front and moved to its side. There was a rusty iron gate that was squeezed between the opening of two trees.

Sasha lifted the gate's latch and helped himself into the home's backyard. Several quiet steps, an easy lock, and some guts gained him entrance inside.

There was laughing coming from the upper floor. The Frenchman and woman. She kept shrieking playfully like he was tickling her.

Sasha traversed the cluttered kitchen. Soiled pots and pans lay thrown about everywhere. A gray tabby cat balanced on the porcelain sink's ledge. The brave kitty licked a slimy coat of crud off of a frying pay and issued a low guttural meow.

Sasha moved close to the walls as he went down the hallway and up the stairs. He timed his movement when he thought the woman upstairs might be laughing. Eventually he reached a spot several feet away from their partially opened bedroom door.

"What will you do with our millions?" The bubbly female asked.

"I'm going to Switzerland."

"You want to be Swiss? I thought you were French?"

"Switzerland is the only place that's free, my love. They don't care what you do, who you screw, or what you believe in. As long as you don't fuck with their banks or corporations you're free from intrusion."

She giggled. "So what are you going to do there?"

He laid on his back staring up at the ceiling in thought.

"Come one, Rinnie. *Tell me.*"

"You'll laugh at me." He had never shared his secret with anyone.

"No I won't." She giggled again. "Now *tell.*"

"Okay, all right." He cleared his throat. "I wish to buy a Chateau in a dairy canton. I want to make a low fat cheese that doesn't taste like shit. I'll start a health food business."

She burst out laughing hysterically.

He slapped her across the ass. "You're very naughty."

She laughed even harder.

They kissed. The house became silent with the exception of the rustling of sheets and sloppy kissing.

A door opened and shut on the first floor.

"Renauld?" Tonya shouted. "Get your ass down here. Your victim almost killed me last night!"

Renauld and his female companion stirred in their bed.

"Shit!"

"Who is it?"

"It's complicated." Renauld pushed her off of the bed and onto the floor. "You can't be seen. Just get dressed...and...uh, hide."

"Renauld!" Tonya yelled. She began to head up stairs.

Sasha looked at the open bathroom door, the partially open bedroom door, and then a hallway closet door. He opted for the last choice and threw himself inside the cramped space without an afterthought. His cell phone began to ring.

Renauld pushed his woman behind the bedroom door which he opened all the way inward. He stood in the open doorway trying to look casual. His equipment dangled out of the open flap in his boxer shorts. His ears detected a faint cell phone ring which he attributed to his visitor.

Tonya reached the top of the stairs and met Renauld's look with a hardened return gaze.

"X...Y...Z," she said

"Pardon?"

"Your barn door is open and you reek of sex."

He glanced down and then righted himself. "Sorry."

"Who was the woman?"

Could she mean the woman behind the door? "Woman?"

"Yes, Renauld. The tramp in your motorboat that ran into us when we were leaving the island early this morning. I don't remember her being a part of our plan."

"That was Shannon." He ran his hand through his hair. His hair gel had lost its power. Sweat from sex had caused it to disintegrate. "She's an associate of mine."

"I've never met her before."

"She works in my glass shop," he lied. Shannon was his new partner. He planned to screw her in more ways than one. To insure his fortune

71

he played human chess with people. Every piece had to be sacrificed except for him. "You're becoming too demanding, my love. Just follow our plan. We're almost home free, okay?"

She nodded.

He outstretched his arms. "Come here."

She came to him and accepted his embrace.

"My little tigress. You know I'll take care of you," he cooed. "I've always taken care of you. We share a special bond, you and me."

Sasha breathed as shallow as possible. His pudgy belly pressed hard against the closet door. One good exhale would blow the thin wood portal open. He pushed his ear against the cell phone ear piece which was up against the wall.

"Hello?" He whispered.

"It's Clayton." There was silence. "You know the guy from the boat crash."

"Call me back in twenty minutes."

The closet was boiling. Sasha wasn't sure but he thought a moth or two was flying around him.

"Why did you come back?" Renauld asked.

"I almost got killed! We were boating and ..."

A sneeze erupted from Renauld's bedroom.

Tonya stepped back.

"No." He protested. "It's not what you think."

Tonya bolted past him into his bedroom.

Shannon stepped out from behind the door. She wore a pair of pink socks and white cotton panties. Her large breasts poked forward at Tonya in naked defiance.

"Hi." She giggled nervously.

Tonya's eyes traveled from Shannon's breasts to Renauld's face and back to the breasts again. She sniffed and left for downstairs. Renauld followed her and Shannon headed into the bathroom. She shut the door and turned on the shower.

Sasha cracked open the closet door. He listened, heard arguing come from downstairs, and a cell phone ring from Renauld's bedroom. He darted out into the hall and made his way to the ringing phone that was inside Renauld's suit coat.

Sasha attempted to impersonate the Frenchman's English-speaking voice. "Ello?"

"I can't meet you," a light, brisk, effeminate voice said.

That's good, he thought. *Keep your words short so you don't arouse suspicion.* "Why?"

"His Holiness won't give me permission to leave the city. He's holding a special meeting with the Cardinals. He wants to discuss new reforms for the Church including the investigation of our P2 Masonic friends."

"Oh." Sasha didn't know if this was supposed to be good or bad. By the sound of the man's voice it sounded bad. "So what now?"

"I don't know." The man kicked a chair hard. "His Holiness plans to announce new decrees. He calls himself, The Redeemer! Can you believe that?! There's no telling what he's planning! It's pure madness. He might even pull the plug on the IOR itself."

"I'm sorry."

"If that happens, it won't affect our arrangement, will it?"

What did that mean? "It depends," he fished.

"We can get a new bank. One with the same discretions. My associate Cardinal Ferroli can arrange it. Nothing needs to stop. I can't afford for us to stop. I'm rather in a bind, I'm afraid."

"Yes?"

"I need one million dollars. Five-hundred thousand in cash."

Uncle didn't respond. *Did he just say one million dollars?!*

"I needed it a week ago. I fear I've procrastinated."

"Why the rush?"

"They're leaning on me."

"Who?"

"A Russian and his friend. They've got me implicated in a murder. It's all over some filthy gypsies. Can you believe it? Hitler should have killed them all."

Sasha cringed. The SS had killed his grandfather in Poland. He wanted to reach through the phone and choke the bastard.

The running shower water in the bathroom stopped. Sasha knew that he had to hurry.

"Are you still there?"

"Yes," Uncle said.

"Can you help me?"

"I'll need product."

"Another painting?"

"Gold. Bring me stuff with solid gold."

"I'll send my usual courier."

"We should meet," Sasha said in his regular voice. The thought of all the gold distracted him.

"Who is this?"

Shannon walked into the room with only a towel wrapped around her waist. Sasha's presence startled her. She picked up her clothes from Renauld's bed. "Who are you?"

"Renauld's driver." Sasha put the phone up to his ear. "Call me back in an hour." He ended the call.

She held her clothes up against her chest. "From the hall you sounded just like Renauld. Since you're not, do you mind?"

Sasha put the phone in his pocket with his own phone and he left without further word. Renauld and Tonya fought in the kitchen. He helped himself out through the home's front door and raced to his rowboat to start its small inboard/outboard motor.

He knew Tonya had been holding out on him but he never imagined that it was like this.

Chapter 10

The Vatican. July, 2004

Cardinal D'Anglese walked among the dead. He was 25 feet beneath the earth in the grottoes of Saint Peter's Bascilica. A long line of Pope's lay entombed on both sides of him. He carried a large rectangular canvas painting case that he normally used for carrying restored paintings. Ancient dust met his nostrils as he approached his destination.

A dark velvet rope cordoned off a small passage that led off from the main underground grotto walkway. D'Anglese traversed the small tunnel until he reached a rusty metal door that boasted an ornate brass handle and latch. As he walked through the doorway he entered an enlarged chamber. Part of him couldn't believe what he was about to do even though he'd done it before.

Industrial light fixtures illuminated the fifteen foot wide, twenty foot long space.

Two Swiss Guards stood watch at the end of the chamber. They were dressed in all blue military fatigues and had accompanying berets. Each man brandished a semi-automatic sidearm and a communication radio on their sides. Neither man took special notice of D'Anglese as he headed for the recessed stone slab-blocked doorway that was positioned between them.

In Latin and Italian an inscription was etched onto the interior door slab that read, "Secret & Sacred."

D'Anglese always enjoyed entering this part of the room. Several clergy over many years had accidentally entered the guarded chamber by mistake and assumed that behind the guarded stone slab lay the sacred remains of Saint Peter himself. They were all wrong. Saint Peter was buried elsewhere but D'Anglese relished the thought that the two Swiss Guard mistakenly believed that they were guarding the man.

D'Anglese approached the Swiss Guard to his left. The guard stepped aside to allow D'Anglese access to a modern security box. The high tech electronic contraption was mounted into the white-and-gray hard rock wall.

D'Anglese produced a plastic card which he kept in a plastic holder in his inside cassock pocket. He inserted his card and waited.

"Voce riconosciment richiestro, per peacere dichiara ilsvo coqnome, il suo nome, e la espressione sacra," a prerecorded voice said from the black metal box speaker. It wanted D'Anglese to give his name and recite the sacred phrase. The box used the latest voice recognition software in its security identification check. The civilian market didn't have it yet. They'd have to wait another ten years. The software had one hundred percent accuracy and could identify you even if you had a cold.

"D'Anglese, Francis L.," he said. "Iesous Christos Theou yios soter." The Greek phrase had been hard for him to continuously remember over the years. I t meant Jesus Christ, Son of God, Savior; but he always had to fight the urge of mixing the Greek with Latin.

The electronic sentry authenticated his voice print.

The huge stone door slab began to slide sideways followed by the low rhythmic hums of the slab's hydraulic pushing/pulling arms.

D'Anglese stepped into a small five foot room that offered another recessed stone slab door.

He waited for the first stone slab to close behind him. The thought of suffocating, should both doors fail when he was stuck between them, terrified him. The Swiss Guard was forbidden to enter the vaults or talk about their existence. If he disappeared for hours, days, or weeks, no one would ever know. They couldn't talk about it.

D'Anglese put his eye up to a retina identification scanner mounted on the wall next to him. A faint stab of pain shot from his eye as a bright white swept over it.

"D'Anglese, Francis L.," the black box states as fact.

"Entra." The non-carved slab slowly slid open.

D'Anglese waited for the vast chamber's ceiling lights to flicker on. As they did a high pitched fan belt scraping air handler came on. The rooms recycled the same air and a carbon scrubber recycled the oxygen. An artificial climate and barely breathable air level was kept in an effort to slow ancient document decay.

D'Anglese hated the place because the low oxygen made him dizzy.

He stepped into the main gallery, knowing that the slab door was on a 15-second timer. The slab began to shut. He looked above the slab to a digital clock that was mounted over it. It was two o'clock in the morning.

He was glad that none of the other four priests who had access to the place were there.

Il Redentore used to work in the vaults for days at a time. The Church's history fascinated him and he always wanted to share his revelations when D'Anglese first started working there. The vaults had no toilet. *Il Redentore* never left on his two and three day benders. D'Anglese always wondered about that.

The main gallery D'Anglese was in was an amazing 600 feet long, 8 feet tall, and a claustrophobic 5 feet wide. Every 50 feet or so on either side were 6 foot tall hallway openings that led to smaller parallel galleries.

There were twenty-one galleries in all. They were originally Etruscan tombs close to the separate resting place of Saint Peter. The *cryptae* used to hold bodies hundreds of years ago until 1513, when Pope Leo X decided to store the Church's treasure there. The bodies were relocated and experts were brought in.

When D'Anglese had first started working there he'd studied the ancient blueprints that the Cardinal who would become *Il Redentore*, showed him.

Leonardo Da Vinci had been commissioned to do the Pope's renovations in the former tomb. The great artist and engineer took to the work by first expanding the empty crypts into wide shelf-like spaces and then he reinforced the ceiling with decorative wood beams. He devised a water-clock and water wheel system to open and close the original stone door slab at specific times of day.

The project had taken him two years to complete. He lived in a studio at the Belvedere as a guest of the Pope. A few of his water studies were left in his general notebook when he left while the engineering papers stayed behind, locked in the vaults.

The Da Vinci door system worked well for over forty years. Eventually the Church was forced to turn to various devote Catholic engineers over the ensuing decades to fix the thing and come up with a better solution.

A barrel-shaped bank vault door was used for a while until a former Pope decided to go modern-classical and restore the original design.

All of the materials in the vaults below were *separate* from the above-ground Vatican Secret Archives which were a part of the Vatican Library.

The Da Vinci vaults were the true secret rooms. No mention of the vaults contents were in any of the Church's card indexes or reference sections. The vaults contained heretical works, records of questionable financial practices and land confiscations carried out by the inquisition and political communiqués from the Jesuits where they played whole kingdoms against one another to carry out a greater plan. There were confiscated books, erotic art works, suppressed pagan teachings, forbidden archeology which disproved many of the church's tortured claims, and diaries of former Pope's which could never see the light of day because the public would never understand. The faithful would become confused and the Church could literally fly apart.

The Prefect of the above ground archives and ninety-five percent of the other clergy were never made privy to the existence of the secret vaults.

D'Anglese waddled down the main gallery. The overhead fluorescent lights hurt his eyes. The rare visitors to the vault never got used to the sudden change in light levels from that of the dark grottos to the sudden brightness of the vaults.

As he walked down the center of the narrow room he eyed the sacred texts and parchments. Each set of documents were stored in their own individual hermetically sealed stainless-steel box. To ensure further protection, clusters of the boxes were placed on each shelf in climatically controlled storage cabinets that were monitored by the central computer's security system. The steel boxes inside of the storage cabinets were all pushed together looking like a label-less compact disc collection turned on its side.

D'Anglese turned down the second hallway passage to his right. It was one of two computer rooms. Both rooms sported a monitor, keyboard, scanner, and hard drive. The hard drives were encapsulated in a steel wire cage which didn't allow access to the openings of the disc drives.

All of the vault's contents had been painstakingly scanned into the computer's hard drive. The process allowed any researcher who was interested in reviewing a stored work little reason to man-handle the original.

D'Anglese accessed the computer to locate a coin collection he'd read about in a 1994 insurance claim. A holocaust survivor had filed it with Krauffer Insurance Corporation, a then new subsidiary of Blackburn & Gossett International. His source inside the global giant said the collection was pawned off to the Church by a fleeing Nazi. It was the price for guaranteed safe-passage to Argentina.

In ten thousand years these coins will still be down here, D'Anglese rationalized to himself. *Helping myself is helping the Church. They don't need a scandal right now. They'll never miss them.*

"Eli Katzenburgh Collection," the computer screen displayed in Italian. "93 pieces. 19th-20th Century. Mint Condition. *Ambulacra II*, Wall B, 3rd Row, No AIIb3-838. Pius XII. 1941."

"B-wall, third row, 838," he said out loud to himself. He could have written it down but he was lazy. "Wall B…3rd row…838."

He lumbered through a maze of passages as quick as his chunky frame would allow. Once he found the current vault, wall, and shelf he produced his magnetic key card. He inserted it into an electronic slot next to the cabinet that he faced. He turned a silver four-pronged handle at the center of the third glass cabinet. A mechanical "click" and a violent hiss of air rushed into the cabinet. The glass window opened up and outward for him.

Like everywhere else there were rows of individually hermetically sealed boxes but these containers were slim and taller.

D'Anglese's chubby fingers skipped along the metallic numbers that rose out of the boxes sides. He located box 838 and stopped. He held his breath and listened.

An air circulation fan squeaked incessantly for another vault room. Its belt had been slipping for years but it wasn't like they could call someone down from maintenance.

Nothing else stirred.

He pulled the box out and laid it down on the smooth rock floor. He activated two cylindrical knobs at the top and bottom of one side and waited for the thin box to pressurize. A faint sucking noise emitted and then halted abruptly. The container was cold and heavy.

D'Anglese broke a plastic seal on the box's side and grabbed a special spindle hook-mounted on a screwdriver handle that was chained to the wall. The same tool was found next to every cabinet wall. He used the tool to pry open the box and remove the plastic coating.

Neatly placed rows of shiny gold and silver coins flashed before his eyes. They were all made in various sizes and pressed into a fancy black felt board. He opened his black canvas painting restoration case and placed the coins at the bottom of it. Sweat burned into the valuable round pieces from his guilty fingerprints.

Relax, he told himself. *They never look at this. They want to forget. Besides, you can't steal something which is already stolen. He sniffed. Here comes your gold Renauld, you stupid Frenchman!*

A full hour had passed when D'Anglese finished his pilfering. In addition to the coins, he'd procured an erotic Renaissance painting titled, *"La Fatale Seduzione,"* The Fatal Seduction; and a water-glass sized gold statuette of Isis. He shoved the statuette down his underpants up under his black cassock.

Part of him felt guilty. The Church had supported him most of his life and yet, another part of him enjoyed the thefts. Most of the brothers hated him and it felt good to kick them. Even when they didn't feel it yet. He figured that they probably never would. The vaults held so much, who would know?

"Working early, Father D'Anglese?" A voice asked in Italian with a Spanish accent.

D'Anglese fell backward into some closed wall cabinets and his butt hit the ground. His heart exploded; pounding relentlessly into the front of his chest. He swallowed hard and gaped upward from the floor.

Bishop Trevelyan stood over him, offering D'Anglese his hand to help him up.

"You surprised me," D'Anglese sputtered. *How much had Trevelyan seen?! Did the coins jingle? Did he hear?*

"I didn't mean too Cardinal." The Bishop was from Spain. He enjoyed the classic Spanish features although he had a bristle mustache and thick TV-screen shaped eyeglasses that intensified his dark brown eyes. "C-Wall, 900's. You're here to restore a painting, Cardinal?"

D'Anglese didn't answer. He hated Bishop Trevelyan. The man was a consummate social climber and his general knowledge of the vaults was uncanny. He was *Il Redentore's* new errand boy.

"Cardinal?"

"Forgive me," D'Anglese recovered. "I'm very tired. I'm afraid I must be leaving." The Frenchman was waiting for him.

D'Anglese felt the statuette's head press sharp into his lower belly. He remained on the ground until the Bishop withdrew his hand.

D'Anglese rose on his own. "What are *you* doing down here so early in the morning, Bishop?"

"I'm here to retrieve some documents for His Holiness." The man glowed with pride. "He hardly sleeps you know. He wants to do so much. The Church is going to be led through some major changes."

D'Anglese grabbed his canvas case and pushed past the Spaniard. "So I hear. Please don't let me stop you."

Bishop Trevelyan watched the Bishop leave. *That's odd, he thought. The Cardinal's stomach was pointy. What could he be wearing that juts out from below his belly like that? It's probably a diaper.* He grinned. *One of the new Velcro types with the flap sticking out.* Some of the Cardinals had problems with incontinence.

A lot of the older Cardinals wore them. Wine and weak bladders had certain disadvantages until modern technology came along.

Chapter 11

Venice, Island of Torcello. July, 2004

Tonya threw Renauld's soiled dishes onto the floor. The fine china shattered into dozens of white fragments. Her black hair danced in front of her glassy green eyes as she picked up more dishes from the stinking sink.

Renauld leaned against the kitchen doorway. He took her rage in and seemed bored.

Shannon called out Renauld's name from upstairs.

Tonya's eyes widened considerable. "You're a bastard! After all I've done for you."

He grinned. He was unashamed and kicked a piece of broken plate across the floor at her playfully.

She waved a plate at him. "So I'm out?"

"No." he lied. "It was just a friendly screw. She means nothing to me."

Her eyes began to water.

"Dear heart, you were never to know. It was an itch I had to scratch. You've had feelings like that. You know how it is." He walked over to her. Broken plates crunched beneath his feet.

She expected him to hug her.

He grabbed a hand-towel instead. A piece of food had jumped up on his knee from the last dish slam. He began to wash it off.

"Renauld!" Shannon shouted. "I'm hungry!"

Tonya shoved him. He responded by hitting her in the arm.

"You're supposed to be off fucking the insurance man!" He said harshly. "You know…get him hooked back on drugs. I have some moves to make soon."

"I'm hungry!" Shannon screamed from upstairs down into the floor.

"Shut up you silly bitch!" Renauld shouted up at the ceiling. "Come downstairs and meet me at our boat."

"You're taking her to lunch?!"

Renauld said nothing.

Tonya stomped on the remnants of the dishes on the floor as she headed for her bedroom. When she first moved in, he pretended to respect her. She was supposed to be insurance that Renauld would give Sasha a cut from Renauld's stolen art source. He kept the kid gloves on for a week and then got her unconsciously drunk.

Tonya's bedroom had peeling flower-pattern wall paper. There was a large closet in the corner next to some boxes where she kept all of her clothes.

She purposely ignored Renauld and began changing clothes. She stripped naked. Her flesh bounced slightly as she lifted each foot separately to slide on a pair of blue jeans.

Renauld lurked in the hallway ogling her.

She put on a white cotton tank top, brown loafers, and a red elastic twist tie around her hair which forced it in a pony-tail. "You can't cut me out," she said over her shoulder. "I'm pregnant."

The house went silent.

"Did you hear me, *dear heart?*"

He stormed into the room and spun her around. "You lie!"

"It's true." She rubbed her stomach. "Eight weeks."

"You've been fucking Jean-Phillipe," he protested. "It's *his*. Your baby is going to be brown and white, like *Gelati.*" The thought of her having an ice cream baby amused him.

"No."

"Okay. Okay. Maybe it's one of your college friends from the University. From the painting class. The sandy-hair American I've seen you with."

"You were my *third*, Renauld. The third out of my whole lousy life!" She shook her head in disbelief. "You..."

"What?"

"You *ruined* me."

She sat on her old bed and the mattress springs groaned. She could remember the sound of his breathing in her ear. His promises. His demands. How clumsy she had felt. He'd been very incessant, if not forceful.

"Do you know what it's like to come home and see your house burned down?"

He looked at his wristwatch. Shannon was waiting in his boat. "It's tragic, yes."

"My mother...father...brother, all dead." She was crying. "I wasn't here for a full week before you came on to me!"

"Single man. Single woman." He waved his hand non-chalantly. "You could have said no to me."

She grabbed a lamp. "I should kill you."

"You won't, my love. After all, I'm the father of your child."

The lamp sailed across the room missing his head by inches.

"I swear to Christ, you women are all crazy!" he pulled out his wallet. "Do you want me to pay for the operation or are you going to give it up for adoption?"

"Oh, I'm keeping the baby," she challenged. "That's why you're going to honor our deal."

"You are crazy." He laughed. "This will never happen! I won't allow it. In fact, I forbid it. It's just that simple." He grabbed four hundred Euros' out of his wallet and tossed them on the floor by her feet. "Get it killed. That's for the plane ticket. I know a good doctor in Nice. He's very discrete. The best."

Tonya charged over to him. She slapped him across the face.

He punched her hard in the stomach. "I'll do it again when your belly's bigger," he promised. "Get the operation!"

"I don't know why you want me to kill this baby but listen carefully. I don't know what the future holds but once I have this baby, he or she will *never* be told about you. *Ever!*"

He began to leave.

"In five, ten or twenty years when you decide that you're a different person who wants roots, you better not show up on my doorstep to meet this child."

He turned and faced her. He took a moment to study her face. "Are you really pregnant?"

She nodded vehemently.

"I see." He turned his back on her. "Go fuck the American."

She fell back onto the bed. *Does he believe,* she thought. *He's got to.*

Renauld headed toward his speedboat. A child was the last thing he wanted. His childhood haunted him.

His father Gerard had been a postman in Paris. He fell from a ladder at work and never got back up. After the accident, he sat at home in a big green chair enjoying state disability payments.

Renauld's mother left soon afterward. She was a Protestant and Gerard was a Catholic when they fell in love. Gerard's parents demanded that she convert and she hated Gerard ever since. Although it was his parents who forced the issue, she resented him for not standing up to them or even launching a protest. Renauld never saw his mother again after she left.

He became his father's go-get-it machine. Eight-year-old Renauld fixed the dinner, did the wash and cleaned the house. His father rarely left the chair. All he would do is eat marshmallows in between meals; ten bags a week for eight years straight. His father died in his fuzzy green chair. He left a horrendous wet-grease-body outline in his wake. It took six strong men to lift his body out of the house. The place reeked of onions and rotting fish.

No, Renauld thought. *I'm not going to be anyone's father. That baby is going to die before its born one way or another.*

Chapter 12

Rome. August, 2004.

Phillip VanAucken met Renauld under the fabricated 18th century Arch of Septimius Severus. The Arch was the entrance to Villa Borghese's *Giardino del Lago*. It was lunchtime and many Italians passed through the Arch to enjoy the artificial boating lake on the other side.

VanAucken was a British ex-patriot who earned his stripes in the American corporate arena as CEO of Blackburn & Gossett. He had learned to play things loose there. After all, the business of insurance was the ultimate scam. Collect thousands of dollars in individual clients' money, hire an army of attorneys with it, and use them to attempt to never give the money back when disaster struck. He loved it.

In the past three years he had played it a little too fast and loose.

He tried to off-set his indiscretions by placing large Black Jack bets in Las Vegas using the company's money. He had managed to lose another twenty million dollars but the casino comped him and he got to see the last show of Siegfried and Roy. One of the handlers took a picture of him petting one of the snow tigers. He had it framed and put in his penthouse office.

The company stock was under-performing. The Securities Exchange Commission had launched an investigation after several whistle blowers sent anonymous letters. Now it appeared as if the Holocaust survivors were going to get wind of the company's ties with insuring Nazi stolen art and the massive lawsuits would be raining down on them, just like the lawsuits against the Swiss.

VanAucken had personally certified the company books for the past three years and he knew under close scrutiny that they wouldn't hold up. He had written off the Black Jack losses as "Speculation in Futures" costs. He figured that he wasn't really lying. Black Jack was just like the stock market. You were knowingly gambling your money in a high risk venture where probability dictates the win/loss ratio. If he had won, he would have paid taxes on the winnings so he figured it wasn't like he was defrauding anybody.

His new plan was to bail. He had already purposely knocked up a Brazilian woman so he could enjoy their archaic immigration non-extradition law. The law states that you can't be extradited back to the country where your alleged crime occurred if you are presently living in Brazil and have impregnated or are the father of a Brazilian child. It was a very pro-family law and it wasn't like he killed anyone. At least not yet.

Renauld appeared stunned to see him standing at the Arch.

"How did you know I would be here?" Renauld asked. His English became thicker with his French accent from being flustered.

"I don't lose track of my investments."

"I don't like it." Renauld pouted. "We have a deal."

"I need you to hurry it along. I couldn't say what needed to be said over the telephone. Be practical."

Renauld held up a paper sack which contained 100,000 Euros in it. He also carried a long thin metal tube that held a rolled up painting in it. "I am being practical. You're delaying me from a very important meeting."

"Yes...sorry chap, but listen. I need you to begin handing the art you sell to Clayton Keasley. Have him place the orders from our usual buyers and divert some of their money into our sting accounts. The Guardia di finanza will be arresting him soon. I plan to disappear and frame him for murder."

Renauld snickered. VanAucken creped him out. The man was average in all physical respects and he wore his straight brown hair in the classic conservative braces-back. He always dressed in Brooks Brothers suits and wore gray neckties.

The man was a thinker. Renauld could tell by the way VanAucken looked at him. It was the same way that a snake stared at a mouse.

"I do not care to hear of all your plans, *Monsieur*. Just tell me what I need to do."

"Get Clayton to move some art, today."

"I'll use the girl."

"Make it happen old boy." VanAucken shook Renauld's hand. "It was good working with you."

Renauld watched the man disappear into a crowd.

Fuck VanAucken, he thought. *Just steal the money and claim it was the girl. He'll be running anyway and you'll be in Switzerland.*

Renauld Faucet surprised Cardinal D'Anglese by approaching him from behind. The Cardinal wore a large gray sweater and brown khakis. He sat on a fancy wood-and-iron bench that faced the calm glass lake and beautiful white stone temple of Aesculapius. An overgrown tree distributed the temple's right side but the Greek god of health could still be seen inside the temple between the front ionic columns.

Several swans frolicked in the water several feet in front of them. D'Anglese brought his large rectangular canvas case with him which he leaned against the bench side.

Renauld slid next to D'Anglese and tossed the paper bag he was carrying into the priest's lap. "One hundred thousand Euro. A friendly down payment."

"Excuse me!" D'Anglese felt up the heavy paper sack. "Where's the rest?!"

"I told you. I couldn't get the rest in cash. This terrorist shit has everyone watching everything."

D'Anglese was flustered. "We agreed on at *least* five hundred thousand, in cash!"

"When was this?"

"On the phone! Your usual number. I told you about the Russian... the one million dollar U.S., and I needed it last week. I told you His Holiness wouldn't let me out of Vatican City."

"I'm sorry, Father. Someone stole my cell phone." He suspected Tonya. She'd lost her mind lately. Shannon was too stupid to have taken it. She was his whore-of-the-month and he planned to ditch her at the airport in Madrid with heroin planted in her purse.

D'Anglese shifted his weight and sat on his hands. "Who stole it?"

"My assistant girl."

He waved his fat hand non-chalantly. "It is of no consequence. Whoever it was doesn't know what's happening."

Sasha strolled down the *Giardino del Lago* walkway with a modestly dressed hooker that he kept to his outside. He wore a golf cap to hide his balding head and he had shaved off his mustache. He stared under the hooker's chin as they strolled and focused his attention on D'Anglese updating Renauld on the Russian blackmail ring and the demand for one million dollars.

Renauld was pleased. D'Anglese would have to hand over a bunch of art for him to sell to get the money. Everything was falling into place perfectly.

"So how goes the Catholic world?" Renauld asked.

"It is absolutely terrible. *Il Redentore* is turning out to be quite the horror."

"What could be so troubling?"

"He has caved in to the carnal world. Last week he announced a new decree that affirms abortion as murder and murder being the greatest of sins." D'Anglese bent over forward. Blood was rushing to his face. "Since many unwanted pregnancies lead to abortion, and this condition results from having sex without contraception, he has declared it a sin *not* to practice contraception unless both parties want conception. Can you believe that? I am incredulous. The man is a radical liberal who must be stopped!"

Renauld grinned. "How *terrible*," he teased. "The nerve. He just saved millions of lives of the unborn and kicked AIDS square in the pants in the third world!"

"The decree is outright acceptance of…of fornication!"

"Like screwing little boys and covering up for each other, eh?"

D'Anglese winced.

"You priests are all the same. You pretend to be such moral people and yet you never practice what you preach."

"You're not Catholic! You can't know what you're talking about."

"My father was Catholic," Renauld's voice raised. "It cost my parents their marriage, which cost my father his life. I prayed and prayed for them. Nothing ever happened. Bills had to be paid above what father's disability check covered. I was practically pushed into crime."

"I'm sorry for your troubles," D'Anglese patronized. "But you can't possibly hold the faith responsible."

"No. The faith is never responsible and that's my point. How can something so flawed truly be the foundation of human beings as the Church tries to claim?"

D'Anglese fidgeted. "I really must be going, Renauld. Can you get me the other four-hundred thousand in the next several days?" He glanced around. Some man and his girlfriend had walked by in front of them four times already. He figured that they worked for Yurgi. "The Russian and his associate will be flying back out here again."

"And?"

"And they are quite perturbed with me. I fear for my safety."

Renauld tried to pet a swan that had approached him. It scurried away. "I'll see what I can do. Let us hope that my next batch of auctioneers are receptive." He reached into his pocket and produced a thin strip of paper. He handed it to D'Anglese.

"There are thirty-thousand Euros in this numbered Swiss Bank account. In forty-eight hours you will have the additional four hundred fifty thousand. Just like before. You'll have to figure out how to convert it into cash on your own."

"We agree on one million US dollars!" D'Anglese's face was flushed between red and purple.

"Your phantom caller did. Not me."

D'Anglese grabbed Renauld's shirt. "They'll kill me!"

"Don't be stupid. You're the cow that makes the mild. They wouldn't dare. They may torture you to let you know that they're not playing, but not to worry, in forty-eight hours your bank account will have one million in it because I had a good auction. I'm just reminding you up front that I only guarantee five hundred thousand."

"Yes, yes. I remember."

"Let's switch the paintings."

Renauld handed over his long metal tube to the disgruntled priest. D'Anglese handed Renauld the big square canvas carrying case.

"The coins you asked for are in the bottom along with the statue."

Renauld grunted. He didn't know what the hell D'Anglese was babbling about and he no longer cared. The priest had just handed him his retirement fund.

"Your artist's work has been slipping," D'Anglese complained. He unscrewed the cap on the thin metal tube. "I hope this canvas at least appears *aged* like the original I just gave you. The last one had no cracks or yellowing. You could tell that it was painted on a brand new canvas!"

"The replicas are only as good as the photos that you sent me." Renauld stood. "They never check the ones you take anyway." He started walking away. "Check the account in forty-eight hours, my friend. Adieu."

D'Anglese stared up into the dark blue sky. A train of pillow-white clouds rolled over him. The sun eased his pains and warmed his skin. He began to stand when a husky Arab gentleman in a gold cap approached and sat down. His girlfriend waved to them and strolled down the path on her own.

D'Anglese didn't pay much notice. He took a deep breath and began to rise from the bench.

"Did you bring my gold, Gypsy killer?"

D'Anglese froze.

The man kept the golf cap's rim down to hide his eyes. "I guess you doubted my tenacity."

"Who…"

"I'm the man who knows, Cardinal. New Orleans. 1996. You had my sister, her husband, and my nephew killed."

"I don't know what you mean."

"Father D'Anglese, I'm the one who loaned my sister the video camera that made the tape. Now, you may not like it but you're going to make me a very rich man." He swung his left arm around to punch D'Anglese in the center of his belly. "Where's my gold?"

D'Anglese began crying; his hefty chest rose and fell violently. His chin rested on his chest as he shook his head "no" from side-to-side.

"You'll pay, you bastard." Sasha grabbed a role of fat from the priest's side and pinched it as hard as he could. "In more ways than one."

"Why?"

"Shut up! We have details to discuss."

Chapter 13

Venice, San Polo. August, 2004.

Renauld and Tonya's third floor workshop apartment stared out from its Venetian Gothic style windows into the bustling *Ruga Vecchia San Giovanni* below. Vegetable, fruit, and seafood stands abounded on both sides of the street.

Evening was drawing near and several of the shops had turned on their lights. A soft rain had passed through an hour earlier and everything smelled fresh.

Clayton approached the apartment building for the fourth time in three days. Tonya kept leaving notes taped to the apartment door apologizing for standing him up. He vowed that this would be his last time visiting her. Sexy green eyes or not, he began to question whether or not she was worth all of the trouble.

Renauld turned out to be quite helpful. He had sent a blond woman named Shannon to greet him at his 57 foot long, *Lagoon 1999* Catamaran, *Rogue's Galley*. She brought along some amazing erotic Renaissance art and asked if he wouldn't mind using his contacts to sell them on behalf of her benefactor. She claimed that Renauld had fallen ill with food poisoning and Jean-Phillipe had returned to Paris. She gave him a series of bank account numbers to deposit the money in.

Clayton couldn't believe his luck. The sale of the art was just like his employer Mr. VanAucken had wanted. Clayton was amazed that the Frenchman had come to him instead of the other way around. He figured that it had to be the girl. Tonya must have sent Renauld his way in return for getting her Uncle off of her back.

Everything was falling into place nicely. He'd have a report for VanAucken in another week.

Clayton was recycling the same three outfits that the company had rented for him. He was dressed in the same Miu Miu whicker-yellow-white wool tweed suit and Van's sneakers.

Clayton noticed a thin man with a three o'clock shadow grown on his face who leaned on a building's faded purple wall. The spot was directly across the street from Tonya's. He'd been there every day Clayton came to enter Tonya's building.

The strange man held a copy of the *Il Corriere della Sera* newspaper. He was pretending to read it but every few seconds he would glance upward, see Clayton staring, and then he would look back at his newspaper.

Clayton loitered outside of the building, openly watching the man. He never turned the page on his paper for over five minutes.

Okay, he thought. I'm under surveillance. He bolted inside of Tonya's apartment building when the man glanced back down at his newspaper again. He made his way up to apartment 9B. There was no note on the door and he no longer cared. Shannon had furnished him with a key. He slid the key into the apartment's modern lock and helped himself inside.

Tonya's apartment was extremely cluttered. Boxes were stacked up everywhere like she never expected to stay.

A radio was on, blasting Italian pop music.

Tonya was in the kitchen making tea. She turned toward Clayton's direction with a fresh made steam kettle and poured the scalding hot water into two tea cups before she looked up. She jumped causing the kettle bottom to scrape the top of the tea cups when she saw him.

Clayton gave a half-wave with his hand and turned off the radio in the common room.

The apartment was simple in design. The lone entrance door opened into hallways that faced the exposed kitchen and common room. A bedroom was off to the left side along with a bathroom. Both doors to the rooms were closed. Unbeknownst to Clayton, the bedroom had been transformed into a painting studio.

Teddy bears littered the common room that he found himself standing in. The fluffy beasts were everywhere; on shelves, tables boxes, and on the couch. Clayton guessed that there were well over two hundred.

Tonya remained in the kitchen. "How did you get the key?"

"Renauld."

"How nice of him."

"I thought so." Clayton picked up a stuffed polar bear.

"No courtesy knock?"

"I figured you'd just give me another note." He tossed the beast onto the couch. "I really just came to get my painting. Your former employer wants me to take it to the Doges' Palace before six o'clock. Someone's supposed to be waiting at the Palace's *Porta della Carta*."

"Yes. The Palace's main gate. It has a marble lion with wings hanging over it. The creature's front paw holds open a marble book."

"Yeah, well, it's a big deal so I've got to get moving." He made his way over to a long pair of velvet curtains, parted them, and peered out into the street below. The man with the newspaper was still standing there looking up toward him and then at the building's ground floor entrance door. "I don't want any complications to arise." He let the curtains shut. Tonya stared at the closed bedroom door and then at Clayton. "How about dinner?"

"You stood me up."

"I had obligations."

He sat down on the couch. His weight crushed some of the teddy bears next to him. His back faced Tonya and the bedroom.

She left the two cups of tea and joined him. He pulled out his antidepressant medication, popped the lid, and dry swallowed one of the pills.

Tonya kneeled down in front of him to get a look into his eyes. "I'm sorry that you felt stood up," she said softly. "Renauld is an asshole. I guess I became too obsessed with him. He's all I had for a very long time. I made him my family, my friend, god...I made him *everything*. It's hard to give up a habit like that."

Clayton knew all about habits.

"Trust me. Do not go and make that sale."

"I can't. It's my job."

She started to say something and caught herself.

"Just bring me the canvas," he said.

94

"Only if you'll have dinner with me."

Sasha delicately opened the bedroom/studio door and peered into Clayton's back. Tonya pretended not to see him. Sasha had heard everything. He figured that this was his chance to screw the Frenchman. It would be the perfect backstabber.

Sasha carried the painting that Clayton was supposed to sell. The canvas picture was contained in a bright orange stainless steel rectangular carrying case. He crept down the hall and out of the apartment. He was heading to the Doges' Palace. He had a stolen painting to sell.

Clayton remained very still. His depression rose inside of him in waves. The tide was coming in and he hoped that the medication would kick it. He was supposed to take his pills regularly but he hated relying on science to carry him through.

"Well?"

"Sure," he mumbled. "Maybe I'll leave you a note this time."

Tonya disappeared into the painting studio/bedroom. She had painted some of her best forgeries there. She grabbed a canvas, wrapped it in a brown tarp, and tied it up in string. She brought it out and put it in his lap. "Take your time getting there."

He was confused by all of her strange hints. "What do you know?"

I know I'll be free of my Uncle, shortly, she thought.

"So now you're the silent one, eh?" Clayton handed her one of her own teddy bears. "I guess we all have our secrets." He snatched the tarp-wrapped painting and left in a hurry.

The man with the newspaper talked into a microphone hidden under his jacket collar and then he started to follow Clayton down the street.

Clayton walked faster. His painting jostled up and down and all about.

The newspaper man spoke urgently into his jacket collar.

Clayton broke out into a full run.

"*Fermate!*" The newspaper man shouted at him. "*Polizia!*"

Clayton shoved an old man to the ground to slow his pursuer.

Boat sirens blared from the nearby canal.

Clayton closed in on the Rialto Bridge. He hurled the painting into the canal as he scaled the bridge's steps. One of the policemen in the police boat under the bridge dove into the canal to save the painting. Their source had claimed that it was very rare.

Clayton was tackled by two undercover policemen as he came down the other side of the bridge. They shoved him hard into the pavement as he wheezed trying to catch his breath.

It's a set-up, his mind screamed. *Renauld used you as his patsy! You're screwed…they've got you with everything…Oh my God, I'm going to do time in an Italian prison!*

"You thought you were *so* smart," a plain clothes officer said to him. "We were onto you last week."

Clayton stared up from the pavement toward the police boat.

The policeman in the craft held the tarp-wrapped painting high in the air like it was the Stanley Cup hockey trophy.

A crowd had gathered on all sides of the bridge.

The policeman cut the string and pulled off the tarp that covered the painting. A plain white canvas stared back at them.

Clayton grinned. "I confess, officer. I've decided to learn how to paint. My girlfriend bought it for me."

"Then why did you run?"

"I was late for an appointment."

The policeman began cursing in Italian at a speed in which Clayton couldn't translate.

"Do I need to call the United States embassy?" Clayton asked.

The head investigator scowled and dismissed him. "Let him go but seize his passport."

Clayton was uncuffed.

Chapter 14

Venice, San Marco. August, 2004

Sasha boarded a black hulled, white roof, water bus at the floating *San Silvestro* water station. The sleek economic transport headed down the Grand Canal stopping at various water stations and point of interest. The trip wouldn't take long before the bus would reach his destination; the Doges' Palace.

Sasha clutched a bright stainless steel carrying case that held the Frenchman's painting. The bus was crowded. The evening throng was heading out to bars and restaurants.

Light blue water danced off of the boat's side as it glided down the canal.

Sasha used his cell phone to dial Renauld's voice mail service. He knew that Renauld only checked it in the morning time. The messages were always left by would-be auctioneers who wanted to know when and where the next sale was.

Renauld's recorded message came on over the phone. "Ello. You have reached…Renauld. Please leave your name, number, and time you wish me to return your call." The phone line beeped three times.

Sasha made sure no one was directly next to him to over-hear. He held the phone out over the open window and began to speak. He wondered if the grumbling boat engine was also being recorded with his voice message.

"Hello, you robbing bastard. Does my voice sound familiar to you?" He laughed. "Good. I want you to know that it was me who fucked you. I stole your painting and now I'm going to sell it to your guy and them I'm going to pocket our money. What do you…"

The message recorder emitted a high sonic tone. The recording had stopped.

Uncle cursed and redialed the service to continue his message. Several people were staring at him. He appeared very strange as he partially hung out of the boat's open window, talking into a cell phone. Many figured his phone had piss-poor reception.

"In two days I'm going to leave you an account number. Start kicking me regular payments of ten percent on all of your future sales. If you refuse…I'll snitch on your fat priest friend to the new Pope. Then no one wins, eh? Be seein' you."

Sasha jumped ship at the *San Marco Vallaresso* water station. He walked past the Archaeology museum that faced the San Marco canal. The view of the pink Veronese marble of the Doges' Palace soothed him.

Pigeons loitered about everywhere. Sasha was weary of stepping on them as he went. He didn't wish to draw undo attention to himself.

The Doges' Palace was finished in the 15th century and had held up well over the years. On the ground level, white Istrian stone columns and arches assailed the eye from two angles. Directly above the arches laid the second story loggia in which each arch of the ground level supported two arches above it. The pink marble was designed in a grid of pink-white diamond shapes and the roof top had pyramid-style spikes set against one another.

Sasha headed to the Palace's main gate; the *Porta della Carta*. A man in his forties held a green duffle bag in his hand. He was standing five feet in front of the Palace's decorative gate door. A Municipal policeman was casually talking to the man as if they were good friends.

Sasha waited for a few minutes.

The Municipal policeman grabbed his radio after hearing something alarming come from it. He patted his friend on the shoulder and began to run past Sasha toward the Grand Canal.

The man with the bag began to leave when Sasha rushed him.

"You're the buyer?" Sasha asked. Renauld's money was on his mind and he couldn't wait for the payoff.

The buyer was taken aback.

"Your bag, the gate here...I'm the guy with the painting that you want."

The man hesitated. "I thought you were blond."

"He's been sacked," Sasha lied. "I'm the new guy. You have to go through me now."

The man tapped the top of Uncle's steel case. "That's the painting?"

Sasha nodded proudly.

"The one taken by the Nazi's?"

"I believe so. Obviously it's illegal and rare as hell."

"Good, good." The man handed Sasha the green bag that he was carrying. "Here's the money."

Sasha gave the man the steel case and unzipped the green bag. There were phone books in it.

When Sasha looked up, he had a gun shoved in his face. The undercover police officer meant business. "Get on your knees! You're under arrest!"

The other policemen had scattered from the radio call for assistance in running down Clayton in San Polo drew policemen everywhere.

The undercover policeman handcuffed Sasha, who was still in deep shock. He searched the old gypsy and discovered Sasha's wallet, passport, and two cell phones.

The cop dangled the cell phones in front of Sasha's eyes.

"I wonder who this will lead to when we trace the addresses to this cell phone redial."

The thought of his vicious message to Renauld bit him like teeth of a rabid bull-shark. The police could now piece together everything. Renauld, D'Anglese, Tonya, and Renauld's new girl. He realized that the meeting was a trap for Clayton and even worse, Tonya knew, yet said nothing as he snuck out of the apartment right in front of her. He felt he should have realized that it was a sting when he saw the buyer talking so casually with is uniformed policeman friend. He felt monumentally stupid. He lowered his head in shame.

"Don't worry," the officer assured him. "You won't be lonely. We've already got your mulatto friend in custody. Your girl played on too many cards in her efforts to ditcher partners. Now you're all going down."

"I'm an American citizen," Sasha responded mechanically. "I have committed no crime and I wish to speak to a representative of my government."

He helped Sasha to his feet. "I think you're a little beyond their help, my friend. But suit yourself. We'll give them a call."

You bitch, he thought of Tonya. *I should have cut our throat in Louisiana when you were orphaned.*

He wondered if the American Embassy would discover that his passport was a forgery. He was Romani. They never kept proper paperwork. A bad feeling hit his stomach. It was over.

Chapter 15

The Vatican. August, 2004

Cardinal D'Anglese sat in the tiny ornate wood-panel confessional in the Pauline Chapel. As a fat man, confined spaces made him uncomfortable. He was sweating profusely.

Cardinal Lucius Ferroli sat in the opposite confessional. He observed D'Anglese through the confessional's ornate grated metal screen.

Ferroli was a frail old man with gray-dark yellow teeth. They were rotting and had been for quite some time. He had a big nose, wrinkled face, and a continuous scowl which was chiseled into his mouth.

Both men wore black trousers, a collarless black shirt, a white clerical collar, and a long white cassock with a red sash.

"Thank you for your *valuable* time," Cardinal Ferroli said in scathing Italian. "I would have mailed you a letter but you know how long it takes our post."

"I'm very sorry, *Monsignore*." D'Anglese patted himself with a lace handkerchief. "I have been extremely preoccupied."

"Off administrating the faith I hope."

D'Anglese wouldn't meet Ferroli's eyes. "Yes. There are a lot of needy people out there."

"This I know, Francis. It is one of the reasons that we are meeting here."

"I'm sorry?"

He sighed. "There has been a scandal, Francis." His old wrinkled hand activated a micro-cassette voice tape recorder as quietly as possible. The slim metal box emitted a faint metallic click. "So far, the news has reached only the inner circle."

"The P2 or…"

"Yes." Taping had its disadvantages. "His Holiness is most displeased. I fear that a lot of stones are about to be uplifted."

More sweat formed on D'Anglese's portly head. He squeezed his gold and ruby crucifix for comfort and said nothing as his former mentor continued.

"A poor forgery has been found in the Secret vaults. The original can not be found. It was a disgusting painting made in the Renaissance era. The subject of an orgy in a Roman bath house. His Holiness has ordered an immediate and full inventory of the vaults' contents. He is personally conducting the investigation."

"Who discovered the forgery, *Monsignore?*"

"Bishop Trevelyan. Yesterday evening."

D'Anglese patted his brow with his hanky. He wondered how much Trevelyan knew what he'd seen. "I'm sure he blames *me.*"

"Your name is one on a short list of suspects, Francis. You are one of four who has access to this area."

D'Anglese put his face a half-inch from the screen. "This is a set-up if I've ever seen one, Father. It was the Spaniard, *Monsignore*! He is a filthy liar and cheat!" D'Anglese's feminine voice became worse with heavy lisps on his s's. "How did he gain access to the vaults in the first place? *Positioning.* That's what I say." His finger pointed upward defiantly. "He's been in *Il Redentore's* pocket from day one! He's been kissing well below His Holiness' ring."

Ferroli swatted the screen with his hand. The iron gate vibrated from the heavy smack. "Control yourself, Francis! Know your place and curb these insults of yours immediately! You cry foul a little too desperately."

"I'm sorry, Monsignore. It's just…"

"I recommended you for this position, Francis. If blame comes, a large portion will be served to me. Cardinal Ciatti will see to that."

Both men paused to collect themselves. The thin confessional seemed as if it was boiling.

"This is a serious matter, Francis. I need to know how bad the situation is. What else can we expect to find missing?"

D'Anglese stood to leave. "I have nothing to do with this."

Ferroli slapped the screen repeatedly. "Sit down, Francis! There's no profit in deceiving me. I know of your...*indiscretions*. They found you once in America and I thought I saved you from yourself. Obviously, someone must have found you again."

D'Anglese sat as commanded. His voice had softened. "I was at the funeral when they buried your mother. I helped you refinance your brother's real estate deals with mother church's money. I thought we were friends."

Ferroli suddenly wished that he hadn't been recording their conversation. "We are friends, Francis." He displayed a faint rotting smile. "That is why we are two old men trapped in a confessional trying to protect one another. What did you think we were doing?"

He didn't answer. The question stunned him. It was the gypsy in the park that bothered him. *Gypsy killer.* That's what it all came down to in the end.

"Francis, you must be careful. His Holiness has ordered the Swiss Guard not to allow you or the other three men to leave the Vatican City until this investigation is over." Ferroli glanced through the grate at D'Anglese. "In effect, you are under Papal arrest. The Swiss Guard will be escorting you to the Papal Audience chamber in three hours from now."

The color drained from D'Anglese's fat face. "I see."

"The Swiss Guards have turned in their Halberds for modern side arms."

D'Anglese swallowed hard. He dropped his handkerchief on the floor oblivious to the sweat beads dripping down his face. A red hot jolt of energy tingled in the pit of his stomach and shot up his spine.

"The audit of the vaults could take over a year," Ferroli assured. "They plan to start with the paintings first. Obviously the financial records, manuscripts, and other works will take up additional time. They must open them from their protective casings in low oxygen for inspection. The Pope wishes to take no chances."

"So what are you saying?"

"I am asking you, if you have anything to confess to me and *only to me*." Ferroli's nose pushed against the black metal screen as he leered at his colleague.

D'Anglese could smell his mentor's rotten breath. He hesitated for a moment. "No, *Monsignore*. My conscience is clean." He sat on his hands. "It was the Spaniard, Bishop Trevelyan."

Ferroli shut off his tape recorder. If he used any of it, he knew he'd have to do some serious editing. "Very well, Francis. I shall leave our fate to providence."

"*Monsignore?*"

"Yes."

"Do you still talk to *the family* that lost the two brothers who helped us?"

Ferroli kicked the panel wall that separated them. "You know not to talk of this! Not ever!"

"I feel that I owe them, *Monsignore*. I just want to make things right."

"You owe them nothing. They did their service for me and they are still in my debt."

"So you could call on them again?"

Ferroli tilted his wrinkled head. "If I needed to. Why would I need to, Francis?"

"You wouldn't…uh…you won't. Not for me." He dry swallowed several times, realizing that his spit had left him. "I was just thinking about the Spaniard."

"You're very considerate, but I feel the Swiss Guard have him well in hand."

"Yes. Well, if that's all, *Monsignore*. I have morning prayers to attend."

"Just remember to act surprised when the Pope tells you the news, Francis. We never had this conversation for both our sakes."

D'Anglese left the steamy confessional. He felt as if he had evaporated away ten pounds.

Ferroli remained behind. Now he knew. D'Anglese was the guilty party. Ferroli liked the man but *Il Redentore* was no fool. The liability that D'Anglese posed to the brotherhood was too great and the IOR subject could not be brought back up if it was to still survive.

He began to contemplate his future orders.

Francis D'Anglese was about to suffer a fatal "accident."

Chapter 16

Venice, San Polo. August, 2004.

Tonya's apartment building had mysteriously caught on fire just as Clayton had been arrested. The building's residents evacuated as an anonymous soul banged on all of the doors urging everyone to get out.

The Venice fire department was called to duty along with the police.

The Chief of the Municipal Police left Clayton standing at the Rialto Bridge after he seized Clayton's passport. The Chief wanted to question him but he had to go and supervise the fire and its associated crowd control. As he was leaving he ordered Clayton to appear at the stationhouse for questioning at noon the next day.

Clayton decided that he better call VanAucken. The investigation had turned into a disaster. The sight of a large red-orange glow and black billowing smoke roused him. He hurried down the *Ruga Degli Oreficil* until he reached the main street of the *Ruga Vecchia San Giovanni*. His heart sank at the view of Tonya's apartment building being engulfed in flames.

A woman with a baseball cap and reflective sunglasses bumped into him. "Excuse me," she said in English. She grabbed his hand and pulled him along. "Keep walking," she urged. She shoved a dark blue booklet into his jacket pocket. "I believe that you lost that."

He started to take it out as she stopped him. "Don't bother. It's your passport."

"But…"

She smiled. "I'm not only a budding arsonist, but I can pick pockets too. I saw him carrying it and figured it was yours."

"Where are we going?"

"My boat. It's parked on the *Rio Delle Beccarie.*"

They threaded their way through the on-coming throng that was heading to the glow in the sky. Everyone liked watching an unfolding disaster whether they admitted it or not. Tonya kept a cheating watch over her shoulder as they maneuvered around each other strolling couples.

"We've got a tail," she said.

Clayton started to peek. She yanked his hand.

"Don't let them know that we know."

Two men were following them. One made no effort to hide a bulky communications radio that he grasped in his hand. He lifted it up and mumbled something in it.

Tonya's boat was a modest fiberglass two-seater with a single long white plastic seat. A large black outboard engine was latched onto the back of it. A purple-yellow gasoline slick floated around the engine in light blue canal water.

She leaped into the boat and brought the engine to life. "Untie us!"

Clayton undid the first rope loop off of a wood mooring when Tonya juiced the throttle. He pulled the second rope off just as the line went taught.

The two men seemed unphased. They both ended up at the spot on the sidewalk where Tonya and Clayton had just been standing. The man with the radio calmly issued orders into his radio.

Tonya urged the boat forward at full speed. Four bridges passed over them as they shot out into the Grand Canal. She forced their nimble craft to heel hard right, up the canal. Tiny canal ways came into view on either side of them. She gunned the craft into the *Rio del Santi Apostoli* and slowed the boat to cruising speed. "We'll keep turning down this small canal way for a couple of hours until they think we've given them the slip."

"Now it's you who keeps rescuing me," Clayton said. "I don't know anything about you."

"Humor me."

"Okay." She grinned the steering-wheel hard. "I was born in a prison. My mother was incarcerated for assault with a deadly weapon. She was released when I was two years old. I never went to school, nor made lasting friends, or lived like an outsider. That was me and my brother Mieko's dream. We wanted to find a place we could call our own, forever."

"Where's your brother now?"

"Dead."

"Oh." He suddenly felt stupid. "What about your parents?"

"They're dead too."

"I'm sorry."

A fast cruising water taxi motored up several feet behind them. One of the passengers held a communications radio in his hand.

"They're tailing us."

Tonya ignored him. She had been wanting to release her thoughts to someone for a long time. "I want to be *normal*, but I don't know what normal is. I want to live a straight life but I've been raised crooked. I don't know where or how to start out, you know?"

"Uh...yeah. I can understand that."

"What about you, Clayton. I bet you lived a normal life."

He started laughing bitterly. "Not even close, sweetie. You're not even in the ball park anymore."

Tonya turned their boat hard left at the last second. Their boat eased down the *Rio di Santa Caterina*. She threw their vessel into reverse, making it virtually stop in place. The canal entrance was blocked and since the water taxi lacked brakes it was forced to drive by them.

Tonya slammed their boat's throttle to full power and the engine roared in protest. They zoomed past a police station and had three more bridges zip overhead. She was making a break for the *Rio di Noale* canal where it split into a fork offering two separate canal choices. She raced to a separate third side canal in hopes of confusing the water taxi that wasn't in sight.

The bullet Clayton had converted to a necklace bounced against his chest. "I'm a disaster."

"I doubt it."

Clayton tossed his plastic bottle of antidepressants into her lap. "Then what do I need these for? To see rainbows and ponies?"

Tonya tried to read the pill container while trying to drive. He was turning out to be someone she hadn't figured him to be.

"I have two daughters," he said softly. "Each one has a different mother and each one hates me."

Tonya saw a slim barge that was tied to a house that was being remodeled. She pulled their boat up to the front of it where she backed up to tie them in. Their boat would be invisible to anyone who happened to look down the canal from the direction that they'd just come.

Clayton studied her face for a reaction. Her features remained static. He fixed his gaze on her green eyes. They captured him and he hated her for it.

"So you're a daddy?"

"Yeah."

"That doesn't sound so terrible."

"I was a junkie, Heroin. My first wife Jessica was a drug rehab counselor. One type of therapeutic session led to the other kind and she tried to hide the pregnancy from me. I found out when she collected as much dirt as she could on me from my psychiatric files and then used them against me to gain sole custody of our daughter, Ashley."

Tonya killed the boat engine. Several pigeons watched them from the demolished house's rooftop.

"So, I tried to get my shit together and moved back in with my parents. I kicked the drug monkey and that's when I met Laura Gold." He groaned. "The last name should have warned me. She saw dollar signs when she met my parents and heard that we owned a newspaper in Boston. I got a job at our paper and in a year I planned to petition the court for joint custody of Ashley."

"Everything looked great until Laura started spending money that I didn't have. I married her after she proposed and I had already leaned on her for my own strength. My debts were mounting and Ashley was getting further away from me. Jessica was poisoning her against me."

The boat rocked back-and-forth gently as Tonya hugged him.

The sun set leaving them in total darkness. The small canal way that they were in was poorly lit. The barge that they were tied to had a half ton of construction rubble cresting out of it. A faint breeze blew plaster dust from it at them.

Clayton's mind was reeling. He was back in Boston in his parents' large house. Laura was moaning behind their bedroom door. He opened it to find her and one of her male friends screwing on his bed. Laura loved it when she saw him catch her.

The man who was enjoying her was a guy he saw her around all of the time. She had told Clayton that he was "just a friend." He never knew why he had accepted that lie. Men and women of the same age could never just be friends without sex entering the picture somewhere. He didn't know who was more deluded. Women for saying the stupid line and believing what they said or the men who bought into it.

The whole experience made him consider grabbing a third wife from India. Over there, the practice of arranged marriages was still the norm. Love hardly ever entered the equation. In India the single women stayed clustered in groups of other women whenever they went anywhere in public. If an Indian girl or woman was seen in the company of any male and no other member of the female sex was right there at her side, it was automatically assumed that something improper occurred. Usually the female offender would get punished with a stick or in more severe cases, stoning. Something in the whole thing appealed to him but then he also realized that for him, that was sick.

"Laura cheated on me," he told Tonya in the dark. "She told me she was pregnant before she started messing around. That was her meal ticket with my parents and her insurance card that the money wouldn't stop."

"You went back to drugs, didn't you?"

"Yup. I got high during the court proceedings. The judge bought her poor-me-I'm-married-to-a-junkie and I've done anything wrong in this marriage, story. He jacked my alimony payments and gave her full custody. To visit my kids I've got to have state supervised visits."

Tonya rubbed his head affectionately. She pulled him close to her. Renauld's words echoed in her mind. *Fuck him and get him strung out on drugs.*

"I stole my parents' art collection, fled to Paris, and sold the shit on the black market to keep me in "H" for a year."

The wholesome image of a Hollywood television family fled Tonya's mind. Outsiders weren't supposed to live this miserable.

"My parents sent a private detective to Paris to find me and bring me back home. Me and him got into it, he stole my "H", and he eventually kidnapped me back to the States. He tossed me into a high class drug rehab clinic where I was held against my will. I didn't want to get clean. They had already taken my kids away and the system is fucked!"

Clayton traveled back in time to family therapy at the clinic. He held a short broken piece of a fluorescent light bulb tube up to his sister's neck. His parents and the doctor gaped in disbelief. They weren't used to psychotic patients at the high society club. Even the rock stars didn't act that crazy.

"I took Kathreen hostage, got the orderly to pop the wards locked exit door, and then I put Kathreen in my parent's car trunk. The spare key was kept in a magnet holder under the rear wheel-well."

Kathreen had screamed, and kicked, and begged. He always wondered why he didn't just let her go. All he wanted was to get high. She was a means to an end.

Tonya stopped hugging him and held his hand. "Okay. So she's in the trunk. Then what?"

"I decided to go downtown to the east side. There's a crack house every three blocks. If there was no "H" then I'd settle for rock."

He remembered driving the Lincoln Town car. The vehicle kept swerving all over the place. He was shaking uncontrollably. Long sweat rings drenched his shirt's armpits. Kathreen kept kicking. The thumping noises were driving him crazy. He looked back over the driver's seat into the car's empty backseat. He failed to see the red stoplight at the four-way intersection. The car barreled ahead. He kept yelling at the empty seat telling her to shut up.

"A pick-up truck slammed into the left back side of us. The police report says that I must have been driving over forty-miles per hour."

"Oh my God!"

"Kathreen lived but she suffered massive head trauma." Clayton's eyes were watering. "She was studying to be a children's doctor. Now she needs help with tying her own shoelaces."

There was a long silence.

Tonya couldn't believe it. Clayton never appeared crazy to her. She didn't know what to feel. "Did you try apologizing to your parents and sister?"

"When I got clean." He sniffed heavily. "Dad tried to punch me and mom couldn't stop crying. They couldn't believe that I showed my face. They wouldn't let me near Kathreen."

"How do you go on?"

Clayton lifted off his necklace bullet and placed it in her hand.

She examined the small cylindrical object with her fingers until her imagination worked it out in the moonless night. "A bullet?"

He remembered sitting on his catamaran over a year ago. It had been raining. He slid the silver projectile into the nickel-plated revolver and fed the gun into his mouth. He pulled the trigger with less effort than he thought it would take. A dull metallic click erupted and he checked the revolver's barrel in disbelief. The hammer had fallen yet the bullet failed to explode in his mouth and empty his brain. He related the grim story to Tonya.

"...and that's when I figured that I must be here for a reason. I keep the bullet as a reminder of that. Phillip VanAucken called me out of the blue two days afterward. He's the CEO of my grandfather's insurance company, Blackburn & Gossett International. He said that he could use me for a special assignment so I started work in Paris. I infiltrated the art world's black market there. I had established contacts with my sale of my parent's stolen art. VanAucken was pleased with my results but no one was arrested. This is my second assignment. He's risking an awful lot by hiring me because my mom now sits on the company's board of directors."

Tonya took her hand away from him.

"You hate me now, don't you?"

"No," she said quietly. "It's just a lot to digest. That's all."

"Tonya."

"Yes?"

"I think I'm in love with you," he blurted out.

The darkness hid her reaction.

He hated himself for saying it. He'd only known her for a few days and yet it felt like he'd known her all of his life. Suddenly he felt very foolish for saying it.

She leaned over, used her hands to find his face, and she kissed him.

Chapter 17

Vatican City. August, 2004

Cardinal D'Anglese sat in an 18th century chair in a small ornate office in the Vatican's Governatorato building. He was doubled over, staring at the floor's oriental carpet, head spinning and trying to think.

A modern phone rested on a dark cherry Rocco desk. The phone's receiver dangled in mid-air over the side of the table.

A lone, tall Swiss Guard entered the tiny office. "Are you feeling ill, Father?"

D'Anglese shot back up in his chair. "Oh, no." he said in his slick effimitive voice. He stretched his arms and forced a fake yawn in the man's direction. "I fear that the *Coda alla Vaccinara* that I ate for lunch mildly disagrees with me. God's punishment for today's over-indulgence."

The tall Swiss Guardsman appeared grim. "I'm sorry."

He gave a wave of his hand. "Don't worry on my account. It's merely indigestion."

"I wasn't referring to *that*, Father. I'm afraid I bring bad news. Your apartment is being dissected today. Commander Occhibelli wishes to know whether you wish to be present during the search or not."

D'Anglese felt a cold chill race up the base of his spine. "What are you searching for and on whose orders?!"

"I can't discuss the specifics, but the order comes from the Holy Father."

"Perhaps a hint." D'Anglese gauged the young man for a reaction. "Did Bishop Trevelyan run away?"

The Swiss Guardsman creped towards him. "What do you mean? What do you know about Bishop Trevelyan?"

D'Anglese contemplated his next move and decided to feed his biting fish some more line. "The Spaniard is a sneak."

"You're referring to the Bishop?"

"Who else." D'Anglese produced a white lace handkerchief from his white cassock and patted his wet forehead. "I'm not one to let loose a wagging tongue, mind you. But let me just give thanks to Our Lord that all the paintings in the Vatican Museum are counted each night."

"What leads you to have such beliefs, Father?"

"He's just shifty," D'Anglese said under his breath. "That's all." He coughed once into his closed-hand and escorted the guard out. "But you didn't hear these tales from me."

"Yes, Father."

"I do not need to be present for this supposed search because I have nothing to hide. Tell *that* to Commander Occhibelli."

"I will."

"Go with God, my child." D'Anglese patted the man on the back heartily and admired his flank.

The man left feeling certain that Cardinal D'Anglese wasn't the man that they were looking for.

D'Anglese shut the gold leaf office door and proceeded back to the phone. He hung the receiver back up and redialed the bank that he used in Switzerland. Cardinal Ferroli had recommended it to him.

The phone rang once on the other end before someone answered. "Good afternoon. UBT Deutch Bank. This is Stephanie speaking. How may I assist you?"

"Yes," D'Anglese's voice cracked. "I talked with you earlier today. I'm the Italian gentleman with the supposed empty bank account. You said that you would check into it for me."

"Let me forward you to my manager, sir. Hold please."

Chamber music assaulted his ear for a few minutes until a new person answered the phone.

A German voice in broken English spoke. "Hello?"

"Yes. I talked to one of your people about an account discrepancy. She told me all of my money's gone. Even the old thirty thousand U.S. dollars that I had parked there."

"Do you have you account number with you, sir?"

D'Anglese retrieved a thin strip of white paper from his cassock. "Yes."

"Please read the number to me, sir."

He was careful to annunciate each digit correctly. "01-03-9TB-11, Blue."

"My numbers concur with your numbers, sir." Uncomfortable pause. "The account is question has been *closed*. The current balance is zero across the field."

D'Anglese's face went bright red although his caller couldn't see it. "I've just lost over one million dollars...and you say you're sorry?!"

"I am very sorry, sir. I must report to you, however, that all is in order here."

D'Anglese slammed the receiver into the phone's cradle. *Bastards! God curse the gnomes of Zurich!*

A timid knock came from behind the office door.

"Entra!"

A young African priest in his twenties entered. He carried a thick brown manila envelope. *"Monsignore?"*

One million dollars, D'Anglese's mind screamed. *How are you going to pay them now?!"*

D'Anglese's heart thumped away rapidly, sending his molten hot blood everywhere at once. He tried to rein-in his heavy breathing as he snatched the envelope from the young priest's hand. "Thank you."

"Are you ill, *Monsignore?*"

"Yes." He rolled his eyes. "I ate the *Coda all Veccinara* for lunch."

The young African priest's Italian wasn't up to speed yet. "Coda alla…"

"Braised oxtail." D'Anglese rubbed his belly. "They smother it in tomato sauce, herbs, and a hint of spice. I drink it with a *Torre Ercolana*. That's red wine. They make it in Lazio with Casanese grapes. The nectar caresses the tongue."

The African clasped his hands in front of himself, unsure of what to do. "I am still getting use to the food here. It is very rich."

"Well?" he issued a *'why are you still here?'* look.

"Uh…the letter I gave to you was brought by courier. I signed for it and went looking for you."

"And now you've found me and I have my package."

The African bowed slightly and left.

D'Anglese tore open the packet only to discover a miserable one-page letter. The document was typed and had no signature.

He held the lone paper close to his failing eyes and read:

D'Anglese. You sick mother fucker. Give us money we talk about. Your time is up. We fly back out here and you know what that means. You can't hide from us.

Everyday that you do not pay we make tape copies. Pretty soon we charge strangers admission to see you in film.

Hope they don't recognize you.

We will be in reach soon. Have money ready if you like your toes.

D'Anglese picked up the phone and dialed for Cardinal Ferroli. The phone rang several times until the Cardinal's aid answered. "Hello?" he said in Italian.

"Is the Cardinal in please?" D'Anglese practically begged. "This is very important."

"I'm sorry but the Cardinal is indisposed. May I ask whose calling?"

"He'll know. Just say someone called."

"Cardinal D'Anglese, is that you?"

He hung up the phone in reply. *He knows it's you. You've called enough over the years. What were you going to do? Say everything? You fool.*

D'Anglese began to pinch the skin between his thumb and forefinger. He exerted more and more pressure. Blood began to seep from it but the pain was a pleasant distraction.

Chapter 18

Venice, Island of Torcello.

Renauld Fouchet's living room was full of furniture ghosts and their dusty white sheets.

Renauld sat in a dull orange lounge chair and stared at the moonless midnight sky which concealed all that was outside of the living room windows. His new "partner" Shannon paced back and forth distracting him. She wore white leather stretch-pants and a black leather jacket. She was ready to travel.

Shannon was pouting. She didn't know why they were still hanging around now that the police were involved. Renauld's contact said they'd be brought in for questioning very soon. Her tips to them had not been very accurate and now a building has burned down.

Shannon stopped pacing and glared at Renauld. Her hand swept out toward the midnight window. "When's your gypsy bitch gonna come, Rinnie?"

Renauld ignored her. He re-read a note he'd drafted ten minutes earlier.

> D'Anglese, my true and faithful friend. I regret what has occurred with the Swiss account. My gypsy girl assistant betrayed me by stealing out account numbers and taking the money with her American boyfriend Clayton Keasley.

My sources tell me that they are hiding in a two-story white plaster house in Torcello. The home is along the small waterway a half a mile South of *Santa Maria dell'Assunta Cathedral.*

The police mistakenly blame me for Keasley's forgeries on the local art market. He is a dirty insurance investigator and I'm afraid his efforts in framing me have been successful.

To protect you and me, I am leaving for Spain immediately. Jean-Phillipe has already been arrested. I am truly sorry my friend. I pray that you can find the right type of people to help recover your funds from these scoundrels. *Adieu.*

Your faithful servant,

Renauld.

Renauld carefully folded the letter, slid it into an envelope, and handed it to Shannon. "Go to the main post office in Cannaregio. Hire a *Posta celere* to take this letter directly to Cardinal D'Anglese at the Vatican."

"*Posta celere?*"

"It's a state courier. If they get nosey then tell them you're in a rush because it involves an urgent, private spiritual matter." He slapped her on the ass. "Get moving."

"Where should I return to?"

"The glass shop."

She leaned forward to kiss him goodbye.

He patted her on the head and pointed at the door.

Shannon sneered and was gone in a hurry.

Renauld waited in the dimly lit room for another hour before Tonya and Clayton stumbled in. They were laughing and having a great time. Renauld waited patiently for them to notice him.

Clayton was helping Tonya off with her coat. She made out Renauld's ear as her eyes searched for the room's light source.

"Ello, my love."

She approached him.

"I see that you've recovered well from our little fight, no?"

119

"Uh-hunh."

"How quickly you move on." He waved at Clayton who stood at the doorway holding Tonya's coat. "My buyer was displeased."

Tonya frowned. "You mean the cop who was *posing* as a buyer?"

"I knew of no such thing," he said quickly. "All I know is that I have tired of this place and I am leaving."

There was an awkward silence. Tonya helped herself to a covered loveseat. Clayton leaned against the wall between the door and living room. His grip tightened on the neck of Tonya's jacket.

"So," Tonya said. "This means you're going to Switzerland to work on your low fat cheese?"

The remark stabbed into him. A sour look spread across his face. "No. That was a silly day dream."

"So where are you going?"

"Brazil. My money will stretch better there now that I am retired."

"I never thought of you as a sun-and-fun guy."

"You keep the Raphael, kitten. That should keep you and the baby well for quiet some time, eh?"

"You promised me more." She winked.

Clayton rolled his right hand around in a semi circle like a helicopter blade. "Fuck it. I give you this house then. Just leave me alone."

Tonya leaned over to hug him.

Renauld pushed her off. He had thoughts of when he had last slept with her and he hoped that D'Anglese killers would do her quickly; but maybe not so fast when it came to Clayton.

Renauld decided that it was time to start the second part of his plan. He addressed Clayton. "I bear you no ill will, my friend. I know you tried to make a sale for me. In return for your good faith I've left you a special cigar box upstairs in my room. Why don't you go upstairs and open it on your own."

Clayton glanced at Tonya for permission. She seemed uneasy.

"Thanks." He walked away down the hall towards the staircase that led upstairs.

Renauld watched him leave and then he turned to Tonya. His eyes hardened. "You're fucking this up, *bitch*. He should be in jail right now and instead it's your Uncle!"

She suppressed a grin.

"There's heroin in that cigar box that I just gave to your new boyfriend," he whispered. "China white. Barely stepped on. Now. You get him high; you fuck him, and send our little robot on a mission. I've got a new painting to plant on him and everything else has been arranged."

Tonya was unusually quiet. She didn't want to do it. Clayton had become human to her. He wasn't an outsider anymore.

Renauld read her face. His hand found her belly. He grabbed at the skin and pinched her hard. "Listen to me. If you don't do this I'll kill you and your bastard baby! There are more people involved in this than you or me. I've got to lose the dogs and this is it. Do you *hear* me?"

"Yes."

"No." He pinched harder.

Her eyes watered. She let out a muffled shriek.

"Do you hear me?"

"Yes. Please..." she grabbed his hand and tried to pull it off.

"Don't fall in love with this piece of shit junkie."

"He's not."

"He will be," Renauld reassured her. "And *soon*."

The thought of being the third woman in Clayton's life who hurts him gnawed at her. The financial aspect of the deal then entered her mind. "If I do this...what's my cut?"

"Forty-percent, my love." He pet her hair. "Just like before."

Clayton came back down the stairs and into the living room with a cigar box tucked under his arm.

She decided to test his honesty. She wouldn't protect a man who claimed to love her but lied to her face. "What's in the box?"

"Uh...cigars."

Tonya turned to face Renauld. "Okay," she said in poor French. "We have a deal."

Chapter 19

Rome. The Columbus Hotel. August, 2004

Svetlana carried dozens of tourist maps in her thin trembling hands. She felt like a fool. She had been dragged onto a plane and flown to Italy in her spandex whore's clothes with nothing else. Once they'd arrived she was forced to talk to different Italian vendors in her native Russian. She was trying to discuss the prices of their tourist maps and Yurgi expected change from the Euros that he gave her. No one understood her.

After hours of frustration she returned to the hotel lobby where she collapsed on a sofa and cried. The hotel concierge noticed her crying and took pity on her. He spent a half an hour attempting to communicate with her to determine what she wanted. Eventually he supplied her with a half-dozen complimentary maps.

She found herself back in front of Yurgi's hotel room; hoping that he wouldn't give her left eye the same dark purple ring around it that her right eye had.

The door opened inward and Yurgi leered out at her from within the room. He was dressed in the same Nike Tiger Wood's jogging suit from the day before. The stench of Vodka swept her nose as he latched onto her wrist and pulled her into the room. He snatched the maps from her and handed them to Big Tony.

"You've done well," Yurgi grunted in his native Russian. He grabbed the back of her neck and pulled her face to his dry lips.

She flinched.

"What is dis shit? I am not mad. You did the wonderful." He grabbed her ass. "Now get the fuck out."

Svetlana produced several silver-and-gold 1 and 2 Euro coins and a red 10 Euro note.

Yurgi looked at her in amazement. "What is 'dis?"

She offered the money. "Your change," she said in Russian.

He grabbed her ass again. "Go buy yourself dinner. It's on me."

She trembled slightly, turned, and left.

Big Tony limped over to the area where they were planning the Vatican Job. He used a stapler that he "borrowed" from the front desk. He opened the maps of Rome and the Vatican that Svetlana had brought and stapled them onto the wall.

Six new maps joined a slurry of postcards that were already fixed into the rose petal and green-leaf lined wall paper.

The postcards depicted the Vatican City's Botanical Gardens, different exterior and interior views of the Vatican museums, St.Peter's Basilica, and a massive fortress on the outside of the Vatican City that lay against the Tiber River called the *Castel Sant'Angelo.*

Big Tony limped to the edge of his bed and sat down to admire his handiwork. Yurgi joined him.

A foul odor crept into the room from the closet-sized bathroom. A few minutes later the toilet flushed and the bathroom door opened. A skinny man with poorly dyed blond hair stepped out.

"Nikoli," Yurgi said. "You are a nasty stinker."

"*Da.*" Nikoli was impressed with himself. He was dressed in a dark blue jogging suit. "No worse than you when we were at Camp 2, in Nadym." He joined the men on the bed.

"Dis is truly incredible," Yurgi said.

"Yeah," Big Tony said. "We musta turned him."

"He gives us no fuck-ing time though." Yurgi took a swig of his Vodka bottle. "We have to take 'dis shit down in *two days* from now." He snorted. "Dis shit is impossible. We will get caught."

"It's gonna take some *balls*," Big Tony bragged. "Who the fuck has balls big enough to even try it. They're never expectin' it. Fuck...I'm

123

dyin' of cancer. If we get pinched, say it was all me." Big Tony grinned. "Tell them I held you at gun point and forced you to do the job. Hell, say whatever you want to lessen the charges. I'll take the weight."

Nikoli saw humor in Big Tony's statement. He laughed like a sea lion on nitrous oxide.

Yurgi examined Big Tony. "You don't look sick."

"You didn't see the blood I was hackin' up all of last night. Pretty soon I'm gonna have ta be put on oxygen." The picture of a steel cylinder, hoses, and a cylindrical carrier hit his mind. "Fuck that."

"Sorry." Yurgi looked to Nikoli. "That's bad shit."

"*Da.*"

"I'm not complainin' so let's go over the blueprint."

Both Russians agreed. Yurgi passed his Vodka bottle to Big Tony. Big Tony took several pulls off of the bottle and reached behind himself to grab six pages of hand-drawn blueprints.

D'Anglese had sent an African priest as a courier to deliver the papers. A note came with the drawings that gave brief history of the secret vaults and Leonardo's work upon them. The rest of the note covered what was drawn in the blueprints.

Big Tony read the technical parts out loud so Yurgi could trace the route on the tourist maps Svetlana brought.

"The priest writes:

The sewage and old water wheel out-take is one meter to the left of Ponte Sant'Angelo, directly under Castel Sant'Angelo itself (See Diagram D). The tunnel travels down the length of the *Borgo Pio* into the Holy City.

The waterway splits in two directly underneath Stanze di Raffaello (See Diagram F). Both the intake and outtake tunnels to the old waterwheel room have been bricked up. This dry room house's the security electronics of the vaults. Access to the electronics room is to the left; there is a square reinforced bank vault door which is locked at all times.

The vault penetration must occur at midnight. You will only have six hours to steal all of the vaults' art.

YOU MUST LEAVE THE TEXTS, RELICS, AND COMPUTERS ALONE.

This is the price you pay. The art alone is valued well over half a billion dollars.

Sell the art through Renauld Fouchet. He has recently left for Spain. His assistant girl should know how to reach him.

My debt to you is now resolved. If you are captured at any point I trust that you will forget my name. I rely on your word that you will burn the tape(s). There is nothing left for me to pay you.

I have paid my penance. Go in peace. You have less than 48 hours." Nikoli watched Big Tony limp up to the hotel room wall. He stapled D'Anglese' letter next to the maps and postcards.

Nikoli put a generic filtered cigarette in his mouth and patted his own pockets for matches. "I am needing to get my contacts moving," he said. "Telephone Company shouldn't be problem. I am friends with their union guy. What else?"

Yurgi handed Nikoli a detailed list of equipment. He snatched the cigarette out of Nikoli's mouth and threw it at the room's brown plastic garbage can. "Tony has lung cancer. The smoke aggravates it, yes?"

Big Tony confirmed his friend's deduction.

"You get every fuck-ing thing on list, okay Nikoli?"

Nikoli scanned the small piece of paper. Handwriting was squeezed in everywhere. Yurgi wanted foam dry suits, pumps, scuba gear, generators, outdoor floodlights, drills, ladders, pulleys and tons of rope and string. At the end of the list was an order for C-4 plastic explosives. Nikoli's eyes balked. "This I do not think I can be getting. Dynamite... perhaps. But C-4 is dangerous. Terrorism has snitches looking for people buying this type of thing. Uh...it's *not* possible."

Yurgi folded his arms. "I say, C-4 *is* possible. Is non-negotiable. You fuck-ing go." He pointed toward the door with his thumb.

Nikoli cursed him under his breath. He retrieved his cigarette from the floor next to the garbage can and left the room in a hurry. The door slammed behind him.

Big Tony focused his attention on the postcard depicting the Castel Sant'Angelo Bridge. He wondered how conspicuous divers in the

Tiber River at twelve o'clock midnight would look. He glanced at his wristwatch; 10:30 PM. They had a little less than a day and over a half before the thing had to go down.

"I have to go to tobacco shop and buy fuck-ing international pay phone cards," Yurgi said. "That bitch Svetlana kept my 10 Euros! Stupid women always spending *my* money!"

"Relax."

"Easy for you to say."

"This is the heist of the friggin' century, Yurg. It's so right, I can feel it. It's like being electrocuted. Have you ever been electrocuted, Yurg?"

"Da." Yurgi lowered himself back until he was lying on the bed staring at the ceiling. "When I was rigging my cousin's video poker. He had bar in Hoboken before he missed his payments. I fixed machines for him so they wouldn't pay out. It shocked the hell out of me."

"Well, this is just like that, ya know? Blam! It just hits you. There's no turnin' back."

"Sure."

"So who are ya gonna get as a crew to help us with this thing?"

"Fuck-ing Colonel Brovosich, my cousin's husband. He used to be Spetnatz in old Soviet military."

"What's that shit, Yurg? The Polish ski team?"

"No. They are Russian mirror image of your Navy SEALs."

"Oh."

"He knows scuba gear, close quarter combat, explosives, and other guerrilla warfare shit. He is Zandor's enforcer now, in Ukraine. I saw him cave man's face-in with folding chair. He can be counted on to keep his mouth shut along with others."

"They're Spet-nazis too?"

"Spetnatz. And da, they are. All except for electronics expert. Is hard to find good talent on such short notice, I tell you."

Big Tony turned on the television set. He wanted to watch a porno but the set didn't offer it. He settled for an Italian game show. "I wish we were all back home."

Yurgi got up to leave. "We will be."

"Hey…"

"Da?"

"Let's say the crew totals ten guys, all right? Ten guys floatin' in the Tiber with tools, and bags, and God knows what else…cops and people are bound to ask a few questions, ya know. What are we gonna say to them?"

"Fiber optic cable broke under water." Yurgi grinned. "We have rush order to fix. That's why we're parking telephone company trucks near dive sight."

Chapter 20

Venice, the Island of Burano.

Clayton Keasley had left Tonya shortly after Renauld had departed. She seemed to be very understanding and kept staring at his new cigar box present. Guilt poked at him through the rest of the night. He had borrowed Tonya's motorboat to make the short trip to Burano where he found a family run hotel to stay in. Tonya had convinced him to face his past.

Clayton laid in his rustic hotel bed still dressed in his rental suit. The clothes lenders were going to be pissed. The designer suit was all but ruined and gave off a faint mold smell. He doubted that they'd be able to get rid of the smell no matter how much chemical fresh scent they used.

He figured that his employer Mr.VanAucken had fired him so he avoided checking his mail. The painting sales had turned out to be a disaster. All he had were bank account numbers, no real names other than Renauld's and a police department that was convinced he was a criminal.

For the past half hour he had tried to figure out the time zone difference between Venice and Boston...

Tonya's words echoed in his mind. "Did you try and apologize to them?"

He loosened his necktie and stared at the open cigar box next to the phone. Four brand new syringes, a metal spoon, cotton swabs, and a cigarette lighter lay up on top of a plastic bag of white-gray heroin. Shivers and goose-bumps raced up and down his body. He hated the fact that somewhere inside of himself he still wanted it. Hell, he needed it.

He used his room phone to dial his parent's home phone number. It rang four times when a familiar slurred female voice answered.

The voice belonged to his sister Kathreen. "Hel-lo?"

He swallowed hard. "Hi," he managed to say. A cold jolt of emotion shot down from the center of his chest. "It's Clayton."

"Hel-lo Clay-ton. How are you?" She asked cheerfully.

Obviously she doesn't recognize you, he thought. "I'm your brother."

"I know...w-ho you are." A little dog barked in the background.

"How are you, Kat?" The heroin caught his attention. He wanted to slam the receiver down into the cradle and shoot up.

"We wa-ent...to a pup-pet show at the mall. Mom bought cotton candy." She spoke very slow and deliberate. The dog kept yapping. "It was stick-y."

Clayton was determined not to start crying. His nose ran and he took slow, controlled deep breaths to help himself remain calm.

"Clay-ton?"

"Yeah, Kat." He sniffed as he began to lose control. "I am *so sorry* sweetie. I uh..." he wiped his eyes with is wrist. "God, I am so sorry."

"Why?"

"Because of the car crash, Kat," he whispered. "I wasn't myself. I should have died. You shouldn't have been locked in the trunk. I should have left you in the parking lot."

"Mom says...it was an accid-ent."

The memories raced through his head at high speed. Rehab, the glass he held up to Kathreen's throat, shoving her in the car trunk, and the crash. When he took her hostage she looked so betrayed.

The memories had been away on vacation for a while. He put the cigar box in his lap. "Do you remember the hospital?"

"Af-ter my operation?" She was still cheerful.

"No. Before the operation and the accident, Kat. When I was in the drug rehab clinic."

"I do-n't remember."

High heel shoes clacked across the kitchen wood floor, bleeding into the receiver. The little dog had run off into another room. "Kathreen," a majestic older woman said. "Who are you talking to?"

"Kathreen!" Clayton shouted into the receiver. "Answer me one question!"

"O-kay."

The older woman questioned her again. "Who are you talking to?"

"I ruined your life, Kat," Clayton hurriedly said. "You were going to be a doctor and I took that from you. I destroyed that. I put you in that trunk and made you the way you are!"

"I know. Dad-dy told me."

He leaned forward, pushing the phone hard against his ear. "Do you forgive me, Kat? Can you?"

The older woman spoke into the phone at him. "Who is this?"

"Put Kathreen back on the phone."

"No."

"You have *no right* to deny me. Kathreen is my sister!"

Silence.

"You have to let me ask her something."

"No." The woman's voice toughened. "I don't."

The little dog returned to the kitchen yapping. Kathreen laughed heartily and chased the little creature around close to their mother.

"I can't believe you called here," his mother said. "You should stay under your rock and leave us alone! Let me guess. You need money. Well, forget it Clayton. You won't get any here and there won't be any. If you show up at our door…I promise that we'll have you arrested."

"Look. That's not why I…"

"Kathreen can't comb her hair, Clayton." She spoke in a hushed tone with her hand cupped to the receiver. "She can't get dressed, drive, cook, date, or live on her own. She'll *never* be an independent woman. Your father and I don't talk. We only pretend to be happy in front of her but even that isn't working anymore."

"I called to apologize."

"Who is going to care for Kathreen when we're gone? Ask yourself that because it keeps me awake at nights just thinking about it."

"I will."

"No. You won't. I've got legal documents that see to that."

"I've changed," he pleaded. The heroin spoon was in his hand.

"Clay-ton!" Kathreen shouted. The dog yapped behind her. "Mom! I wan-na talk to Clay-ton."

"Promise me something, if you really love your sister."

"Okay."

"Never…I mean *never* call here again."

"I'll try."

"No. You won't." She hung up the phone.

He listened to the hollow of the dial tone for several moments and then he hung up slowly. His hands were sweaty. He felt the strong urge to get high. He undid the plastic baggy that held the heroin and put some onto his spoon. He activated the cigarette lighter he had and held the flame under the spoon gingerly. Slowly it began to bubble.

You've come too far for this, he thought.

The emotional pain squeezed him.

The spoon now held a fine light-gray liquid. He grabbed for a syringe.

Chapter 21

The Vatican, Vatican Museum.

Inside of the Vatican museum stood an architectural masterpiece designed by Guiseppe Momo. The great work was a pair of grand spiral staircases which were set within each other to form a giant double helix.

The steps on each staircase were extremely long and flat. Ornate leaf and vine stonework decorated the interior white marble wall face of both stairs. Each stairway overlooked a large glass sphere at the center of the ground floor. One staircase was built for patrons to walk up while the other existed for them to walk down.

Cardinal D'Anglese started the stroll down the top descending staircase with Cardinal Ferroli at his side. Both men were dressed in plain black underclothes with outer white and black. They each wore red skull caps on their heads. It was late evening. The museum was closed to the public leaving the two men alone. They kept a watchful eye out for any Swiss Guardsmen who might appear and overhear them.

Cardinal Ferroli secretly activated his tape recorder from inside his cassock. He was quite ill and attempting to beat the flu virus that afflicted him. "What did His Holiness say to you?" Ferroli wheezed.

D'Anglese stopped on a step to face his old boss. "He says that I am the number one suspect, *Monsignore*! I asked for time to prove my innocence and he's consented so far. I'm not sure he knows what he wants to do with me, even if I turned out to be guilty. Which I'm not."

Cardinal Ferroli sucked in a bit of air through his rotting teeth which made a faint inverse whistle. "He plans to make you an example, Francis."

Their footsteps echoed throughout the double helix as they began walking down the stairs again.

"I've had the Spaniard followed," D'Anglese said with his effimitive lisp thickening. "He's working with an American confidence man calling himself Clayton Keasley. There's also a gypsy girl, Keasley's assistant, and their associate Renauld Fouchet."

"I do not understand, Francis. What is this relationship?"

"Uh…" D'Anglese jowls flapped. "They are all in cahoots together, *Monsignore*. They are selling mother church's stolen treasures through illegal auctions in Venice." He leaned hard against the marble stair rail. "The Spaniard feared detection as greed took hold of him. He purposely stole works of art that I had been logged-in as restoring on our computer card system. He came forward to His Holiness in an effort to frame me for his evil acts!"

Cardinal Ferroli's lips arched backward revealing his gray-dark yellow teeth. His wrinkled head moved up and down in avid agreement. "I like this story of yours, Francis. Very…believable."

D'Anglese grabbed the old man's arm and squeezed it. "It's not a story, *Monsignore*! I am being framed."

Ferroli slapped D'Anglese's heavy paw off of him. "We are allies, you and I. You needn't convince me."

D'Anglese said nothing.

Ferroli's wheezing was getting louder. "What would you have me do, Francis?"

"I need your *family* friends to get rid of the gypsy girl and American. If the Holy Father has the Swiss Guard retrieve them then there is no telling what they'll say to save their Spanish friend." D'Anglese was so excited that he had moved two steps ahead of Ferroli. He talked over his shoulder as if Ferroli were only one step behind him. "I also need your friends to capture the Frenchman Renauld, *alive*."

"You ask much of me, Francis."

"Not more than you've asked from me in the past, *Monsignore*." D'Anglese was hinting of their days together at the IOR. He had laundered more than a little money for certain nefarious third parties.

The old man held his tongue. D'Anglese was out of control.

"I need your family friends to encourage the Frenchman to reveal his Swiss bank account numbers."

"To what end, Francis?"

D'Anglese was livid. "We have the Swiss bank transfer a large sum of money from Renauld's accounts into the IOR under *Bishop Trevelyan's* name…"

"The news of such a large cash transfer into a single priest's account will reach Il Redentore's ears almost immediately." Ferroli reasoned. "Suspicion will transfer to him."

"Of course, *Monsignore*. And the matter will take care of itself."

"If I decide to follow your plan, Francis." Ferroli wanted to remind D'Anglese of the folly which led to the whole mess. "You've risked much for so little."

D'Anglese's face froze in place, he stopped, and Ferroli caught up with him. He turned and moved within an eyelash of the old man's face. "I laundered *millions* for you over the years, *Monsignore*. Millions! I have many old documents left over from our era together. *Sensitive documents* which might hint about the fate of certain funds which were supposed to go to our charities."

"*If Il Redentore* isn't initially interested, I'm sure your good friend Cardinal Ciatti will be." He raised his eyebrows and pushed his finger into the old man's chest. "I wonder how His Holiness would view that. The theft from our charities, I mean."

Ferroli's shoulders slumped profoundly. He leaned against the stair rail. "Kindly remove your dagger from my throat, Francis." Cardinal Ferroli gazed up at him from his stooped position.

"I carry no dagger, *Monsignore*." D'Anglese patted his mentor's shoulder. "I merely remind you that I carry an olive branch of peace."

"Indeed," Ferroli coughed. "Then let us enter this endeavor together. Friends once again."

D'Anglese kneeled at once, grabbed his mentor's hand, and kissed his ring as a sign of appreciation and respect.

I should have killed you, Ferroli thought. *Sentiment is for fools.*

"Have your men seek out the girl and the American at once," D'Anglese ordered more than suggested. "They are hiding in a house on the island of Torcello in the Venetian Lagoon."

"I shall make it so. Let us speak no more of this matter until it is complete."

"One more thing, *Monsignore*."

"Yes, Francis?"

"I need a fast acting poison to put down a very large dog. I know this is an unusual request, but it is for one of my parishioners."

"How large is this...dog, Francis?"

"About two hundred pounds."

"Indeed."

Chapter 22

Rome.

Big Tony was dressed in a stolen red-and-gray Telecom Italia jumpsuit. He sat behind the wheel of a stolen phone company truck which was parked on the *Lungotevere Castello* that over-looked the twenty foot wide, one-hundred-fifty foot long grass and gravel river bank below. The truck's digital dashboard clock indicated that it was 11:30 PM.

The Tiber River ran swiftly below. The square base and circular tower of Castel Sant'Angelo stood proudly behind Big Tony and the phone truck.

Large square-shaped outdoor floodlights lit up the castle and street. A fine mist fell from the sky creating a weak misty fog.

Nikoli had made twenty separate trips in assembling the group's equipment. He and Big Tony had decided to set up the gear on the river bank taking pains to be as conspicuous as possible. To accomplish their plan they arranged five portable bright yellow construction floodlights which illuminated the surrounding equipment and running water.

There were four construction tents near the floodlights, a pair of long wood benches, one large air compressor, dozens of scuba tanks, and coils of ropes and hoses.

A long chain ladder dangled from the telephone truck's street over the side of the old wall down to the river bank.

A thick aluminum ladder was installed on the edge of the grassy river bank. The ladder descended deep into the river.

A dozen men stood around in the new "construction area" dressed in scuba dry suits. Yurgi mingled among them and held laminated paperwork and drawings that he'd taken from the hotel room wall.

Big Tony abandoned the telephone truck on the street and clumsily made his way down the chain ladder to join Yurgi and the group.

"Where we at?" Big Tony yelled over the roar of the generators and air compressor.

The mist from the sky bounced off of everything making all of the men and equipment appear as if they were submersed in a clam chowder soup.

"We are fuck-ing with underwater metal grate to river's sewer." Big Tony launched himself up on his tip-toes to be closer to Yurgi's ear. "Dat shit is put in tough for sure, I tell you! The Colonel says we should use explosives but I say, is too early."

To simplify the operation everyone was given a number which was written on the arm of their dry suit. The procedure allowed everyone to refer to one another without having to learn each other's names. Most of the men were from different units. Some were retired, some still active. They had all stepped off of a plane from Russia only two hours earlier. They were all rolling dice on not getting an embolism or blood clot.

"The grate's gonna throw us off schedule!" Big Tony shouted.

"Dis I know." Yurgi threw his hands up in the air. He barked orders in Russian to the Colonel and his men.

The Colonel grabbed two of his former soldiers and prepared to go to work underwater on the grate again.

"Where's Nikoli?" Big Tony inquired...

Yurgi led him by the arm to a large brown tent that was set up next to the scuba tanks. He lifted up the flap allowing him and Big Tony to step inside.

A stack of ropes on wood spools was in the corner of tent along with a stack of metal carrying boxes. Yurgi pulled a dark brown tarp off of a lump on the floor. Nikoli's soaking wet naked corpse lay in the fetal position on the floor. There was no sign of blood or a struggle.

"The Colonel put him in a sleeper hold and then we drown him in river." Yurgi pulled the tarp back over him. "We put body in river right before we leave. Hopefully it will float several miles before the sun rises."

"This is crazy."

"Da, but we must keep going. I have bitch-slut-whore alimony payments to make. Besides, dis shit is my day job."

"I'm worried about the cops though, Yurg."

"We use the numbers now. Call me number One."

"Okay," he rolled his eyes. "I'm worried about the cops, Number One."

"Dey are block away." Yurgi seemed pleased with himself. "Who the fuck pulls something so crazy right next to police station?"

"Us?"

"You're fuck-ing right." Yurgi pulled a gold chained medallion out from under his dry suit's neck and kissed it. "We do dis shit."

Big Tony left Yurgi in the tent.

Two Russian men climbed down the thick aluminum ladder into the dark river.

Number Three was an Asian man and the last minute hired electronics expert. He hurried over to the ladder to hand the two men their rubber foot fins.

Both men put on their fins and grabbed a rope that was tied to the ladder to keep them from being swept away by the heavy river current. They joined the underwater welder.

Bright white-blue flashes flickered downstream several feet away from the water ladder. They were cutting out the grates.

Big Tony watched the Castel Sant'Angelo Bridge for rubber-neckers. The underwater light provided quite a spectacle.

Big Tony winced as the telephone company jumpsuit rode up his ass. The garment was a size too small but he forced it on anyway.

Nikoli had employed a young Italian woman to pose as a telephone company employee and answer any questions that curious people might ask. She hovered around the chain ladder at the top street level. Occasionally, she'd look down at Big Tony and give a thumbs-up sign; all clear.

Big Tony figured that Nikoli might be screwing her. She was wiry with big breasts, a slim waist, and long curly brown hair. He figured that Nikoli told her what was going down because she was way too focused and motivated for someone who was hired for such a low level task.

He knew that Yurgi planned to have her killed after the goods were loaded. Nikoli was outfit, so to Big Tony his death was acceptable. Guys who ran with the mob understood that one day they may have to pay a price but the girl was different. He wondered if he should warn her or maybe send her away before the trucks were loaded. He decided that he was getting ahead of himself.

Chapter 23

Venice, Island of Torcello.

Clayton had flushed the heroin that Renauld had given in the hotel room toilet. He emptied the syringe that he had prepared into his pillow and threw the rest of the paraphernalia into the canal.

The boat drive to Torcello that morning had been agonizing. He couldn't sleep after disposing of the drugs and he felt like he was trapped inside of a skin that he couldn't wear anymore even though it was his own.

He had Tonya's red boat's throttle maxed out during the entire trip. A deep part of him wished that a barge would emerge out of nowhere and hit him head on at full speed.

Clayton's past leaped onto him and wouldn't let go. He felt like his two ex-wives Jessica and Laura were seated beside him, his two daughters sat in their lap staring at him, and Kathreen was beside him with her hand on his shoulder. There was nowhere for him to turn. He felt claustrophobic. His mind wanted a pleasant distraction, his body wanted a fix, and his soul cried out for relief. None of the three were available to him.

Clayton parked Tonya's speedboat in front of Renauld's house. The specters from the boat followed him to the home's front door. He rubbed his eyes slowly and then patted his lucky necklace. He was shaking all over but it wasn't too cold outside.

Tonya heard the boat pull up. She greeted him at the door and led him into the living room where they'd gathered the night before. She offered him a seat on the uncovered couch.

She'd been busy packing. Boxes lay everywhere along with waded balls of *La Stampa* newspaper.

She wore a stylish blue-jean skirt, shin-high brown leather boots, and a bright red shirt that complimented her figure.

Clayton was a mess. He reeked of cheap deodorant and mint mouth wash. He wore the same crinkled and molding rental suit. H e fell into the couch with a grunt.

She moved over to him and ran her hand through his hair. "So, what happened?"

"I called Kathreen."

"She blames you?"

"Worse." He focused his attention on the living room window. "She's indifferent."

Tonya sat on the couch's overstuffed arm. They were quiet for a while. A small bird flew by outside of the window.

"I asked her to forgive me Tonya. I was robbed of her response and told never to call there again. My mom hung up on me." He pulled his legs up onto the couch, leaving his empty shoes on the floor. "I wanted to get lit so bad. Your boss gave me some H. It was in the cigar box. I'm sorry I lied to you."

She kissed him on the forehead and pulled him close. "I'm sorry too. I should have followed you there or made you stay."

She felt so warm to him. The smell of her perfume calmed him. He wanted time to freeze in that moment forever.

"Why didn't you?" She asked softly.

"Why didn't I what?"

"Get high."

"Because it would mean Kathreen's sacrifice would have meant nothing if I had."

She crooked her head slightly and moved in to meet his lips. He received her kiss with a slightly opening of the mouth. They tasted each other's passion and confirmed that there needed to be more.

He reached for the hair at the base of her head and slid his hand in to caress her. His other hand traced up and down the side of her face to enjoy the smoothness of her skin. He didn't want to rush but he could feel a tidal wave of desire rushing fast toward his self restraint.

She encouraged him to start kissing her neck. Her free hand pulled off his suit jacket and worked on undoing his necktie. He traveled from her neck back to her mouth.

They kissed for an eternity. She grasped his hand from behind her head and guided it onto her breasts. He mouth curled up into a smile. She fell backward onto the couch to lay flat. He used his thumbs to slowly pull off her bright red shirt.

Clayton's hand traveled up her thigh into the cave of her denim skirt. He undid he skirt's brass button and its long concealed zipper. The blue denim shield fell away to reveal his rough hand massaging her warm fleshy mound through the soft cotton fabric of her gray panties.

She pushed him over the edge with a hard savage thrust of her sex in his hand.

They couldn't hold back their lust any longer. They lost their underclothes in seconds much in the same way a snake sheds its skin. Instinctively, as if in an afterthought. Waves of ecstasy hit him as he put himself inside of her. Her head rolled to one side, her mouth hung partially open.

Greed consumed them. She wrapped her legs around his waist and grabbed his bottom. She concentrated on the feelings and warmth that radiated between them. Her black bangs spilled over her face in between physical jerks and sweat.

Their breathing was heavy. Labored. They lost themselves in each other as their senses heightened. Tonya opened her eyes and stared into Clayton's soul. She had found him, and he was coming to her. A molten wave of electric energy washed through her as she let out a stifled gasp. They reached fulfillment at the exact time.

Chapter 24

The Vatican. The Papal Audience Chamber.

Il Redentore sat in his gold and red velvet chair awaiting the first business of the day. The Pope's garments were all white and in the center of his chest dangled a solid gold pectoral cross. He wore a red ruby ring on his right hand and *the fisherman's ring* on his left.

Il Redentore was an exceptionally tall man with thick white hair and a graceful thin frame. Now that he was Pope, he enjoyed walking around the Vatican's Botanical Gardens much like his successor John Paul the Second, used to do.

It was eleven o'clock in the morning when Cardinal Ciatti, the Pope's perfect, entered the Grand Papal Audience Chamber with Swiss Guard Commander Occhibelli. They both greeted *Il Redentore* by bending down, kissing his ruby ring, and saying, "Your Holiness."

The rest of the ornate chamber was empty except for the Pope's four Swiss Guard who stood directly behind him.

Cardinal Ciatti was seventy-three years old and was developing a case of hard hearing. The young forty-year-old Commander allowed Ciatti to speak first.

"Your Holiness, I bid you good health but I fear that I bring you bad news. The cancer which has plagued our church has reached deeper than expected." Ciatti handed the Pope a hand written paper. "The Inventory has revealed five paintings in our vault which are poor forgeries, one painting which is an exceptional forgery, and two paintings whose authenticity we cannot discern."

"Only one-fifth of the paintings which have been accessed under Cardinal D'Anglese have been checked, Your Holiness," Commander Occhibelli said. "Other items also have yet to be examined. I believe that we should place Cardinal D'Anglese under arrest."

Il Redentore remained stoic. He had been elected Pope for almost a year now and he still wasn't used to making open and direct decisions. His radical decrees were a different matter. He'd been formulating them in his mind for years before becoming Pope.

"Your Holiness?" Ciatti prompted.

"It pains me to think that some wayward soul would steal from the children of mother church. What need could possibly force a man to be so needy?" *Il Redentore* rose from his seat slowly. "There will be no arrests as of yet, gentlemen. I wish to give the offender or offender's conscience time to force them into confession so that we may forgive them."

Commander Occhibelli forgot his place and lost his composure. *"Forgive him?!"*

Cardinal Ciatti was just as indignant but he held his tongue. Both man wanted blood. They felt like fools.

"Your Holiness," Occhibelli said gingerly. He talked to *Il Redentore* as if he were talking to a child. "Cardinal D'Anglese answers to our first inquiry were *far* from helpful. He was evasive, if not downright deceptive. He blames Bishop Trevelyan for everything."

Ciatti chimed in. "If D'Anglese is responsible then I *guarantee* that *Cardinal Ferroli knows.*" Ciatti's finger pointed toward the ceiling. "He should be *questioned.*"

Cardinal Ferroli was the last name that *Il Redentore* wanted to hear. The P2's had been a constant thorn in his side since his acceptance of the Holy Office. The Vatican's IOR was back to its usual tricks. He feared that a call for an official investigation might lead to his having a "sudden" and fatal heart attack, fall, or other contrived medical complication. Vatican Law made an autopsy of any fallen Pope almost impossible. There were some things that he knew better than to step in front of.

The thought that Ferroli could be involved un-nerved him.

Il Redentore planned to remake the church. The taint from being linked to a guilty Ferroli would destroy that idea. His new enemies would see to that. He decided that he might join the P2 group to thwart their attempts at forming a coalition against him. If they took him down, they'd go down too.

"Bring me Cardinal D'Anglese and Bishop Trevelyan." The Pope addressed Commander Occhibelli. "I wish to question them both further. Just remember. Treat them well. They are still *not* under arrest."

Ciatti couldn't help himself. "Should I speak to Cardinal Ferroli, Your Holiness?"

"You will talk to no one." The Pope snapped.

Cardinal Ciatti half-bowed in obedience.

Il Redentore started to wonder if it was time to employ a food and drink taster to all of his upcoming meals. He kept his paranoia in check. Such a move would send the wrong message to all quarters.

Chapter 25

The Vatican. Saint Martha's House.

Bishop Trevelyan lived in the *Domus Sanctae Marthae;* a hotel-like building built in the mid-1900's to house visiting Cardinals and Bishops. Bishop Trevelyan had been offered other housing in the Holy See but he preferred St. Martha's for its modest modern bedroom and bath, plus its basic simplicity. The accommodations made him focus more on his tasks for the church and less on his private living.

Cardinal D'Anglese had taken the Spaniard Bishop by surprise when he showed up at his door unexpectedly.

D'Anglese stood in the hallway holding a large paper sack in his bloated hand. "Bishop Trevelyan," he said in his friendly affirmative voice. "In the spirit of brotherhood, I wish to break bread with you and discuss our misunderstanding."

The Spaniard invited the plump man inside. D'Anglese inspected the outside hallway, saw no one, and so he proceeded inside.

As Trevelyan closed the door, D'Anglese invited himself over to a small round table where he began unloading his paper sack. There was a short squat plastic thermos, two china teacups, and two pie slices of *Torta di Limone;* a rich yellow and white topped dessert prepared with lemons and cream.

D'Anglese set the china cups next to the pie slices and then he opened the thermos. The pleasant odor of steaming hot Espresso filled the room.

D'Anglese beady hazel eyes examined both cups that he bought. The cup on his right had brown-green powder in it. The left cup was empty.

He poured the steamy espresso into the powder cup, turned, and gave it to the Spaniard.

Bishop Trevelyan examined the light brown coffee as D'Anglese poured himself some from the thermos. The portly visitor immediately began to sip the drink he had to put aside the Spaniard's suspicions.

D'Anglese lifted up his cup in a mock toast. "To new beginnings and a poor misunderstanding." He took a deep sip and pushed a piece of pie on the table in the Spaniard's direction.

Trevelyan peered into his foreign cup of coffee and then he glanced upward to study D'Anglese smug face. The fat priest seemed concerned that he hadn't taken a sip.

Trevelyan decided to humor the man by taking a drink of the espresso. His face contorted. The espresso was very bitter.

"It's good, yes?"

The Spaniard took another polite sip.

"Have some *Torta di Limone.* I have a special friend in the bakery who bakes for me sometimes. He made it special."

The Spaniard was glad to be able to put the cup down. He didn't wish to offend a superior who had come to start a friendship. He took the Cardinal's pastry and ate from it. The pie was very rich and had a slight bitter taste like the espresso. He attributed the bitterness to the pie's lemons.

Both men ate their pie and drank their espresso in silence. The Spaniard kept waiting for D'Anglese to make his peace.

D'Anglese kept waiting and continuously looked at his wrist-watch. He had called Cardinal Ferroli before he had left for the Spaniard's and told Ferroli that Trevelyan wished to confess to them. They were to come at three-o'clock.

A lingering doubt kept worrying him that the old man might come over early or bring someone along with him.

A half hour passed.

The Spaniard had finished his pie and most his coffee. He rested his knees against the table in front of them and leaned back in his chair. He appeared rather comical with light brown espresso foam caking across the lower line of his thick black mustache.

"Well?" The Spaniard finally asked. "I hope that you come over here with more than dessert in mind."

"Indeed I have, Bishop," D'Anglese gloated. "Indeed …*I have.*"

"Forgive me, but I 'm afraid that's rather diabolical sounding."

"Why did you run to *Il Redentore* first when you discovered the thefts in the vaults instead of coming to me?"

"I felt…that uh…it was my duty." He lurched forward. There was a dragging-nails-across-the-interior-stomach-lining sensation coming from the center of his belly. He felt dizzy and hot. His muscles started contracting and convulsing. "I'm afraid the *Torta di Limone* doesn't agree with me, Cardinal."

"It shouldn't, my dear Bishop." D'Anglese rose. "It's poison."

Trevelyan's eyes widened. He lunged at D'Anglese. "You!"

The Spaniard slid off the Cardinal's round belly and onto the modern carpet floor. He curled up into a ball and shook violently as his own body attacked itself. A strange course plant taste stuck in the back of his mouth and his heart raced away faster and faster. Several minute later his heart stopped beating. The last image that his eyes beheld was Cardinal D'Anglese prodding him with his fat foot.

A frail knock uttered from outside of the Spaniard's room door.

D'Anglese hovered over Trevelyan's corpse not quite believing what he'd done.

All there is…is the plan, he thought. *You must follow your plan!*

D'Anglese took a deep breath and retrieved a long black stainless steel dagger with a double razor edge to it. The knife had a hilt to protect the stabbing hand. He grasped the blade's handle firmly and carefully hid the dagger behind his flabby back.

A second rapping at the door occurred.

D'Anglese kicked the Spaniard over to the bathroom wall so that when he opened the door, Cardinal Ferroli wouldn't see the body on the floor.

A third rapping came when D'Anglese finally answered.

Ferroli was shocked to see that D'Anglese was already there.

"Where is Bishop Trevelyan, Francis?"

D'Anglese motioned Ferroli inside. "The bishop is most upset, I'm afraid. In fact, I believe that my early arrival may have prevented his suicide."

Ferroli entered slowly. D'Anglese carefully shut and locked the door. He added the additional security of a short slide-in-a-door-groove gold chain.

"Bishop Trevelyan?" Ferroli called out.

No answer.

D'Anglese turned from the closed door to face his mentor's back. His hand sweat from squeezing the dagger. He'd known Cardinal Ferroli for decades. The thought of plunging a piece of cold steel into the man was alien and repugnant but now all of his options were gone.

Ferroli reached the point in the room where if he bothered to look directly to his right, he'd see Trevelyan's body laid out on the floor.

D'Anglese gathered strength, raised his dagger pointed upward, and charged toward the old man as fast as his heavy frame would allow him.

He shoved the knife into the old man's lower right back. The sheer force of his charge caused both men to fall to the floor. D'Anglese found himself on top of Ferroli. He had lost the grip on the dagger but his fat gut had pushed the handle in deeper with the fall. "I'm so sorry," he kept whispering.

Ferroli moaned as he fell. D'Anglese weight crushed the air from his lungs.

D'Anglese rose from the old man's back, spotted the dagger handle in growing spots of dark red blood, and he retrieved it to plunge the knife into the old man again and again.

He picked his stabbing spots carefully. He hoped to destroy a major organ on every thrust. He went twice for the heart, twice for the lungs, and once for the liver. He slashed the old man's throat as an afterthought and emitted a strange girlish giggle.

The dark and bright red signature of human blood was everywhere. A dozen red specks traveled in a vertical line up the white wall to the ceiling. The dagger was soaked along with D'Anglese hands, face, and white Cossack. Ferroli was even more bloody.

D'Anglese mouth was gaping open. He was sucking in more and more oxygen which has him quite dizzy. He had the taste of copper in his mouth and he kept swallowing hard, trying not to puke. A sudden sharp pain erupted from the center of his chest.

A series of heavy, thunderous knocks came from outside of the room.

"Bishop Trevelyan," a 26-year-old called out. "Swiss Guard! Open your door please."

No one screamed, D'Anglese thought. *They shouldn't be here. I have to frame the Spaniard, but I'm covered in blood!*

More knocks followed. "Bishop Trevelyan?"

D'Anglese crawled over to the table and tossed the poison coffee cup over by Ferroli. He grabbed Trevelyan and pulled his limp body over to wipe the knife handle off on. He put the knife in the Spaniard's dead hand.

"Help me!" D'Anglese screamed. "For the love of God, Trevelyan's a madman!" He clasped his hand over the Spaniard's to maintain the grip on the knife and dabbed the lifeless appendage into Ferroli's blood.

"Break it in!" Boot-stomps started in on the door, but the door was very sturdy.

D'Anglese used the Spaniard's dead knife-holding hand to stab himself in the leg and free arm. Despite the adrenaline coursing through him the dagger wounds crippled him.

The door gave way partially to the Swiss Guard's kicks but it still held because of the tiny chain.

D'Anglese pulled the Spaniard on top of him and used the dead man's knife-in-hand to stab himself in the side. The final act was excruciating. D'Anglese started screaming in mock terror. "Get off! Get off me you madman! Somebody help me!"

The door slammed inward, allowing six Swiss Guardsmen to rush in. Their radios were alive with security chatter indicating that more help was on the way.

The first two Swiss Guard ran up on the dead Spaniard and yanked him off of D'Anglese.

"Poison," D'Anglese gasped. He craned his neck to focus on the empty coffee cup that lay on the floor. "He filled it with poison, drank it, and then tried to kill me and the Cardinal!"

One of the Swiss Guardsmen felt for a pulse on Trevelyan. "He's still warm, but he's dead." He reached over and examined Ferroli. "No pulse. He's dead too."

"I'm dying," D'Anglese whispered. He was turning a sickly pale. "Don't blame the Cardinal. If I die before I speak to His Holiness… tell him…the Spaniard confessed to everything. His French cohort has fled to Brazil." He faked passing out.

"Aiuto!" The Swiss Guardsman shouted into his radio.

"Chiama un medico!"

Another Swiss Guardsman reached for the dagger that still stuck in D'Anglese side.

"Leave it," the other Guard said in Italian. "That's evidence and removing it might cause more damage to his injuries. Remember your training!"

"Okay, okay! Let's get him out of here now or we're going to loose him."

D'Anglese listened to the Swiss Guard initial reactions. Everything was working out wonderfully.

Chapter 26

The Vatican, Deep Underground.

The Tiber River's water was cold even with the dry suits that they were all wearing. The underwater swim up the Vatican's ancient sewage tunnel had been extremely demanding. The tunnel was very tight in places where bricks and rubble had fallen from the circular tube ceiling. The debris rested in strange piles that they had to clear all the way back out of the tunnel or swim over.

The journey wasn't for the claustrophobic. Air bubbles from the scuba regulators lay trapped in the tunnel's ceiling and green slime from algae colonies covered everything.

Big Tony hated the swim because his waterproof flashlight kept blinking on and off. He would see a furry of big and tiny bubbles directly in his flashlight's path, then darkness for a few seconds, and then he'd see the fins from the man swimming in the tunnel in front of him waving inches from his face.

He felt relieved to finally be able to swim through a freshly broken brick-and-mortar tunnel plug. He followed the bubbles and artificial light upwards into a large granular stone room.

He spit out his rubber regulator and reached over his shoulder to turn off his tank's air flow.

Ten men floated in a wide semicircle and their flashlights danced all over the white stone ceiling.

Against the far granular stone wall was a large metal electronics box that had a metal walkway under it. The short walkway started form the electronics box and ended at a locked vault door that was places into the left wall.

A rusty iron waterwheel skeleton wreck rested in the wall opposite of the vault door.

Yurgi swam over to Big Tony and splashed the foggy brown-green water at him. "We fuck-ing made it! Let's loot 'dis bitch."

"Big Tony raised his arm out of the water to peek at his cheep wristwatch; 1:46 am. He was surprised that it was still working. "We're runnin' late, Yurg."

"Fuck schedule! One painting will make heist total success, I tell you."

"It's your clam bake, Yurg. I'm just here ta eat."

"*Da.*" Yurgi started barking orders in Russian.

The Asian man produced an inflatable rubber raft which instantly filled with air from an activated canister. He let his air tanks sink to the bottom and climbed aboard the floating raft.

The water in the room was continuously rising slowly. The water alone was one foot under the metal walkway and three feet beneath the electronics box.

Number Four, a skinny Russian with a block shaped head, handed the Asian a squat metal cylinder. He took the cylinder into the raft, unscrewed its top, and emptied its contents onto a thin wet fabric cloth that lay on the raft's inner bottom.

Bog tony watched the man intently. He was curious to see whether the smart yellow man could beat the rising water's self-imposing deadline.

The Asian assembled a modern handle-activated push-drill. He studied the electronic box's screws, found a matching bit, and set it in the push drill's mouth. He moved the raft over to the walkway and climbed out, pulling the raft with him.

He placed the bit into the first screw and pumped his drill handle in and out. The screw came out as the drill bit twisted from the kinetic recoil. He had all of the screws out and the cover panel lying beside him in the raft in less than three minutes time.

The water tickled the bottom of the metal walkway with its tiny waves.

He studied the electronic box's maze of square circuit boards, red-yellow-blue-black wires, and clocks of green and red LED lights. He stepped into the raft as the water rose through the grill to touch his feet. He studied the technological soup for awhile and talked to himself in Mandarin Chinese.

After a hesitant fifteen minute study session he attacked the box with shiny gold alligator clips that were both attached to a single wire. He clipped on to a green wire and then onto a red wire going to a LED block. He reproduced the same technique over a dozen times. All of the lights stayed green as he did further wire bypassing and high wire trickery.

The water had risen a foot-and-a-half away from the bottom of the electronics' box. He used crude sign language, warning the men not to make any waves; least the water should spill into the electronics' bay, tipping their hands.

Yurgi's impatience began to show as the Asian spent over twenty minutes on the thing in addition to his initial fifteen minute study session. Yurgi questioned the man in Russian. He had recruited him from northern Mongolia because of his work for the Chinese space program.

The Asian shrugged his shoulders and gave a lengthy sing-song sounding reply.

Yurgi relaxed and watched him make last minute adjustments.

"What did he say, Yurg?"

"He fuck-ing says they have oxygen alarm, humidity alarm, heat detection, motion sensors, and fucking invisible laser beams all inside of vaults."

"Oh."

"Fuck yes, *oh*." Yurgi mocked. "He say he has system bypassed but worries about water shorting out our fix."

Big Tony stared at the Asian and then back to Yurgi. "Shit. So what's it all come down to then?"

"Fuck-ing ACME tire sealing foam."

Big Tony snorted. The revelation was insane.

"We must hope 'dis shit holds tough."

The Asian retrieved a bright yellow can of tire foam with a red hose attached to the top nozzle. He placed a specially machined spigot onto the end of the red attachment and raised the spigot end up carefully to begin spraying a fuzzy white spray across the metal edges of the box. He sprayed as quickly as possible.

The water was only inches away from reaching the bottom of the electronics box.

The foam expanded outward into a white marshmallow lined mushroom. He grabbed the cover panel from the raft, pushed it onto the box, and used the push-drill to reinstall the screws.

The screws went in hard, fighting the pressure caused by the expanding foam.

Once the panel was mounted he sprayed the screw-tops in white foam along with the cover-lid's edges. He spoke to Yurgi in Russian as he finished.

Yurgi raised his first in triumph. "If system fails, our friend has electronic beeper which trips on box failure to warn us."

"Great."

"*Da.*" Yurgi ordered the Spenatz Colonel into action. They were told to drill into the rock wall next to the reinforced steel vault door, place C-4 explosives in the new holes, and blast their way in.

Number 4 and Number 8 disappeared underwater to grab the drills.

"How much higher is the water gonna rise, Yurg?"

The idea hadn't entered the ambitions little Russian's mind. "I don't fucking know. We swim down three meters or so. We swim two-hundred meters horizontal. Chamber is below water line. So... oh shit."

Both men stared at each other as the revelation hit.

"Old Leonardo's wheel used *water current* for power," Big Tony deducted. "This room used to be submerged! The door is a *modern* addition!"

Yurgi groaned. "Dis place will fill up."

"Minus the air pockets and air pressure in here. That's probably why we aren't completely flooded out yet.

"We need to open scuba tanks to fill room with more air pressure," Yurgi said in Russian to the Spetnatz Colonel. He gave the Colonel further instructions.

Two more divers submerged beneath the stone room's water line.

"What did ya tell him, Yurgi?"

"I tell them to get water pump and long hose to pump out water. We start pimping this shit to slow flooding. They will also start extra tank relay. One man brings in full air tank while other swims out previous empty. Man outside takes empty and refills with air compressor."

"Sounds good."

Yurgi grabbed at Tony's back. "Let me see your air tank."

"Why?"

"I'm going to undo regulator and let all our tanks air out."

"That's fuckin' crazy, Yurg!"

"But necessary. Don't worry," he lied. "We'll have every-one's tank replenished before we leave."

Chapter 27

Venice, The island of Torcello.

A polite knock came from the front door of Renauld's old house. Clayton and Tonya lay stretched out on the couch in the living room. They were enjoying the remains of the breakfast that they'd made together. Bacon omelets, croissants, and warm orange juice. Renalud's refrigerator had died. It was late afternoon.

Clayton pulled himself off of the couch and approached the door. The knocking became more incessant.

"*Si?*" Clayton called out from behind the door with a heavy American accent.

"*Para l'Italino Lei?*" A smug voice questioned.

He wondered if the cops had tracked him down and decided not to open the door. "I speak just a little, but English would be much better."

"O-kay then," the smug Italian voice said in poor broken English. "Mr. Kea-sley? I am from …da…po-lice…de-part-ment."

"Un-hunnh, and?" He snapped his fingers to alert Tonya.

"Uh…and…a sir. We…uh…wish to talk-ed with you. Open the doors please."

Tonya crept over to the living room window. She squat down and peeked up out of the bottom of the window glass.

Four men dressed in everyday street clothes stood about. One man smoked a hand rolled cigarette and kept an eye out for onlookers. Each man brandished a semi-automatic pistol in their hands.

She snuck back to Clayton and mouthed the words, "Not cops." She kept shaking her head "no" repeatedly.

"A Mr. Kea-sley, sir. Please...open your doors for questioning, please."

"Puo parlare piu lentamente, per favor?" Clayton shouted through the door in almost perfect Italian. He had asked the man to talk more slowly. It was all he could think of to buy more time.

He grabbed Tonya's hand. They tried to make a dash out the back through the kitchen. A man loomed outside staring into the kitchen from a window in the garden.

Clayton figured that they were surrounded. They were hoping to have him walk right into their arms.

The men outside of the door didn't like being made fools of. Clayton's perfect Italian tipped them off that he expected something. Two of them began attempting to kick in the front door.

Clayton and Tonya ran upstairs. She ran into the bathroom as he headed into the bedroom.

Tonya grabbed a flask of rubbing alcohol form Renauld's medicine cabinet. She brought it out of the hallway and poured in onto the floor and walls on either side. "I need a match!"

Clayton had Renauld's bed sheets in his hands. He was tearing them into sections to make a rope. A jump from the second floor wouldn't kill them but he wanted to be able to make a healthy escape.

He glanced around for some matches, rushed over to Renauld's dresser table, and started pulling out small drawers. The third drawer held the matches. Renauld liked lighting candles in his bedroom when entertaining.

The downstairs doorway caved in with a thunderous crash. Glass broke from the downstairs kitchen. Footsteps abounded from below.

Clayton tossed the matches to Tonya who stood in the bedroom doorway.

She made it to the alcohol puddles and lit the matchbook. She placed the flaming cardboard book into the puddle and jumped back as it erupted into a small steady fire.

The first thug didn't aim when he took a shot in Tonya's direction. The bullet whizzed by her right ear and hit the ceiling. The man half-stumbled on the last top step.

Tonya scrambled down the hallway and dove into Renauld's old bedroom. Clayton slammed the door shut and pulled the dresser against the door to block it. The smoke form the fire hit their noses.

The fire wasn't an inferno but it was burning nicely and the killers would be forced to deal with it.

"Smart girl." Clayton acknowledged. He went back to tearing sheets.

Three gunshots rang out from the hallway making their door shudder. Two penny size bullets were high in the center, while the third disappeared into the back of the dresser barricade.

Tonya peeped out over the balcony.

A hit-man below raised his gun and fired. The bullet pierced a piece of tile above her head causing it to fly.

She returned to the room to search for a weapon.

Clayton had fashioned a half-ass sheet-rope ladder. He tied one end of the rope around a thick table leg and turned it sideways. He planned to drop the sheet between two stone rail supports that held up the balcony rail and prayed that it would hold.

Tonya raced past him with a television set held high above her head. She stepped out on the balcony and tossed the set in the spot where she had last seen the hit-man standing. His shot rang out and hit her in the elbow as the television descended down on top of him.

The 1960s era television hit him square in the head. The glass screen broke across his face as he fell backward to the ground and didn't move.

Tonya slumped to the balcony floor, grabbing her elbow.

Clayton pulled her up and handed her the end of his sheet ladder. "Can you use one hand?!"

"I can try." She noticed that her boat was parked only ten feet away from them. It was worth the gamble.

The killers kept firing into the door from the hallway. One of them shouted out for the guy who was supposed to be covering the outside windows. He wanted to know if Clayton or Tonya had tried to jump yet. The fire was growing.

Tonya used her good arm and hand to wrap the sheet around for a good grip. Clayton helped her gingerly over the side and then strained to lower her gently using his own power.

The bedroom door jolted inward but the dresser barricade made it hold. One of the thugs had jumped through the fire and was now trying to knock-in the bullet-hole Swiss-cheese door.

Tonya made it to the ground safely and headed straight for her little red speedboat. She held her elbow as she went. The bleeding wasn't too bad.

Clayton positioned himself over the side as a killer ran out of the front door under him to grab Tonya. Clayton abandoned the sheet-rope and dove onto the man's head feet first. The man's gun flew into the bushes as his hand flew backward to deal with Clayton's debilitating weight.

Clayton's left foot broke the killer's nose which in turn sprained Clayton's ankle. The thug grabbed at his face and moaned in pain.

Clayton made it to the boat when one of the killers's shot him from the balcony window where they'd just came from.

The bullet hit Clayton high in the back shoulder. A two-inch hole exploded out from the front of his chest as the bullet exited. He stumbled forward and fell into Tonya's boat.

She launched the little craft at full speed.

The assassins broke out of Renauld's house as quickly as they'd entered. They poured into their purple speedboat and started after their prey. *The family* didn't tolerate a failure of this magnitude. If they screwed the job up then their man at the Vatican would definitely be displeased. Heads would roll.

"Who are they?" Tonya asked Clayton incredulously.

"I don't know. I thought they were friends of yours."

She looked over her shoulder down the canal. Trees, boats, and an old house whizzed by. A purple speedboat charged forward at the far end of the horizon. "Whoever they are, they're awfully persistent," Tanya yelled out through the course wind. She pushed down on the maxed out throttle hoping that it would somehow give them a little more speed. "We'll head for the parking lots and train station in *Santa Croce* in the *Piazzale Roma*. They'd be stupid to take pot shots in the Grand Canal. The police boats would be on them in seconds."

"Yeah." Clayton put pressure on the front gunshot exit wound with his opposite hand. "But we need to get medical attention."

"Take the wheel." She moved out of the driver's seat while still steering.

Clayton took the wheel with his good hand and slid into the driver's chair. He was shivering and his strength was draining quickly.

Tonya wasn't in much better shape. She used her good hand to reach under the seat and locate an old beach towel that she'd brought when she and Renauld had gone to the posh beach of the Lido. She used her feet and good hand to rip it down the middle.

Waves in the open lagoon forced their boat to bounce up and down violently. It couldn't be helped. They were forced to remain at full speed even though the assassin's boat slowly closed in on them.

Onion shaped domes, tall square bell towers, and a blend of floating Gothic-Byzantine-Baroque architecture reassured her. They were closing in on the main city of Venice extremely fast.

A long sleek white-and-black *motorscafo* sped past them transporting a gaggle of gawking tourists and naturalized Venetians.

Tonya used the towel pieces to temporarily dress her elbow and Clayton's shoulder. Their boat rapidly approached the *Canal delle Sacche.*

The assassins risked firing their guns several more times.

One of their bullets hit the butt of Tonya's boat throwing a triangular piece of fiberglass into the air.

"Keep your eyes peeled for a small canal entrance," Tonya shouted over the rumbling boat engine.

Clayton pointed their boat toward an area where a crowded gondola was coming out. A man in a striped shirt and black pants balanced on the back of the long canoe boat. He pushed a tall pole to push the craft forward.

"We'll make it," Clayton said.

Another bullet streaked past them hitting a Japanese tourist in the throat. He fell forward out of the gondola that he'd been standing in outward into the canal.

Apparently the assassins didn't care about the police anymore.

Chapter 28

Rome.

Cardinal D'Anglese was rushed from Bishop Trevelyn's room at the Vatican straight out to the *Ospedale Del Celio* in Rome. The best surgeon that the hospital had to offer operated on the failing Cardinal for two hours. After the surgery they placed him in a special communicable disease isolation room for recovery. An overhead fluorescent light washed out the color on D'Anglese skin making him appear deathly.

The hospital nurse signaled *Il Redentore* and the Swiss Guard Commander that D'Anglese had finally awakened. Both men thanked her as she left. The Pope's bodyguards remained in the hallway as the two men went in to visit.

"It was the Spaniard!" D'Anglese insisted in his effeminate voice as they entered his hospital room. "I never would have visited him if I had even suspected that he could be so violent."

Commander Occhibelli's face was flush. His voice was curt if not icy. "The Bishop *was dead* when my men pulled him off of you."

D'Anglese averted the Commander's gaze. His eyes pleaded for sympathy from the Pope. "The Spaniard heard the Swiss Guard kicking in the door. He left me bleeding on the floor to go and drink a cup of poison! I called for assistance as he returned to finish the job of murdering me! Thank goodness the poison acted quickly on him or I would be dead right now."

"Indeed." The Pope sat in a chair next to D'Anglese. He held the obese man's sausage hand in an effort to comfort him. He didn't believe D'Anglese story any more than Occhibelli but he played the game to discover the truth. Whatever that truth may be.

Occhibelli moved close to the recovering Cardinal. "Why did Bishop Trevelyn have poison in a tea cup, Cardinal? Why not just ingest the poison straight from the carrying container?"

"How would I know? I'm not in the Spaniard's mind. Clearly he was mad."

"We never found the poison's original container, Cardinal," Occhibelli's voice raised. "What we did find was another tea cup that matched the cup Bishop Trevelyn drank the poison from." He waited.

There was an uncomfortable silence.

D'Anglese eyes bulged and his jowls shuddered. "And?!"

"And….how odd that the man has no other china cups to speak of. Nothing that matches those two cups."

"I don't care for your tone." D'Anglese turned his attention to *Il Redentore*. "Your Holiness, do I have to listen to these ridiculous heavy-handed allegations?"

The Pope patted his hand saying nothing.

"Did you have tea with the Bishop, Cardinal?" Occhibelli pressed.

"Tea? Why no." D'Anglese stared at the Holy Father, ignoring his interrogator but answering the man's questions at the same time. "No, I did not."

"So why were you there then? My investigation reveals that you and the Bishop *hate* each other," the Commander growled. "I believe you implicated him in the theft of the paintings in the vaults to one of my Swiss Guardsmen. I believe that you said to him that you weren't one to spread rumors."

"Yes. It's true that we disagreed often, Commander. But *hate*? Hate is a very powerful word. I was at the Bishop's residence merely to assist Cardinal Ferroli whom had sources supplying him with information which implicated the Bishop in stealing and selling stolen art. That's all I was told."

Occhibelli grabbed the bed rail and held it so hard his knuckles turned red. "I'm sure it was."

D'Anglese mind began turning various scenarios around until a great one presented itself. "Oh my," he gasped out loud in self-realization.

Occhibelli's grip on the bed rail eased. "What?"

"Perhaps the Spaniard planned to poison Cardinal Ferroli!" He clapped his chubby hands together and then winced from the shooting pain in his side. "That must have been the reason that the poison was in the cup and why their were no other cups. After the Cardinal fell he must have planned on destroying the cups and implication of poisoning. The only reason his plan failed was due to my unexpected appearance at the Cardinal's request!"

Commander Occhibelli's mouth hung partially open. He shook his head in disgust and left the room slamming the door.

Il Redentore patted D'Anglese hand again. "You must forgive him my son. Two priests have died under his command. He can only be frustrated."

"Of course, Holy Father," D'Anglese gloated. "I forgive him."

Chapter 29

The Vatican. Deep Underground.

Three Russian ex-commandos finished placing C-4 explosives into the six holes that they had just finished drilling into the stone wall. The process had taken almost an hour.

The water had risen halfway up the foam-sealed electronics box.

The three demolition men wired up the explosives with thin blue wire and told Yurgi to get everyone ready.

Yurgi looked to Big Tony. "We must swim to bottom of this chamber, hold breath, and blow up wall."

"Sounds dangerous as hell."

"Da." Yurgi told the other men to get ready.

A minute later all of the men sucked in a deep breath of air and dove to the bottom. The Colonel turned the handle on a friction activated detonator as he swam to join them.

A huge blast rumbled above them sending large and small chunks of cement raining into the water and down on top of them. Bubbles and dust destroyed the water's visibility so that nothing in the water could be seen at all.

No one saw the huge chunk of wall sink on top of the Asian man. He was pinned under the mammoth rock and his lungs couldn't help but suck in the river-sewer water.

Big Tony swam up to the chamber surface to breath. The air was covered in thick dust and he started coughing heavily. He barely made out the silhouette of the Colonel who swam two-feet in front of him.

Yurgi's distinct voice kept cursing someone in Russian. He kept telling them that they were morons for using too much explosive.

An arduous stench of burning mildew and hay hit their noses. Gray and black smoke filled the chamber from the gaping hole in the left wall.

The Colonel found a half-filled scuba tank and passed the regulator around so each man could take a breath of uncorrupted air.

"What the hell is causing that smell?" Big Tony asked his friend.

"Fuck-ing smoking cow pies or some shit. In Siberia, they use cow shit for coal. Smell is very similar, I tell you."

Two of the demolition men made it up to the large hole in the wall. They climbed up into it and pushed rocks and debris down into the water.

Yurgi wanted to be the first inside of the vaults. Black and gray smoke still poured out filling their chamber. He had two men help him up and inside.

"Yurg! The water..."

The addition of new air spaces caused dramatic changes in the chamber air pressure. The water started rising quickly. The smoke began to blow back through the hole it had come from, creating a reverse air vacuum.

"We'll need our scuba tanks now," Yurgi said. He gave the order in Russian.

The vault Yurgi was entering was pitch black. He switched on his flashlight and stepped inside. He grabbed a matted smoking material from inside and brought it out into the chamber for them all to see.

Big Tony swam over to him. "What the hell?"

"Is fuck-ing ancient tapestry." Yurgi dropped it into the water. "They're all fuck-ing smoking." He grinned. "They would all be impossible to fence anyway."

The Colonel handed Yurgi a bag of tools and a large pair of bolt cutters.

Yurgi disappeared into the hole again. He side-stepped the ripped steel tapestry holders and started tossing the remaining hanging ones into the water. "Piece of shit rugs!"

The men pushed the ruined ancient murals down into the filthy brown-green-gray water in hopes of putting out the smoldering fires and getting rid of them as an obstruction. The chamber stank of mold, dust, and a substance close to gobs of burning hair.

Yurgi disappeared into a tangle of more hanging tapestries. Seconds later came a series of dull thumps. He was slamming into the tapestry locker's thin protective door trying to make it burst inward. Finally it gave way from a hastily placed karate kick and an old Russian curse word.

"Tony! You come now. Right now!"

"Yeah." Big Tony ditched the community scuba tank and joined Yurgi inside of the tapestry locker. Tiny burning embers popped and hissed around his head as he bumped into Yurgi from behind.

The sub-vault that they had broken into was trashed. The tapestry locker door lay on the floor under two-feet of quickly rising water. Smoke was everywhere making Yurgi and Big Tony's flashlight beams look more like laser beams than open light. The vaults were icy cold.

Yurgi took off into another sub-vault attempting to reach the main gallery. "We must find main doors," he said.

Tony stumbled behind him. The water had risen to their knees.

After a hurried search both men discovered the inner stone slab entrance/exit door with its little metal box attached to the wall.

Yurgi put his flashlight into the cruddy water illuminating the shape of his feet. "Stick your head down there, Big Tony."

Big Tony did as he was instructed and felt around on the rough floor. His fingers felt a thin metal lip and then inverted metal ridges. "It's metal."

"*Da*. Is grate to hydraulics on power doors," Yurgi said. He lifted a crowbar out of his tool bag and had Big Tony place the bar's teeth into the grate's lip. He shoved down hard.

Big Tony grabbed the grate and pulled it aside. He felt down into the spot where the grate was covering. "I feel...four hoses. They're pretty big."

"Fuck-ing cut them."

"With what, Yurg?"

"Bolt cutters."

"They might be electric lines!" Big Tony stepped back. The water around his knees made a sloshing sound. "Just a little cut in the cable could fry us all, Yurg! We're fuckin' standin' in three feet of water fer Christ's sake!"

"Is hydraulics," Yurgi insisted. "You cut cables or they come through doors! Priest's note says first thing to do is cut cables. His shit has been money so far."

Big Tony stared at his partner and imagined what might happen if he refused. He would be gambling his life on a last minute instruction made by a blackmailed pedophile priest. Surely it was meant to be a death trap.

He was dying of cancer so he figured that electrocution wasn't the worst way to go. "Fuck it." He put the bolt cutters down into the muck, placed the dual metallic teeth over the first cable, and cut. Blackish-blue fluid squirted up to the cruddy water's surface like squid ink. A hot blast of air exhaled through Big Tony's nose as he laughed to himself in relief. "One down, three more to go."

The water had risen another foot.

"Let's go Tony. We're fuck-ing way behind."

"Da, da," Big Tony mocked. "I'm working on it."

Another hour had died by the time Yurgi's men had the looting assembly line going. Yurgi, Big Tony, and the Colonel were taking large paintings that were stored in hermetically sealed casings out of their containers and handing them to the three men.

The latter would take the bulky oversize canvases that were handed to them and roll them up in plastic air-tight tubes. The men brought a pile of miscellaneous equipment with them that they carried in small bags. They didn't know what they'd need so they brought special items for just-in-case scenarios. The irony was that the water had risen up high on their chests and the bags kept sinking from sight. They were spending more time relocating their equipment bags than properly stowing away paintings.

Four men worked on their own, grabbing hermetically sealed boxes that were of size to fit down the tunnel. They would collect a stack of slime boxes, bring them into the electronics box chamber, and then pass them off to the relay men. The tunnel men would put the boxes in a large net sack. The sack was tied to a very long rope which ran down the tunnel and out into the Tiber River to the next man.

The sack would be untied and tossed up onto the Castel Sant'Angelo river bank among all of their fake telephone company equipment.

They had abandoned the scuba air tank relay idea after realizing that they'd never get enough air in the vaults to stop the flooding. A few emergency air tanks were brought in so the men could exit without drowning if the vaults all become flooded.

The whole crew had been down in the vaults for well over six hours. The dead Asian man who laid under a boulder and a pile of burnt tapestries had been beeping for over an hour. The foam had given way and the alarm had sounded. The crew continued stealing totally unaware.

Yurgi and Big Tony discovered the rare parchments, inquisition records, Papal diaries, and Jesuit communiqué containers after the paintings and relics were looted. Yurgi had the crew start removing them as quickly as possible.

"I thought the priest said not to touch this stuff," Big Tony said.

"He said a lot of things. Book worms pay big cash money for 'dis." Yurgi shined his flashlight in Big Tony's face. "If you had papers you never wanted world to see but you couldn't bring yourself to burn them, where would you put them?"

"Some place no one would ever find them."

"*Da.* Now we have more than video tape for insurance." Yurgi grinned.

The water was clearing. It had risen up to their throats. Yurgi inflated his scuba jacket to keep his head above water.

The rest of the crew had their scuba gear on to operate underwater in their continuous stealing.

Seven o'clock in the morning was quickly upon them. The paintings had all been grabbed; most of the parchments, ancient coins, small erotic marble statuettes, and a computer hard drive were taken.

Once the vaults were ninety-five percent flooded, Yurgi and Big Tony were forced to revert back to using their scuba gear and fins. Their swim around the newly emptied corridor shelves was surreal. Debris floated everywhere.

Big Tony discovered a vault room with an ornate gold leaf and hand carved *cassone*; a Renaissance chest in excellent condition minus the new water damage. He tried to open it with his right hand as his left focused the flashlight on it. A flurry of air bubbles expounded from his regulator from the effort. The chest was locked.

He used his stainless steel diver's knife to jimmy open the lock. Tiny wood splinters floated away from the lock as the lid rose up; sucking in several dozen gallons of water.

Inside the long coffin-like container he discovered stacks of fired clay cuneiform tablets written in an ancient language. On top of the tablets was a three foot long solid gold statue of Isis cradling a baby boy in her arms that lay on its side. The statue was very old and mirrored a marble statue of the Virgin Mary and the baby Jesus that was in the same chest.

On the outside of the *cassone* were two solid-black Madonna's resting on both sides.

Big Tony left to find the rest of the crew. He wanted the tablets and statues taken by hand since the coffin chest was too big for the sewer tunnel.

Yurgi swam by himself down the farthest vault rooms to make sure that they hadn't overlooked anything.

I bet they're shitting, he thought proudly to himself as he swam. The image of water trickling under the slab excited him. *How do you open a stone door that won't open, without drawing attention to a place that's not supposed to exist?*

Yurgi left a water-proof package tied to the foam-lined electronics box as he swam out.

A bright yellow square tent hung over the aluminum ladder that led out of the Tiber River. The casual observer watched as a bogus phone company employee walked to the tent and then came back out with two very large duffle bags. Obviously they were merely packing up phone repair equipment.

When the entire crew was about to leave in the trucks a friendly local policeman stopped by to direct traffic for them.

Chapter 30

The Vatican. Deep Underground.

The muffled boom from behind the main secret vault door alarmed the two Swiss Guard who were on duty. Dust rained down from the rock ceiling over them creating a fine chalky mist.

"What was that?!" The junior guard asked his senior in awe.

The older man cocked his ear and waited for the sound of the alarm. "Wait...." The repeating low electronic chime never sounded. He waited five minutes and then called for Commander Occhibelli on his radio. "031 to 1..."

"031 to 1..." The senior guard repeated into his radio.

"1 is off duty, 031," the radio switchboard operator answered.

"Please wake him immediately," the senior Swiss Guard requested.

"What is your emergency?"

"Just wake him up and tell him to report to 031."

"I don't have you listed on the duty chart 031. What is your location?"

"He'll know. Just wake him. Now!"

The senior guard put his radio down and turned to stare at the stone slab. He wondered what could have caused the horrendous noise and what exactly did the Church keep behind the double-stone slab doors.

Commander Occhibelli took a half hour getting down to the secret vault entrance. The senior guard related the events to him.

"But the alarm didn't sound after the noise?" Occhibelli asked.

"No, sir."

"No other disturbance to report?"

"No, sir. But I figured that you or one of the clergy should enter and check anyway. I've held this post for eight years and this has never happened before."

Occhibelli rubbed his eyes. He was still waking up. "I'm not allowed in the vaults either. As far as the priests are concerned, Trevelyn's dead, D'Anglese is in the hospital, and His Holiness is sleeping."

"What about the fourth Cardinal, Commander," the Senior Guard asked.

"He's in charge of the vault inventory auditing. I can't wake him up for something like this. He's been down here all day already. The alarms would have sounded if there was trouble. I'm not going to sound the alarm on something you *thought* you heard. Keep me posted if there are any further developments."

They saluted each other.

Occhibelli left for his bedroom. He returned several hours to face another nightmare.

A series of fine sprays of water squirted out from the edges of the recessed slab door.

Occhibelli couldn't believe his eyes. "For how long?"

"For the past thirty-minutes, sir."

"I've got to go and wake the Cardinal."

"Shouldn't we wake His Holiness, Commander," the senior guard asked with a hint of sarcasm.

"No. Not until we know what's going on. I'm guessing a water main burst above us and is traveling down. The Cardinal's card will open the door and then we'll see." Occhibelli glanced at his wristwatch; it was a little after six o'clock. He began to leave to wake the Cardinal when the vault alarm sounded.

"I guess its figured out that there's water inside," the senior guard said.

Occhibelli felt sick. Something was wrong and all of his senses were now screaming it. He left to go get the Cardinal.

More water started spraying from the slabs side corners.

Chapter 31

Venice, Cannaregio.

Clayton turned the boat around the tight 17th century Baroque-style house's corner; shooting down a narrow residential canal way. Tonya was partially turned in her seat watching the after effects of the Japanese tourist who had been shot in the throat. The man grabbed at his neck and fell forward out of the gondola into the water. The purple assassin's boat hit him and the front end of the gondola that he'd been standing in as the killers' sped past. The pole-pusher dived in to save the floating tourist.

The scene went out of Tonya's view after they turned the corner around the house but the assassins were only a hundred feet away. The boat slowed to turn the tight corner and regained its spot in the chase.

To everyone's right was the *Fondamenta Case Nuove sidewalk.*

Clayton and Tonya's boat flew under two low bridges. The canal narrowed dramatically.

The assassin's boat closed within thirty feet of them. People and buildings whizzed by in a blur of color.

There was no time to warn Tonya. Clayton swayed their boat hard to the left. The little craft scraped along a building's wall leaving a wide lane for the killer's boat to come up along side.

Clayton saw the sidewalk ending up in front of them. He banked their boat hard right, still at full power. Their boat groaned from the heavy horsepower it was ordered to continuously extend as the craft's bow hit the sidewalk head on.

The boat lurched forward; slowing and speeding at the same time. The fiberglass skid across the concrete. Pedestrians dove out of the way as the boat pitched over to Tonya's passenger side and the street raced by with buildings, pigeons, and a tall church tower.

Clayton and Tonya were thrown into the boat's dashboard causing the windshield window to crack.

The horrendous screeching caused by their boat's hull sliding came to an abrupt end. The boat had stopped two feet in front of an old post office building.

Tonya felt a warm trickle come from her nose and mouth. Her hand confirmed that she had a severe nose bleed.

Clayton shook her. "We gotta go! They're coming!"

She turned and saw the assassins hopping out of their purple boat onto the *Fondamenta Case Nuove* sidewalk.

Clayton bailed out first and anxiously began running up the street while carefully minding his rear shoulder/chest wound. Tonya leaped out and joined him. She carried her hurt elbow arm with her good hand ensuring that she wouldn't hurt it further.

She took the lead. "Come on! I know this place. There's a water bus station up on the next street. The *Ponte dei Tre Archi* stop."

They shuffle-ran to the *Fondamenta Di Cannaregio*, hung a right, and hurried toward a light blue-and-yellow roof trimmed *vaporetto* station which hovered on the water a few feet from the sidewalk. A smart steel pole plank way attached the station to the sidewalk.

A group of people were boarding a forty-foot long white steel water bus.

Sirens from the *Polizia Municipale* boats became louder from the canal that they'd driven out of.

Only one assassin followed them. He walked at a leisurely pace, keeping a fierce focus on them.

"Accelerato?" Tonya asked a waterbus steward who was about to chain off the coats entrance/exist way.

"No."

"*Quaranta uno?*"

"*Si*," he answered.

Tonya grabbed Clayton and escorted him onto the boat. "This bus is going to take us to the outer islands."

"You've got a spot for us to hide?"

"Uh…yeah."

The steward pointed to their wounds with a look of concern.

"No," she said. She led Clayton into a crowd of curious people.

The steward began to rechain the boat's boarding entrance when the assassin brushed past him with an air of self importance.

The steward mumbled under his breath and secured the chain as the waterbus engine hummed to life. The unwieldy passenger vessel moved forward into the *Canal di Cannaregio*.

The assassins trailed behind them in their low-riding purple speedboat. One of the three men in the boat held a bright green colored cell phone up to his ear.

Clayton and Tonya leaned up against the steel and wood rail located in the rear of the boat over the propeller.

"Don't we need tickets?" Clayton asked her.

"The only person who checks the tickets is the inspectors and they rarely board the boats for ticket inspections."

"So what if they show up today and catch us?"

"We pay an obscene fine."

"I didn't bring my wallet."

She directed her green eyes to point out the man who had boarded the boat in hopes of killing them. He talked into a tiny silver cell phone to give the purple boat updates. Tonya nudged Clayton in the ribs. "I think we have enough to worry about, don't you?"

Clayton didn't respond. He tried to be invisible.

The assassin was a thin man with a stubble beard. He wore all black square-lenses glasses and sported a bulge in the upper area of his brown leather jacket. He sat on a weather proof cushion bench ten feet away from them.

A heavy-set blonde woman wearing an American flag t-shirt and blue jeans, offered the only buffer between them.

"He's going to shoot us," Clayton whispered. His bullet necklace suddenly felt unlucky. "I'm ready for this. If he shoots…I'll take it and you jump over the side. Just tell my sister I am truly sorry."

"You can tell her yourself." She kissed him. "I've got a plan."

Chapter 32

Rome. *Ospedale Del Celio.*

Cardinal Francis D'Anglese lay in his hospital bed making efforts to befriend *Il Redentore.* The Supreme Pontiff seemed far from receptive but he still held D'Anglese hand in a gesture of support. It was morning. The Pope had returned for a second visit but left Commander Occhibelli behind.

The Commander had left the Pope an urgent note telling him that an incident had occurred in the vaults and that a full report would be given at noon.

The Pope leaned back in the plain plastic hospital chair with his eyes closed in contemplation. He opened his heart to God asking Him for the way he should use to reach Cardinal D'Anglese. The hospital room was freezing and smelled of antiseptic.

D'Anglese watched the Pope rest in his chair. He absolutely hated the man.

Soon the double-crossing Frenchman will be dead, D'Anglese thought proudly. *Him, the gypsy whore, and the American. Ferroli's dead. Trevelyan disgraced. The vault should be stripped of all its art by now, the tape should be destroyed, and I'll be free of this once and for all as they fumble forever with unraveling the chaos.*

D'Anglese eyed the fisherman's ring on *Il Redentore's* finger. He dug deep within himself to curb the urge in ripping it off of the old man's hand. There was a rage within him that kept tearing at his insides. He was loosing control and for whatever the reason, *Il Redentore* always brought it to the surface.

Oh how you're lucky, Il Redentore! If Trevelyan wasn't dead...I could've killed you too. He saw himself standing over the Pope's lifeless body in the Papal apartments. *Oh my ...it must have been Bishop Trevelyan.*

"Why did you become a priest, Francis?" The Pope spoke without opening his eyes.

"To...uh...*help* people, Holy Father," D'Anglese replied with a slight lisp.

"So, your reason wasn't to be closer to God?" He opened his eyes to study D'Anglese face.

"We can all be close to God, Your Holiness. I just wanted to serve Him on a daily basis."

"And have you, Francis?"

"Have I what, Holy Father?"

"Have you *served* Him?"

D'Anglese took a moment to respond. The memory of stabbing Cardinal Ferroli entered his mind. The poisoning of the Bishop. The looting of the vaults and the liberties he took with the gypsy family that led to the whole mess.

"Yes. Holy Father. I believe I have."

"But how, Francis? How?"

"By aiding mother church, Holy Father." He withdrew his hand from *Il Redentore's*. "I have served in numerous parishes in the Americas, in His name. I assisted Cardinal Ferroli in his real estate dealing on behalf of His church. I administered well over the secret vaults until Satan recruited the Spaniard and used him to destroy my good name."

"Your call to return to Rome came at an opportune time, I hear."

D'Anglese sat up in his bed, careful not to upset his wounds. "What do you mean by that comment, Holy Father?"

"I mean, Francis, that when his former Holiness, John Paul the Second, sent me to America, this was to sort out the indiscretions of some of our...troubled brothers. Your name was one of several which continued to come to my attention."

"Indiscretions?"

"Of the carnal nature." *Il Redentore* could tell a lot by the injured priest's reactions. He remembered seeing D'Anglese file a decade ago. It was one of the thicker ones and the number of witnesses who complained to the Diocese was overwhelming. The crisis went away on its own after they moved him. "Tell me, Francis. What parishes did you work for and how long did you work there?"

"Oh there were many, Holy Father."

"Please. Name a few to humor an old man."

"Very Well." D'Anglese waved his hand in the air dismissively. "I administered the faith in Chicago for four years, then I transferred to Boston for two years, then I felt a need for a change and volunteered to go to Alberque, New Mexico for a year and a half."

"And then?"

"Uhmm…then I was ordered to Buffalo for a year, then back to Boston for six months, New York City for a year, Quebec for six, and I finished in Mexico City having served two years there before being recalled to Rome."

"Why so much moving, Francis?"

He giggled nervously. "Restless spirit, I guess, Holy Father." His lisp became more apparent. "I enjoyed administering the faith."

That's what I feared, Il Redentore though to himself.

"Why are you asking me these things, Holy Father?"

"Because you are wounded, Francis. I wish to help you heal yourself."

"Thank you, but my stitches are holding wonderfully." He patted his fat belly close to his stitches.

"I'm not referring to that type of wound, Francis."

Il Redentore reached over to pat D'Anglese heart area. "I'm talking of wounds which run much deeper."

D'Anglese looked away. For the first time in his life he wanted to tell. He fought it. "I'm sorry, Holy Father, but my wounds are only mortal."

Both men remained silent for the next hour.

The Pope decided that he wouldn't leave until Francis opened up to him. He was about to order one of the Swiss Guard's in the hallway to find him some tea when Commander Occhibelli burst in.

"Your Holiness," Occhibelli wheezed. He had been running and was catching his breath. "I must...speak to you...outside...immediately."

"Please speak in here, Commander. Francis can and will remain discreet. After all, he's worked for Cardinal Ferroli."

D'Anglese eyes widened at the accusation.

The Commander issued a deadly look to the mending Cardinal. "Very well." His gaze returned to the Pope. "The Basilica of Saint Peter's grottoes have flooded out. The water is coming form inside of the Secret Vaults and continues to come in. The slab doors won't open and we have no way of getting inside without explosives or heavy demolition equipment. Obviously the use of such material might alert others to the existence of the secret area unless creative measures are taken." He leered at D'Anglese and clinched his fist. "I have reason to believe that further foul play has occurred. Perhaps someone wishes to make an investigation of the vaults inventory all but impossible. The alarm sounded early this morning. The timing was perfect."

D'Anglese tried to conjure up the image of decapitated dogs nailed to the ceiling, to keep from smiling. Everything had gone off as planned.

You have to remain serious, he thought. *Look somber. Act surprised at hearing the news.*

"You've worked in the vault before," *Il Redentore* addressed D'Anglese "What do you make of this?"

"A technical glitch form all of the recent use, I'm sure." D'Anglese tried to dismiss it. "Nothing the brave Swiss Guard can't handle, Holy Father."

"You smug bastard!" Occhibelli broke protocol. He grabbed D'Anglese leg and tightened his grip considerably. "Don't think you're free and clear, my friend! Your confidant Cardinal Ferroli liked to tape record conversations with his subordinates. *"Did you know that?"*

D'Anglese froze. The pain in his leg was nothing compared to the sinking feeling in his chest.

"My boys found *hundreds* of cassette tapes, Cardinal. We're starting on the most current dates and moving backward."

D'Anglese suddenly became very pale.

Chapter 33

Mestre.

Yurgi Svoboccen was an expert at smuggling. His favorite trick was to point customs in the wrong direction with a fake tip while he snuck his goods in or out of the host country's back door.

The commercial shipping port of Mestre was located in Northeast Italy, overlooking the vast Venetian lagoon. It was perfect for his plan. Mestre was hundreds of miles north of Rome and large cargo container ships frequently visited it.

Twelve hours had passed since they fled Rome with their vast haul. The sun set as evening arrived and their trucks transported over ten thousand years of irreplaceable history. Yurgi hoped the loot was worth twice its weight in gold.

The large container ship, *Hiusho Morkki*, lay moored to the Mestre loading dock awaiting the placement of its remaining cargo. Five rows high of orange, blue, and white steel cargo containers lay stacked up on top of each other like adult-sized Legos resting on the ships outside deck.

Seagulls flew over the ship in a natural hover pattern desperately searching for food.

Yurgi had his men lay out a green artificial turf carpet on the roof of an orange container which was stacked on the ship's edge. He brought up some cheap metal lawn chairs and positioned them on the turf so that they faced the busy port. He planned to use his new Eagle driver to whack golf balls into the ocean during the long voyage to Vladivostok. He was dressed back in his Tiger Woods clothes. He'd felt naked without them.

Svetlana brought Yurgi two pails filled with golf balls. After she set them down she clung to Yurgi's arm like a lock-jawed pit-bull. She hated Italy and didn't want to be left behind. People kept leering at her wherever she went. She didn't realize that her white fur coat and black spandex pants screamed for peoples' attention. She felt ugly and foreign and the ship couldn't leave fast enough.

Big Tony sat in one of Yurgi's lawn chairs watching the workers on the dock go about their business. Enormous four-legged cargo container cranes positioned themselves over the trucks to grapple onto the truck containers and haul them up onto the ship.

The puffy gray clouds disappeared as the dock yard's remaining floodlights kicked on, washing out everything that reached their artificial light.

Big Tony had bought a cheap tobacco store AM/FM radio near the docks when they arrived earlier. He had been listening to the radio for any news of the robbery. Eventually a story came out over Vatican radio. He was surprised it had taken them so long to finally release the information. The church had given them a twelve hour head start.

"Damn."

"What do they say?" Yurgi asked him.

Big Tony turned off the radio. "They're claimin to the public that a storage closet in the Vatican museum has been robbed this mornin'. The Italian state police discovered an over-turned rental car on the outskirts of *Citotavecchia*. I think that's in Southern Italy. Anyway, they say the driver is nowhere to be found but three of the Vatican's stolen paintings were recovered along with some coins." Big Tony got up out of his chair and approached his friend. "I thought you said all of the score was stayin' together until we got ta Russia ta divide it?"

"*Da.*"

"So what gives?"

"Is decoy. I set it up so they think we're trying to get out of Southern Italy with goods instead of North. They can't afford not to send the bulk of customs agents down south even if they expect ruse."

"Well, in case you're interested, the Vatican says they're offering a large cash reward to whoever returns their stiff. No questioned asked."

"Fuck that." Yurgi grabbed Svetlana's ass. "I got everything I need right here. Why risk it."

"So where are the rest of the guys?"

"In containers guarding loot."

"Won't they start stealin' stuff, Yurg?"

"I lock them in. We strip search them as we let them out," he lied.

The massive ship that they were on began to vibrate and rumble as its twin brass props slowly came under power.

The *Hiusho Morkki* was over a football field wide and almost two and a half football fields long. The steel bow of the ship rose six stories high from the water line. The bridge where the captain and crew controlled the ship was directly behind the container that Yurgi, Svetlana, and Big Tony were on. To get to their spot Yurgi and his guests would climb off of the outside bridge walkway rail and drop a foot below onto their Astroturf container.

The vessel felt like a ghost ship as it journeyed out into the lagoon at night. Asian deckhands rarely showed their faces. The containers were stacked so close and tight on the main deck that there was little room for anyone.

The lights of Venice shined on in the darkness in front of them. The beautiful ancient city appeared electric at night. The wind picked up and carried the moisture and smell of the slat water to them.

Yurgi wondered if the Colonel had killed the other men yet. He was skilled but sentiment from having served with some of them might slow him at an inopportune time. Yurgi was certain that the other men wouldn't see it coming but the other men did have the same elite military training too. He felt uneasy.

Yurgi's cell phone rang as Svetlana placed a golf ball on a makeshift tee for him.

"*Da?*" He answered.

"I hope you were successful in your business venture, Mr. Svoboccen. You've turned out to be a wise investment."

"Who the fuck is this?"

The voice had a nasal pitch to it and a peculiar familiarity to it. "No names, *Mr. Svoboccen*, but Talli says to tell you, hello."

Yurgi snatched his golf club from the turf and tossed it back down. "Fuck me! Is bitch-slut-whore- and Hollywood lawyer-to-stars, *da*?"

"*Da*...er, yes, Mr. Svoboccen. And I am putting you on notice. We know and *we plan to collect*."

"Dis is bullshit! I don't know of what you mean."

"We've been keeping track of you the whole time. As smart investors do. So, unless you wish to have a long chat with Interpol... I suggest that you immediately agree to an increase in your ex-wife's alimony payments."

Yurgi's blood pressure pushed hard on the veins in his neck. "Fuck you!"

"No, Mr. Svoboccen. I'm afraid it is us who are about to *fuck you*."

"You are fuck-ing ruthless, Sal. You tell me who told you or no deal." He walked over to Svetlana, grasped her skinny throat, and began choking her.

She knew better than to fight.

"*You* told us, Mr. Svoboccen."

"Bullshit!" He looked at Svetlana. "It was whore."

"We had a man who sat on top of the shopping mall roof top across the street from your miniature golf course business. He uses a line-of-sight parabolic dish. We have dozens of your outfit conversations. You are a producer, Mr. Svoboccen. Money opportunities seem to find you like your friend did that one night, but hey. If you're broke then you're broke. I'm sure the Church would pay for information...just like the FBI, if I were to..."

"Five percent." Yurgi let go of Svetlana's throat.

She fell to the turf hacking and gasping.

"I believe that *thirty* is much more appropriate."

"Thirty?!" Yurgi smacked the top of his forehead with his open hand. "You're fucking crazy!"

"Talli." Sal purposely spoke loud so that Yurgi could hear his conversation over the phone. "Can you find me the phone number for Interpol in my Rolodex?"

"I thought you said we were going to screw him again and go to Hawaii," a faint female voice complained in the background.

"You *promised me*, Sal."

"Okay, okay," Yurgi conceded. "Thirty."

"We'll see you soon?"

"*Da.*"

"Make it in two weeks. Talli will love to see you again."

Yurgi groaned. 'This I know, Sal. She is pig."

She grunted away in the background as if she were running on a treadmill. "Ask him if he still dresses like Tiger Woods," she said laughing hysterically.

Yurgi hung up before he could be questioned for her amusement. He turned to Big Tony. He didn't like what he was going to have to do to the man. Big Tony was the closet thing to a true friend that he had ever had, but business was business.

"Problems, Yurg?"

"*Nyet.* Is nothing."

"Was it your ex-wife?"

"No. Is her lawyer-to-da-stars." Yurgi picked up his golf club. "He crushes my balls."

Chapter 34

Venice, Island of Murano.

Clayton and Tonya decided to pick their opportunity carefully. The waterbus approached Murano and began to make its various stops at different *vaporetto* stations. They approached the *Colonna* stop in the *Cannale dei Maran*.

The purple assassin boat kept as close as possible, riding the water bus's white frothy wake.

Tonya left Clayton leaning on the back rail facing the assassin who sat several feet in front of him. She pushed through the throng of passengers and made her way to the driver of the boat.

The boat was only a minute away from reaching the edge of the dock. Clayton approached the obese tourist woman who wore the American flag t-shirt. He had to stall for time and keep her between him and the assassin. "Excuse me," he addressed her. "But is that an *American* flag t-shirt that you're wearing?"

Her eyes narrowed. No one could be that stupid. She assumed that he was some sort of lunatic. "I really wouldn't know."

"My brother has a shirt like that."

"That's nice." She started to leave.

Clayton grabbed her by the shoulders. "Wait! Can I get a picture of me with you and your t-shirt?"

"Now look here, mister..."

The boat landing came up along side of their boat. The assassin started reaching for his gun from under his jacket.

Tonya grabbed the waterbus's throttle and yanked it back in full reverse.

Everyone stuttered backward from the immediate jolt and shift in momentum. The bus backed into the purple boat sending the nose of the low riding craft underneath the butt of the bus and into its propeller. The assassins jumped out of their dying boat into the canal around them.

Clayton shoved the fat women onto the lap of the startled sitting assassin in front of him. He reached away to deboard with Tonya. They both shoved people into each other and made it out of the waterbus onto the *Fondamenta Serenella* sidewalk.

"Let's go, Clayton! Renauld's got a place real close to here."

Clayton half hobbled and half ran as they made their way up the *Fondamenta dei Vetrai*, across a stone bridge and onto the *Fondamenta Daniele Manin*.

Venetian glass stores were everywhere. Murano was the center of the 13th century glass making industry. All of the dying buildings hinted of their former greatness.

A faded yellow plaster building with two large showcase windows on the ground level greeted them as Tonya ran inside.

The assassins recovered from their error quickly and weren't too far behind.

Tonya closed the decorative iron-and-stained glass door after Clayton hurried in behind her. She turned the door's silver deadbolt latch to lock it.

Clayton wasn't holding up well. He had a new sickly gray-and-white skin tone. He swayed back and forth in place, dangerously close to tipping into the Venetian glass display case.

"*Buon giorno,*" a young woman in gray denim coveralls addressed them. She worked in the back of the store next to a big dusty brick furnace which was glowing red hot. The young woman had long onyx-black hair and a voice that sounded slightly familiar. She had a long metal pole stuck into the furnace with a large ball of molten glass attached to the end of it. She stood with her back toward them.

"Hi." Tonya gave a weak wave to her. "You've got to get out of here. There are men outside who want to kill us!"

The woman kept her back to them and removed her thick brown leather gloves. She seemed unusually calm. "Should I make a call?"

"No. Just take Clayton upstairs and hide."

"You weren't supposed to show up yet."

Tonya led Clayton over to the woman. "Just take him."

The woman took his hand and escorted Clayton up along a spiral staircase over in the corner opposite the furnace.

Two assassins stayed glued on either side of the store's display window peering inside. They had already tried to open the locked door and decided to regroup. They didn't dare start openly shooting people with a police station only six blocks and a canal away from them. They needed time to ensure the liquidation of each and every one of their assigned targets.

A third assassin went around to the narrow alleyway behind the shop. He attempted to open the store's faded green steel back door but Tonya had already locked it.

The fourth assassin left the scene to scrounge up a get-away boat for easy egress if shooting started.

Tonya rushed over to an old 1950-era push-lever cash register which was on a desk close to the display cases. She reached under the desk and pulled out a .22 pistol. She pulled back the gun's sliding mechanism to ensure that the spring fed magazine had loaded a bullet into the barrel.

She trotted over to the furnace and wedged the tiny gun between her pants and stomach. The cold steel made her belly ripple.

She snatched the molten glass ball out of the furnace with her good hand, positioned herself next to the backdoor, and suspended the glob of thousand degree glass above the doorway using the pole and floor to offset the ball's weight.

She balanced on one foot and used the point of her shoe to kick off the locking bar on the backdoor. The task made a tell-tale noise.

As she recovered her foot and almost lost her balance, the green metal door swung inward.

A stocky man with a gun dashed in and squeezed off two blind shots.

Tonya led the scorching gooey glass slob arc downward on top of the man's head and face. The killer's skin made an eerie sizzling sound and his shrieking almost ruptured her eardrums.

The smell of burning flesh assaulted her nose as she ran back to the door he'd come form and locked it.

The man's body was on the ground, feet pumping in and out in quick rapid jerks, the glowing translucent orange liquid turned Smokey black over his head. His hands were stuck; trapped in the hardened mass after his desperate attempt to slide the fire gel from his head and face. He ceased twitching and lay perfectly still. Smoke rolled off of the ruinous mound that was the remains of his head.

Tonya returned to the front of the store, crouching low as she went. Only one assassin remained peering through the widow. The other had disappeared.

"Tonya?" Clayton called out from upstairs.

"Be patient," she ordered.

The assassin who was staring through the window was attempting to see what had happened.

Tonya raised her .22 and shot through the window at him twice. Two quarter-sized circles broke into the glass close to the center of the skinny killer's chest.

The assassin's hands swatted forward as if he were waving off a killer bumble-bee, before he slid forward into the window dead.

The body in front of the store on the sidewalk was bound to draw attention.

Tonya dashed up the spiral stairs to retrieve Clayton.

At the top of the stairs, Renauld and Philip VanAucken greeted her. Clayton lay face down on the wood floor with Renauld's foot placed on the back of his neck.

The shop girl that they had met when they initially came inside was Shannon, Renauld's new girlfriend. She had dyed her hair black for when they cross the border into Switzerland. She acknowledged Tonya with a sly wink and watched the street below from the large second floor circular window.

Tonya smiled. She wasn't surprised.

Chapter 35

The Vatican, Beneath Saint Peter' Bascilica.

One of the Swiss Guards informed the Pope that their was something he needed to see immediately.

Il Redentore didn't like being rushed out of the *Ospedale Del Ceilo* and hurried back to the Vatican but the Swiss Guard had given a cryptic warning that the church had been stolen. How does one steal a whole church? Obviously they had all gone mad.

Commander Occhibelli met *Il Redentore* and his ten man Swiss Guard entourage at the *Arco delle Campane* entrance to the heart of Vatican City. Occhibelli ordered the Swiss Guard to form a human square around the Pope.

Eventually they led *Il Redentore* through the great Saint Peter's Bascilica past the astonished tourists and visiting faithful toward the entrance to the subterranean grottoes.

The Pope traveled down the narrow stairway first, followed by Commander Occhibelli, the Pope's two Prefects, Cardinal Ciatti and Cardinal Bitono. The ten Swiss Guard remained at the top of the grottoe's stairway entrance in a protective semi-circle.

A faded gold- and-blue tile mosaic of a saintly angel with wings and a halo watched over them as they descended.

Commander Occhibelli stopped on the last step where water started to spill over. "The grottoes are completely flooded, Your Holiness. River water from the Tiber touches the tomb of Saint Peter himself."

Il Redentore said nothing. He decided to sit on the ancient steps. The two prefects behind him wondered what they should do; sit or stand.

Cardinal Ciatti stood while Cardinal Bitono sat.

Neither man wished to break Papal protocol.

Commander Occhibelli continued in his situation report to the Holy Father. "The chambers of the Secret and Sacred have been robbed, Holy Father. The grottoes flooded out after we used explosives to blow apart the vault's main door slabs. The force of the on rushing water nearly drowned five of my men. If we had been any closer in the grottoe, most of us would be dead."

"How do you know that the chambers have been robbed and not just flooded?" Cardinal Ciatti asked.

"Because the *Polizia Municipale* called and notified us that we should send to help to them in their investigation of debris discovered along the Tiber's river banks. Our men have recovered over one hundred rare parchments that were scattered along the river with trash. The documents were written in Latin and a majority of them were written by the hand of Pope Alexander the Third. They were his commands to launch a campaign against the heretics at the Council of Tours; at least that's what our translator read."

"I hope this translator was Catholic," Cardinal Bitono said. "These papers mark the birth of the inquisition."

"He was one of our priests," the Commander reassured. "Bishop Dotaen."

"Those documents don't exist!" Cardinal Ciatti exclaimed. "The Church lost a majority of all documentation pertaining to the inquisition through poor restoration and a flood. I know this to be true because I run the Secret Archives."

"Which is why you weren't made aware of the vaults existence until the initial thefts occurred," *Il Redentore* answered. "The man who holds your position must never know of the sensitive documents that we posses. Think. You write the bibliographies, keep the central index, and direct approved scholars toward documents in our above-ground achieves. If you knew of the other files, you might error and mention something contained in them on paper or to a researcher by mistake." The Pope shook his head. "The Jesuits have done enough lying in the past to hold us well into the future."

"So I was lied to about the existence of documents related to the inquisition?"

"Yes, among other things." *Il Redentore* looked over his shoulder to make eye contact with the man. "It was necessary to protect Mother Church from her enemies." *Il Redentore* was becoming short of breath. His chest began hurting.

"What threats do the inquisitions documents pose, Holy Father?" Cardinal Bitono asked. He couldn't help himself. "They occurred will over one hundred years ago."

The Pope winced. He was feeling dizzy but he forced himself to deal with the crisis. "Have you been to America, Cardinal Bitono? The land of lawsuits and litigation."

"No, Holy Father."

"But you are aware of what happened to the Swiss Banks recently?"

"I'm not sure."

"The Jews sued them for reparations over money that holocaust survivors and victims lost in World War II. The banks wouldn't return their money to them after the war because the survivors didn't have the paperwork. Lawyers sued on behalf of the original survivors and now mostly the descendants of the wronged get awarded damages." He loosened his white collar.

Cardinal Bitono looked like a dazed animal frozen in a hunter's spotlight. *Il Redentore's* explanation was foreign to him.

"The world has generally forgotten what occurred during the *centuries* of the inquisition. People of noble birth and title were falsely accused of committing acts of heresy. In reality we encouraged them to level charges against one another to strengthen Mother Church's overall authority. Kings and Queens put their whole kingdoms in our hands. The Church would arrest the rival enemies of these people, torture them into a bogus confession, and seize all of their land and properties for Mother Church. The accuser would get a small percent of the seized properties in turn. If the accused was very lucky and didn't refute the charges, he or she was occasionally freed from our dungeons exiled and penniless."

Commander Occhibelli looked away as the Pope continued to explain.

"Once the aristocracy destroyed each other and we had the remaining rulers safe in hand we moved onto squeeze the peasantry. The *auto-da-fe* became public entertainment. People would espouse their faith to the Lord of Hosts by cheering as a fellow human being was burned alive in front of them. It wasn't just men who burned but also women and children. This is the true reason that European pagans converted so quickly to Christianity."

Cardinal Bitono still didn't have a clue.

"Ninety-nine percent of people killed, imprisoned, and tortured were not guilty of any crime. They were killed on the threat they didn't believe in the same idea. Our own documents show the absurdity of the tribunals reasoning and execution. Our Priests knew what they were doing was wrong and yet, the tortures and killings continued for over a century. The Church's wealth...the real money that has put gold leaf on our chapel walls, gold in our crosses and cups, and our vast real estate holdings come from blood and conquest, not the benevolent teachings of Jesus as our apologist friends now claim." His mouth was becoming dry. The dizziness still washed over him.

"No." Cardinal Bitono thought the Pope's view as far too critical. "You can't claim that..."

"To error is human, Cardinal Bitono," the Pope interrupted him. "But we the Church have issued a doctrine which says that *I and former Pope's are infallible on matters concerning faith and morals.* This means that even today, Catholics must view the inquisition as a just and righteous process since its goal was moral and spiritual purification ordered by a former Pope."

Commander Occhibelli appeared quite ill. He wanted to leave but he couldn't step over the Holy Father. The Pope was wrong. Occhibelli's church didn't kill and torture people. That was in the past, done by misguided holy men. He was a solider acting on the behalf of God to assist the Pope in helping God's children. The inquisition was a mistake best left in the past.

He didn't notice *Il Redentore* rubbing his chest in discomfort.

"Think Cardinal Bitono," The Pope said. "What happens when the records of the lands and estates we seized reach the eyes of the general public?"

"They will bring the church's past into a native light?"

"Yes. But Europe and South America will be thrown into chaos. *We* will be sued for reparations and *we* will have to compensate descendants of those wronged. Arguably, whole governments could sue us. The old tortures will be brought forward to the public's mind again. Burning human beings alive. Setting fire to their feet, making them ingest boiling water, suspending them from the ceiling by ropes in such a way that their arms are torn form their sockets, life impressments with a trial, the rape of women and children by members of the tribunal and others who assist them! Need I continue?" The Pope was sweating.

"Surely there can't be that many descendents, Holy Father," Cardinal Ciatti said. He acted cold toward the Pope.

"The inquisition lasted hundreds of years and tortured and killed hundreds of thousands of innocent people. Perhaps even a million. Can you imagine? That's unpardonable no matter what the rationale. Now we no longer control the truth. The records are out there, somewhere. We don't have documents which hold every name or transgression but records taken offer concrete evidence of what we knew, who was affected and how, what properties the Church confiscated illegally as a result. Such lawsuits could cost us *billions*." He leaned against the wall. "I'm afraid that I'm not feeling well."

The men were silent for awhile. Each man stewed in the revelation and no one seemed to hear him.

A Swiss Guard scuba diver surfaced at the grottoe stairs. The brown-green water swirled around him forma new back feeding current. He saluted, his hand dancing out of the water and almost hitting his plastic eye goggles. "Commander," he said after spitting out his breathing regulator. "We found a dead Chinese man in the chamber the thieves deactivated the alarms in. A rock from the wall trapped him underwater. He drowned. We're still in the process of searching the tunnel."

"Tunnel?" *Il Redentore* asked.

"Yes," Commander Occhibelli responded. He realized that he'd failed to update them with a full report. "The thieves used a sewage tunnel that feeds out into the Leonardo room and bypassed our alarm system. No one could have done this without inside help and detailed blueprints. As you are all aware, not even I was allowed back there or made aware of the vaults layout until now."

The scuba diver handed a vacuum-sealed plastic bag to Commander Occhibelli. Inside the foggy bag was a recently damaged VHS tape. The blast from the second slab sent stone fragments through the tape's casing. "I found it in the vault, sir. It was tied to the inner electronics box."

"How much appears missing?" The Commander asked.

"We're guessing everything, sir. Hoffman is in the Leonardo room rigging a seal to plug the water hole. We should be able to pump out the water in the vaults and grottoes within several hours."

"Good job. Stay here and await the pumps."

"Yes, sir."

Commander Occhibelli addressed the Pope. "Holy Father, every minute we sit here the thieves gain ground. Once they reach the safety of their destination, the Church's property will most likely be divided up and scattered throughout the world. Recovery will become all but impossible. I suggest we release a public statement of some sort."

"We can't do that!" Cardinal Ciatti balked. "People will ask questions. They'll want to know what exactly was stolen."

"Let the Jesuits handle the inquiries," *Il Redentore* said. "They'll give them proper answers. Tell them the request comes from me."

"Yes, Your Holiness." Bitono got up from sitting on the steps and began leaving.

The Pope called out him with an after thought. "Oh Cardinal Bitono, have the Jesuits alert the world media and tell them that the Vatican is a sovereign state. As such, I give my word that no one who assists us in the recovery of our stolen property will be persecuted. Furthermore, we will offer a large reward. No questions will be asked."

"Yes, Holy Father."

"Also, recall every Bishop and Cardinal of the Sacred College who is outside of the Holy city. Order them to come to the Vatican within the next forty-eight hours. We will be conducting an emergency meeting on the future of this church."

Cardinal Bitono climbed the last step and disappeared from view.

The Pope rose. He remained partially hunched over. "Commander Occhibelli. Do you believe that anyone is trying to assassinate me?"

Occhibelli's mouth dropped partially open. He managed to say no. "Why?"

"I wish you to reduce my body guards to one man and reduce the overall security of the Holy City to a handful of men. You can use all of the extra man power to search the ports and likely boarder crossings that the thieves might use to escape with our collections." He sighed. "As for me, I must visit my personal physician. I'm not feeling well. I believe I'm having an anxiety attack."

Occhibelli remained still. The Pope suddenly appeared much older and frail to him. The notion of leaving one soldier to protect the Holy Father from a laundry list of enemies seemed absurd.

He's right, Occhibelli thought. *Who tries to kill the Pope on a weekday here at home?*

"Commander?"

"Yes, Holy Father."

"Find out what is on that VHS tape without our history being recovered; we may not have a Church very shortly."

Chapter 36

Venice, Murano.

Renauld Fouchet enjoyed standing on the back of Clayton Keasley's neck. Clayton was wheezing. Drool oozed out of his mouth onto the dusty lumber floor.

VanAucken put his wedding ring and wallet inside of Clayton's jacket pocket.

"People are gathering outside of the shop," Shannon said form the big circular window. "You guys need to hurry this up." Visions of vacationing in Hawaii with Renauld swam around in her head.

Old plywood crates and boxes lay about cluttering the glass shop's second floor. The wood containers had springy spiral wood shaving spilling out of them which were used to protect the shop's creations when they were mailed out.

Tonya finished her ascent up the spiral staircase, unmoved at Renauld and VanAucken's appearance. She rounded the corner of the corkscrew stairs hand railing and disappeared behind a stack of large crates.

"You should have put her in jail when you had the chance." Renauld put more pressure on his neck. "It's crazy what a piece of ass will do to a man, no?" He ran his hand over his own slicked back hair. "I can speak of much experience on this."

"You hired the killers that came after us?" Clayton asked softly.

"No. They're no friends of mine," Renauld snorted. His French accent almost made his English unintelligible. "I would wager that they were hired on half of my good friend the priest."

"That was your supplier? A priest at the Vatican?"

"*Oui.*"

"How?"

"He approached me. I was selling fake holy relics and Renaissance paintings at my backroom auctions. Since I had already created a market for the black market Renaissance, the sale of the real thing was quite easy. I used Tonya to paint copies of the real Renaissance paintings which the priests would place back in the Vatican's vault. In this way they never missed anything at a casual glance."

"That's where I come in," VanAucken bragged. "Your family ordered an audit of my company last year. My certified books did not stand the muster, so I developed a quick retirement plan. One of our insurance customers got burned by Renauld here, I hunted him down, and we made an arrangement. He already had started his authentic art auctions of the Vatican's paintings so we both needed a bagman when we decided to get out. We wanted you arrested to link you directly to the painting scam but the police investigator's suspicion will do just as well."

"Why tell me now?"

"Because you're not going to leave this room alive, old boy." VanAucken

produced a glass vial with blood in it. He punctured the top of the vial and purposely put drops of blood on Clayton's jacket sleeve and collar.

"What are you doing?"

"It's very simple, really. When they discover your corpse they'll find my wedding ring and wallet in your pocket and my blood on your jacket. For insurance purposes the company already has my DNA. When the police run the blood splotches on your jacket they'll make the link and naturally assume that I fell victim to foul play. Meanwhile I'll be headed to *Rio de Janeiro* to start living the good life. I know a really great plastic surgeon there."

Tonya returned out form behind the crates and boxes. She carried a medium-sized canvas luggage bag with a thick brown leather carrying strap.

"It's all there?" Renauld asked her.

She unzipped the canvas top and peeled it back for Renauld to see. Stacks of orange-and-white 50 Euro notes slid about wrapped together in neat stacks with banker's bands.

"A police boat has pulled up outside!" Shannon yelled. She looked at Renauld. "We've gotta go baby!" She stamped her foot.

"Go downstairs and watch the back alleyway," Tonya volunteered. "Me and Renauld have unfinished business anyway." She zipped back up the canvas bag.

"I don't get it," Clayton said.

Renauld retrieved a Ruger pistol form under his jacket. He aimed it at Clayton's head. "What's not to get?"

"The sack of money. You're giving it to Tonya?"

"That slut wishes." He took the gun's safety off. "The cops will find the money with you. A dirty insurance investigator who is linked to his employer's disappearance, stolen art markets, and a bag of cash. Your renewed drug habit and sordid history will take care of everything else."

VanAucken fidgeted. "Kill him already."

Shannon left for downstairs.

Tonya joined Renauld's side and put her arm around his shoulder. Her green eyes had turned Cobra cold; deadly and calculating.

"Wait!" Clayton pleaded.

Renauld found himself hesitating. He'd never killed a man before.

Clayton gawked at Tonya. "He treats you like shit! You're his property. Didn't that time we spent together mean anything to you? *I love you*, Tonya!"

She didn't blink.

Shannon reached the backdoor downstairs and opened it. An enraged assassin greeted her outside by swinging the butt of his gun upside her head.

She fell to the cement floor with a slight whimper. The thug whacked her in the head two more times to silence her.

"Would you mind turning your head at an angle, please," Renauld asked Clayton politely. "The gunshot wound needs to appear self inflicted."

"*Kill him already*," VanAucken ordered. He had traveled to the circular window to watch the street below.

"What about your baby Tonya? Do you really think Renauld would be a good father? Do you honestly believe that he'll stick around?" He laughed bitterly. It had been awhile but now Clayton wanted to live to see tomorrow.

The police pounded on the entrance door down on the first floor. They commanded for someone to open the door in angry Italian.

Tonya arched her left foot back, aimed, and then brought her foot rushing toward and up in a hard core soccer kick. Her Italian pointed steel-toe-boot found its mark; smashing into Renauld's dangling testicles.

The dull thump caused by the contact didn't do justice to the severity of the injury.

The Frenchman gasped as he dropped his gun and doubled-over from unimaginable pain.

She kicked him again just to make sure.

VanAucken and Clayton stared at the abandoned gun that lay naked on the floor. Clayton was much closer to it than his advisory so VanAucken made the only play that he could. He bolted over and down the spiral stairway.

Clayton grabbed the firearm and sat upright.

Renauld coughed violently. His body was balled up in the fetal position with his hands holding his family jewels.

"There is no baby," Tonya said triumphantly. "I figured it was the best way to get rid of an old friend while still getting paid."

Renauld coughed. "Whore!"

The assassin punched VanAucken out of reflex and then used the butt of his gun to knock the man in the head.

The police kept banging on the front door. The sound of new police sirens approaching through the open back door encouraged the assassin to retreat from the building. He decided to wait in the alleyway.

"The cops are coming," Tonya said.

"I know you lied to him, but why to me?"

She reached for Clayton's arm. "Later. We have to leave."

Renauld sprang up and half-heartedly lunged at Tonya. His slicked-back hair swung about in a tangle as he grabbed Tonya's throat and carried her toward the window facing the street.

Her eyes bulged from the sudden attack. She kneed him in the groin again and spun him around by the time they reached the window. Her hit caused him to release his grasp on her.

Renauld's body followed the momentum of Tonya's shove causing him to break through the large round window and plunge below to the crowed street.

Tonya threw an open block of Euros out the window behind him shortly after the fall.

The horrified crowd was on top of the raining money in an instant throwing the police attempt to storm the shop and secure Renauld's withering body impossible.

Clayton hurried down the spiral stairs first. He held the Ruger out like a madman. He was at a point where he didn't care who he had to shoot to get free of the whole thing.

Tonya shadowed him with her drawn .22 pistol.

The unconscious body of Shannon lay between them and the open backdoor.

VanAucken stood, leaning against a glass display case that was tipping badly. Beads of blood dripped from a jagged gash on his forehead. He was attempting to make it to the front door.

Tonya picked up the woman's body, propped it up against the inner doorway, and waved her unconscious arm out the door.

Three shots rang out from down the alleyway. One bullet blew off of the woman's pinky finger.

The police out front came alive as the shots fired. They figured that the shots were aimed at them as the crowd out front scattered. The police saw VanAucken stumbling toward the front door with his hands outstretched. The shop was dark so they assumed he was aiming a gun at them. They opened fire.

Half dozen bullets flew through the front window sending shattered glass fragments everywhere. Ricochets blasted nearby blowning glass vases into pieces.

"One of our friends is still out there," Tonya warned to Clayton. VanAucken's body fell to the floor.

201

"Were you in the military or something?" Clayton asked. Tonya's melee skills shocked him.

"Worse." She grinned. "I'm a gypsy."

He ran; she thought about the assassin. *The gunshots have spooked him. Cops are everywhere.*

She waved Shannon's hand out of the door again. Nothing.

She stuck Shannon's face out of the door by holding her hair. Shannon moaned. She was coming around; her finger nub was shooting out blood.

Tonya dropped her to the ground.

The Italian police were breaking in the remnants of the shattered window. They had dealt with Italian mob wars before and history showed that it was best for everyone if they proceeded slowly. Their job was to pick up the pieces and turn the evidence over to the prosecutor. By then, politics came into play and it was out of their hands.

Tonya grabbed Clayton's side and helped him into the alley. "Lets go."

Gunshots rang out from up the alleyway by the street entrance. The police were fighting it out with the assassin.

Tonya tried several backdoors to other shops until they found a door to a furniture store that was open. They both stumbled in as a little glass door with bars activated a little door bell.

"*Si?*" an old woman in the front of the furniture store called out to them in the back.

"*Sto soltanto guardando,*" Tonya replied.

"*Va bene.*" The old woman didn't mind people who were just looking.

Tonya locked the door behind them; she took both of their guns, whipped off the fingerprints, and stashed them in a dresser drawer.

"We'll have to buy something expensive to encourage her not to sell us out."

Clayton had a strange smirk across his face. He just watched her intently and considered himself grateful.

She stomped her foot playfully. "What?!"

He remained quiet. His eyes slightly watered.

"What are you staring at?"

"You're *not* pregnant."

"No." she cocked her head.

"But you could get pregnant."

"So…" He nodded, grinned, and fixed his eyes on her belly.

"Clayton Keasley. You are impossible."

Chapter 37

The Vatican, Saint Peter's Bascilica.

Two days had passed since the Pope ordered a call for the Sacred College's Catholic Bishops and Cardinals to come to the Holy City.

Il Redentore still lived, leaving the Cardinals to wonder why they were needed so urgently.

The P2 Brotherhood held a secret vote on the fate of the modern Pope. Their brother, Cardinal Ferroli, was dead. This meant that they had lost direct control over *Il Redentore*. A black marble was a vote for his death. A white marble was a vote for life.

Given the rumor coming out of the Papal apartments and *Il Redentore's* latest comments denouncing the church's past, left one white marble in the voting box in a sea of black.

The dark work was planned to take place at *Il Redentore's* grand meeting. Cardinal Ciatti informed them that the Pope planned to have no bodyguards in the room. Commander Occhibelli was preoccupied in the town of *Civitavecchia*, searching for the man who rented the car that flipped over and had some of the Vatican's paintings in it.

The brotherhood's plan was simple. Their assassin, an Arab man who did freelance work for the intelligence community, would do the hit with a very loud and dramatic AK-47 assault rifle. He would come out of the grottoes into the Basilica, thus bypassing security. His hiding space would be a former Papal grave. After the hit they would properly discover an oxygen tank in the stone lid coffin and claim he placed himself there during the vault robbery.

His escape would be just as easy. A gypsy had been arrested in Venice who could pass as an Arab. The brotherhood planned to announce *Il Redentore's* assassin's arrest and use the gypsy as a patsy. America didn't claim him as a citizen and he lived a life without an official paper trail. Their man in the Venice Police department brought the prisoner to Rome. His "Capture" was a car drive away.

Saint Peter's Basilica had been searched by the Swiss Guard several times after its closing to ensure that no one from the public had lingered behind.

The visiting Cardinals and Bishops began filtering into the ornate marble church at ten o'clock in the evening. Sets of black iron candle labras were brought in to add illumination for all of the folding chair aisles that had been set up.

The Basilica was 610 feet long with an ornate Baroque canopy at the far end of it. The decorative gold and paint canopy sat in the center of Michelangelo's 136 foot high dome, overlooking the rows of temporary seats.

A storm of faint footsteps echoed throughout the Basilica as more and more clergy poured inside.

Cardinal Ciatti stepped up on the raised platform that the Baroque canopy was built on and announced that the Pope would be coming out shortly.

The clergy began taking their places wondering what the emergency was about.

The Pope ordered the Swiss Guard who remained in Vatican City to seal off the Basilica from outside. Under no circumstances were they to enter or allow any one to leave the Basilica during the meeting. No matter what they heard.

After the doors were locked and barricaded, *Il Redentore* walked into the grand church without escort or fanfare. He wore has all-white formal attire and a mask of grim determination.

All of the clergy stood from their chairs as he walked past them.

Il Redentore ascended the canopy platform and approached a microphone that had been erected for him. He paused to study the sea of wrinkled faces that watched him. Either these men would allow him to lead them into the Church's new future or he knew that within several weeks he'd be dying "peacefully" in his sleep.

"Brothers," *Il Redentore's* voice trembled. "The very heart of our church has been ripped from its body and now only undisclosure keeps us alive."

"All we have is this." He held open his hands to encompass the basilica. "A beautiful corpse of art and architecture. If you bother to look around you will notice that there are no Swiss Guard inside of the basilica."

Several dozen old and middle-aged necks craned around in various directions to confirm the Pontiff's observation.

Il Redentore's voice strengthened. "The truth is going to be spoken here on this night and there will be no fleeing from it." The Pope had their full attention now.

Cardinal Bitono had been promoted as interm head of the P2 Lodge. He sat next to Giovanni, his Number Two man. Bitono whispered to him, "This is it. He plans to attack us openly and evoke mass excommunication."

"We must act quickly," Giovanni replied.

Bitono pressed a button on a transmitter in his pocket. "Be ready. The signal has been sent."

"I may be the Holy Father," *Il Redentore* said. "But on this night I invite you to openly question what I have to say because *all* of the arguments must be considered given the end result against the Church. Therefore, if tonight, you wish to disagree with me on something I've said or if you want to make a comment, please stand up and wait for me to acknowledge you. We cannot have people all speaking out at once, so I implore you to follow this procedure."

The Pope stomped on the red carpet beneath his feet. Nearby underground in the grottoes, the Arab assassin pushed off his partially closed stone lid coffin with a metal bar.

"Directly below me is Saint Peter's tomb," the Pope said. "At this tomb is the stone in which Saint Peter said, *upon this rock I will build my church.*"

There were numerous smiles. The clergy love hearing the story of the founder of their church.

"Unfortunately, the church that Peter built is made of mud and not rock. A look beneath the surface of this construction will reveal that it was built on a plague of lies."

Two-third of the clergy shot up out of their chairs. Several more priests sprouted up a few seconds after. No one sat back down.

"Brothers," *Il Redentore* said softly. The electric Public Address speakers hummed from feedback. "I am *conflicted*. Many in this room elected me Holy Father and leader of this Church. For this, I am indebted to you and am grateful." He took a deep breath. "The moment that the Chapel chimney gave white smoke and I took my name, The Redeemer, I took a personal pledge of service to hundreds of millions of the faithful. I promised to help them help themselves find and maintain a true relationship with God."

Angry faces burned into him. The Pope wondered if his message would get through.

The assassin checked and double checked his AK-47. He put on his specially cut mask and gas mask. Three canisters of CS nerve gas lay on top of the coffin lid. Form the neck down he was dressed like a priest.

"I said my comment about the church being built on mud because *we* have all maintained an organization built on deception with the rationale that this is acceptable because it helps people."

"No!" Several dozen clergy protested.

"Liar!" A bold Bishop in his 40's shouted. "How could you?"

"Believe me when I say that I don't make these statements lightly!" The Pope yelled back. "In our museum here that we have open to the public, we offer an extensive Egyptian wing with works that are over 4,000 years old. Ask yourselves, why would mother church care about Egyptian art or culture with so many cultures that are available to display?"

No one sat down and more began to stand.

"Tell me if anything I'm about to mention doesn't sound familiar," *Il Redentore* said. "Osiris, Isis, and Horus. Now please keep in mind, the records I'm about to mention *predate the Christ story by well over seven thousand years!* Osiris was called the Good Sheppard, the King of Kings, and the Resurrection and the Life. Osiris arrival was announced by three wise men and the star of Sirius.

To the Egyptians, Osiris was the god-man who suffered, died, rose from the dead again, and reigns eternally in Heaven. The Egyptians felt that they would inherit eternal life as he had. To commune with Osiris, Egyptians partook of eating his flesh through cakes of wheat."

A handful of standing clergy sat down. They were older members so they could have simply run out of stamina.

The assassin unferreled a small prayer rug on the damp mud-rock floor. He wished to make a prayer for success and his own personal safety before he departed his mission. He viewed the assignments randomly handed to him as the exercise of God's will. The company encouraged this view from its trainees.

"Horus, Osiris son, was born on December 25th of the virgin Isis-Meri in a manger. Three wise man were there along with a star in the East which announced his birth. Horus's earthly father was *Seb*, which is Egyptian for the name Joseph. When Horus was 12, he was a child teacher at the Temple and then he disappeared for eighteen years only to resurface at age thirty to be baptized by *Anup the Baptizer* who was later decapitated." The Pope snickered. "Am I beginning to make my point with you or have you all suffered deafness?"

Twenty sat down. Those who remained standing appeared physically ill.

"Horus was called the K-R-S-T, or Anointed One. *Horus* walked on water and performed miracles such as raising *El-Azarus* from the dead and exorcising demons. *Horus* had twelve disciples including two men named John in Egyptian who acted as his witness. *Horus* came to fulfill the Law and he was supposed to reign for one thousand years. *Horus* war crucified between two thieves, buried for three days in a tomb, and then resurrected." The Pope spoke with a tone of resignation.

Cardinal Bitono nudged his associate in the arm and whispered urgently to him. "We have to call it off, Giovanni!"

"Why?"

"He's making our teachings known. He's trying to lead them to the light."

"Did you truly send the signal?"

"Of course I did."

"Then it's too late."

Cardinal Bitono wanted to scream out a warning to *Il Redentore*. He was trying to do what the brotherhood had been attempting to do for over a hundred years. Reveal the truth and bring about change. The brotherhood's error had always been utilizing the principle of the means justifying the ends. They felt that they had no choice. Their enemies were fierce and they were fighting 1,754 years of false history and doctrine.

"On the walls of the Temple at Luxor are the images of Thoth, announcing to the Virgin Isis that she will conceive Horus; Kneph, the 'Holy Ghost,' impregnating her by immaculate conception; and Horus being attended by three kings bearing gifts. These engravings are over *3,500 years old*. These teachings were well known even in Rome during the beginning of the created "historical" Jesus's lifetime. Christians were persecuted by the ancient Romans because they were making public the ancient teachings of the Egyptian mystery schools which were only to be taught to initiate! They were *not* persecuted because Christianity had some new teaching that no one had heard before. So, do we dare call this Egyptian chronology a coincidence?"

"I wish to be heard!" A 40-year-old Bishop from Peru shouted.

The Pope pointed directly at him and nodded.

"My name is Bishop Jaxier Diaz," the man announced with pride. "I only recognize Jesus Christ as my King and Savior! I have dedicated my life in the service of our Lord and I have witnessed the miracles of the Holy Spirit work through people." The Bishop rocked back-and-forth in place. "How could *you*, of all people, Holy Father, cast doubt on this? I do not care of ancient rocks forgotten in sand. *I Know* that Jesus Christ lived, died for our sins, and returned to offer the promise of eternal life to those who would follow *Him*."

Numerous young priests nodded in agreement while older clergy rolled their eyes and sat down. The thousands of lit candles cast the basilica in an eerier orange-red glow.

"You deny what I say?" *Il Redentore* asked.

"Yes, Holy Father."

"You do not believe that the inscriptions truly exist?! I have seen them with my own eyes. There are pictures of them in prominent magazines and journals. Our own Egyptologist makes reference to them in papers that are no longer in our vaults."

"They exist, Holy father. But I assure you it is the work of the Devil."

"I see, Bishop. When confronted with truth, blame Satan."

A gaggle of young priest sat down. Bishop Diaz had spoken well for them.

"Have you had time to visit *The Lapidary Gallery* here in the Vatican

Museum, Bishop?"

"No, Holy Father."

"Do you know what's there?"

"This gallery," he interpreted. "Is closed to the general public because it contains early inscriptions from pagan and Christian catacombs." The Pontiff grinned. "Odd that we wouldn't let the public see old catacomb paintings and carvings, unless there was nothing to see. *Literally.*"

The Bishop showed the Pope a questioning face.

The assassin finished his prayer and readied himself for his mission. He began to slowly walk through the grottoes to the stairs.

"Christian scholars and scientist have desperately been trying to discover the evidence of a historical living and breathing Jesus for the last thousand years or so. They find nothing or 'discover' items which prove later to be forgeries. Sometimes the forgeries turn out to be created by the scholars themselves. Now we see a passionate depiction of the Jesus story in the form of a popular movie and so everyone say it *must* be true.

Don't you find it highly unusual, Bishop, that *Jesus*, a miracle worker, savior, and great spiritual teacher, dies and comes back to life only to have no one mention him, no one write about him, and no one spread his teachings for one-hundred-fifty years after he's gone? Why was there no art right after the curcification to record this momentous alleged real-life event? Did it take one-hundred-fifty years for people to learn how paint and sculpt again?"

The Bishop's eyes showed pain. "Why are you doing this, Holy Father?"

"The catacomb art in the closed Lapidary Gallery has depictions of the baby Horus being held by the virgin mother Isis. Our legend that the disciples of Jesus carried his teachings directly to Saint Peter's church and that there has been a continuous, unbroken succession form the crucifixion to the present is totally false.

The Gnostics knew that Jesus was a mythical being which was based on the teachings of the Egyptians Osiris, Isis, and Horus mystery schools along with the aspects taken from the Persian god Mithra. This is the reason the first Popes saw to it that the Gnostics were branded heretics and killed."

"I ask you again, Holy Father. Why do you say these things?!"

"Because the proof of the deception has been stolen right out from under our very feet. Very soon the world will have texts, tablets, and old papal diaries which will reveal all unless there is a miracle. There are documents in the Index of Forbidden Books in which the office of the Inquisition forbids the faithful to read or posses the Holy Bible!"

A majority of the clergy sat down.

Il Redentore leaned against one of the decorative canopy poles. He hated saying what he'd said. So many people were already disillusioned. Now the infection spread to the younger clergy who still believed in making a difference in the world under the banner of Christ.

The assassin reached the top of the grottoes steps. He put a CS-gas canister in his hand and put the AK-47 assault rifle strap over his head so that he could fire the weapon accurately with one hand.

"Many of you here who have done serious study in the archives and through logical reasoning have deduced that there are serious problems with the Bible."

"I know of no such *problems*, Holy father," Bishop Diaz defended.

"Do you believe that *the word of God* through his son *is infallible* if the son truly existed on this Earth?"

"Yes, Holy father."

"Then why do we keep correcting it?"

"We didn't correct the Bible!"

"Yes. We did. At the end of the 2nd century the canonical gospels were forged from two pagan religions; that of the Egyptian mystery school and that of Mirtha. The twenty-seven New Testament booklets incorporated in our Bible *were taken from over two-hundred admitted forgeries in an attempt to create a historical, living, breathing Jesus.* The first 'gospels' contradicted themselves so much that Emperor Anastasias ordered them retouched. *The Council of Nicea had them destroyed to adopt their new version.* In the eleventh centuries we have the Bible corrected again!

There are cuneiform tablets from Mesopotamia that predate the Old Testament. They tell the story of a deluge and ark but the characters and names are different. There are letters and diaries of old Popes stating policy changes of the Church burned and abandon certain books, declared certain group heretics, and discuss the benefits of the inquisition. *All of them make reference to the Church's knowledge that Jesus Christ is a myth;* based on an esoteric ideal. Pope Leo X said, 'What profit has not that fable of Christ brought us.' This is the reason that these documents were locked away. Even from the clergy."

Bishop Diaz was saddened. "Other Popes knew?"

"Some of you are less shocked than you appear. The truth has been released from our vaults for those who bother to listen when it surfaces. I wonder where people will be without organized, institutional faith. Lost? Hopeless? Desperate? So many will deny the truth even though it exists in our own Catholic Encyclopedia."

Bishop Diaz stormed up the aisle toward *Il Redentore* on the podium. "What would you have us do?! The Church needs its legends! Our existence is based on the idea!"

The assassin prepared to break from the steps in a disciplined run. He wouldn't fire until he was within five feet of his target.

"We need to rebuild the Church," the Pope said. "On principles of self-enlightenment, divine realization, and spiritual science."

"Oh my God," Cardinal Bitono said to his subordinate. "We have to call it off! *Il Redentore* is attempting to install the Brotherhood!"

Chapter 38

Adriatic Sea.

The *Hiusho Morkki* cargo container ship had been out to sea for three days before Yurgi's orders were carried out.

Big Tony and Svetlana joined Yurgi on the artificial turf roof container at ten o'clock in the morning.

The sky was cloudless and the sun was already out radiating heat in full force.

Yurgi had been whacking golf balls into the ocean when they arrived. Svetlana was dressed in a two-piece yellow bikini. The wind blew in sudden fits causing her to have large Goosebumps pop up across her skin. She put on a pair of cheap sunglasses and laid out on one of Yurgi's lawn chairs.

Big Tony was dressed in jeans and an Italy flag logo t-shirt. He lounged out in a chair next to Svetlana. She had taken a liking to him instantly. Big Tony would open ship doors for her to enter first and he assisted her with her chair whenever she sat at the ship dining room table. They couldn't speak to each other without Yurgi translating for them but they had a great time playing charades in guessing what the other was saying. She liked his limp. She thought it made him look helpless instead of imposing. Time passed quickly.

Yurgi shanked a golf ball, sending it short into he water below them. "At least two more weeks on dis boat," he complained. "I hate not seeing any land."

"But your golf swing is improving," Big Tony said.

"No, is shit." Yurgi chinked his golf club handle. "I hit over thousand balls and no fuck-ing improvement, I tell you."

Gunshots rumbled from three containers below them. Seagulls that rested next to the outer container near the rail flew off. The robbery crew volunteered to do the voyage in the container together so as not to raise suspicion. The Colonel had offered the suggestion to them.

Yurgi turned to face Big Tony. He knew his friend wouldn't take the revelation well. "We visit my brother in Russia. Dis you already know." More gunshots rang out from below. "He doesn't like a lot of visitors."

Big Tony remained quiet. He'd seen guys stabbed up in the federal penitentiary. If it didn't directly involve you, you kept you mouth shut. Business is business and he wanted to stay alive.

Yurgi surveyed the ship for any crewmen or deckhands. When he was satisfied that no one was around, he said something to Svetlana in a low forceful tone.

She scrambled out of her chair and away from Big Tony.

As Big Tony turned his head to gauge Svetlana's sudden departure, Yurgi spun around swinging his titanium golf club upside Big Tony's head.

A dull crack sounded as Big Tony spilled onto the plastic grass in a limp heap.

Svetlana began crying.

Yurgi dropped his club and open-hand slapped her across the face.

Big Tony dug deep within himself to summon the energy to attack. The ground was spinning even though he was lying still. He vomited all over his shirt as he rose to his feet slowly. He had a funny taste in his mouth and his ears were ringing. He staggered forward and backward as he tried to regain his bearings.

Yurgi's back was to him as he punished Svetlana for not keeping her place.

She was *his* girl; prostitute or not. He expected total loyalty. He slapped her again. He was breathing hard and became excited at seeing her helpless on the ground. He figured Big Tony was dead.

"Take your swimsuit off," he ordered.

Big tony stumbled forward and wrapped Yurgi in a bear hug.

"Son of bitch! Let me go!"

Big Tony's vision was so blurry he couldn't determine his position. He planned to hurl Yurgi off of the container, over the side, and into the ocean. He tried to execute it by dragging Yurgi over to where he thought the edge of the container was and mistook the distance.

Both men flew over the side and traveled through the air for a long time.

The ocean was light blue and white from the massive ship's hull slamming through it. Big Tony released his hold on Yurgi as they both broke through the ocean water's surface. They traveled deep under the water caused by the height of their fall. Tiny bubbles floated up all around them.

A deadly mechanical hiss greeted their ears as the ship's massive twin propellers neared and passed them.

Big Tony used everything he had to gather up the strength for a return swim to the surface. The water was cold and helped in reviving him.

Yurgi was a terrible swimmer. He thrashed about wildly, trying to remember how his Uncle had instructed him to swim when he was eight years old. Yurgi was a hustler. The majority of his life was spent on robbing and chasing after money. None of that ever involved swimming.

Svetlana lay on the prickly plastic grass and stared out into the ocean.

Did I just see them fall over the side? She thought. *I should tell them to stop the ship*! Her face still stung from the slapping. *Or maybe not.*

Svetlana got off of the fake grass quickly, climbed up onto the ship's exterior bridge walkway, and then she grabbed a bright orange circle life-saver floatation ring from the wall. She threw it over the side of the ship as hard as she could.

The bright orange ring skidded along the waves below and slowly disappeared behind her.

For Tony, she thought. *Good luck to you.*

Svetlana climbed back over the rail and onto the container with the plastic grass and chairs. She kicked Yurgi's golf clubs over the side along with his bucket of golf balls. She lay back down in the deck chair and worked on her tan.

"Yurgi?" She heard herself saying to Yurgi's brother in the future in Odessa. "No. I don't know where he is. He told me that him and his American friend had business to discuss and sent me inside of the ship. I never saw them again. Hey, you don't think they fell over the side by accident, do you?"

Chapter 39

The Vatican, Saint Peter's Basilica.

The assassin closed with grim determination. He dropped to one knee to take aim at a priest running up the aisle toward the canopy. He figured that the man might be undercover security. Several of the priests now noticed him. He was thirty feet from the Pope's side.

The Pontiff didn't see him and continued in his speech attempting to hurry his points before the clergy revolted.

"People wish to develop a personal relationship with God. With this relationship a person generally becomes an improved, enlightened human being who will benefit us all. This was *the promise* whether it comes from the mouth of Osiris, Isis, Horus, Mithra, Krishna, Buddha, or Jesus. We concern ourselves with *exact* and tortured interruptions of conflicting messages *which were not meant to be taken as literal.* They are mystical and a blueprint toward understanding that each one of us is a part of God. He is us and we are Him; the ancient I Am That I Am. How have we lost sight of that for the veneration of bones, myths, created, proofs, and profits?!

The word is infected with a sickness and it is false religion. Everyone is quick in proving that *their* Bible's God and Savior is the one and only, and that all others are false. Yet, no one among us is saved no matter who we believe in. How many have died as victims of wars fought in religion's name? The faithful keep waiting for the return of a fable to save them when they can save themselves here and now!

No more worshipping of the fictional figures within the aisle when he saw the gun pointed at him. The bullet hit the young Bishop in the left eye. The gun's report echoed in the Basilica like a stick of exploding dynamite.

With a deft commando move the killer pulled the pin on a CS-gas canister and hurled it toward the center of the nearest grouping of clergy. The dark mustard yellow gas shot out everywhere.

Il Redentore saw the hit man and realized that his message to the church was dead from inception. He couldn't fight history, but he remained stubborn to the end. He spoke into the microphone as the assassin approached within five feet and took a firing position.

The Pope's hand swept in a circle incorporating the entire Basilica. "If we are to survive, we must renounce all of this."

The killer's AK-47 unloaded twelve bullets center mass into *Il Redentore's* chest. The sound of the rifle's continual firing screamed out in the dome like Zeus's thunder.

Il Redentore was tossed backwards off of the canopy and onto the marble floor.

The assassin activated and threw out two more CS-gas canisters. The basilica filled with acrid smoke which obscured everyone's vision. The assassin fired a volley over the clergy heads.

The herd of freighted old men stampeded toward the barricaded doors.

The CS-gas had a terrible effect on the older clergy.

Several priests had been trampled in the rush to get to the doors. Others were crushed in the gathering throng that pushed and pounded against the doors.

The assassin threw his gun to the floor and discarded his gas mask. No one could see him in the thick yellow-white clouds. He headed toward them. He slipped out with the frantic priests as the doors were opened. The Swiss Guards didn't dare hold them back. The surge of the holy crowd's flight was unnatural.

Cardinal Bitono and Giovanni immediately rushed to the Holy Father. They could hardly see him through the gas but they could make out a large pool of blood.

Cardinal Bitono spoke softly in his ear, "Holy Father?"

Il Redentore hovered next to him staring down at the lifeless shell of his old physical body. He regretted not being able to finish his message. He had wanted them to start a new church. One where no more religious policing by worrying about what one's neighbor believed in. No more self superiorty by holding oneself higher through the judgment of another. He wanted a church that taught the lessons of community, compassion, and self-fulfillment through service to God and others. Above all, he wanted to end the monopoly held on God and the imagined authority the few derived from it.

"You should have told us what you were going to do," Cardinal Bitono cried softly. "We could have helped. Our goals are the same."

Il Redentore began to travel backward through his life like physically reliving pictures in time. He especially loved his childhood. Walking his dog, picking olives, swimming in the ocean, and playing with his friends. How long it had been. How wonderful. Everything seemed so simple then.

Chapter 40

Adriatic Sea.

The Rogue's Gallery was a sleek fifty-seven foot long catamaran that was built in 1999. The ship was a rich man's toy that Clayton's grandfather gave to him in hopes that he would sail his troubles away. His grandfather had circumnavigated the globe twice and belonged to several prominent yacht clubs. He didn't wish to talk to Clayton until his grandson got it together, a time period he'd said Clayton would know.

Clayton left Tonya to pilot the catamaran with its big chrome steering wheel that was mounted high up at the back right side of the boat. She wore a floppy white fisherman's cap, a red bikini top, and denim cut-off shorts. Her elbow wound was dressed and treated by a newly made doctor in Mestre. He had been a medical student at Venice University where Tonya took painting classes. She and the student were good friends.

The new doctor had also treated Clayton but worried that he might not have done everything correctly given the severity of the wound. The doctor had to steal two pints of blood form his hospital's blood bank to help Clayton recover. Both surgeries were done late at night and kept off the books. Clayton paid the man ten thousand Euros form the bank accounts that Renauld and VanAucken had given him. He still had one hundred thousand Euros left.

Clayton came out of the ship's galley bringing Tonya a plastic bottle of orange juice.

She enjoyed steering the cat into large waves and watching the cutting effects of the boat's twin hulls after they bit into the beautiful dark blue water.

Clayton kissed her on the neck and sat down next to her on the white cushion mini bench. He wore a large gray shirt to cover the bandages on his chest and shoulder wound and a pair of baggy sweat shorts. The high noon sun washed them in it's warm orange glow and cast sleepy black shadows across the boat's hardware. He had thrown his lucky bullet necklace into the ocean an hour earlier.

"You're a natural at this," he said.

"I had a great teacher."

"One whole day of instruction and now you're better than me."

"I hope you're not holding a grudge, Mr. Keasley." She laughed.

"No. But now you can do all of the steering. He rested his hands on her waist and put his chin on her right shoulder. "We can go wherever you want. Just steer the way."

They spent the afternoon enjoying the cloudless blue sky and smooth sailing. Tonya kept searching the water ahead for a freak wave that she could crash the boat into but she came up empty.

Clayton prepared lunch on a portable wood tray and brought the meal out to her. Tuna fish sandwiches, chips, and salad.

She teased him about the lunch. "Not exactly gourmet, is it?"

"If it's not a TV dinner then this is all I can make form scratch, okay?" He dashed the end of her nose with his tuna sandwich. "Critic."

She hurled a tiny cherry tomato at him which hit his throat and rolled down his shirt.

"No fair!"

She pointed off of the port bow. "Hey, look."

A stocky man with caked blood over half of his face floated in the ocean with a bright orange life-ring under his armpits. His eyes were closed but his arms kept moving, as if treading water.

Clayton made his way forward. "Swing it around, Tonya. I'll drop the sails and you start the motor."

Tonya began to turn the boat in a wide circle. There were only two of them to operate the boat so Clayton told her to play it safe.

Tonya screamed out to the man. "Hello! Hey! Are you awake?! Can you hear me?!"

The stranger managed a faint wave of his hand.

A short time later they had him aboard wrapped up in a dry blanket and his head wound bandaged up as best they could. The man came in and out of consciousness.

Clayton attempted some polite questioning in Italian. "Who are you?"

"Tony," the man replied in English.

"Tony who?"

"Uhhh... I don't remember." He winced. "I got hit upside the friggin' head with a fuckin' golf club, all right?!"

Clayton picked up on the man's New York accent. "So you're American?" He felt stupid asking.

"I don't remember," Big Tony lied.

Tonya pointed to a series of fresh fingernail scratches across the left side of Big Tony's face. "That's not good."

Clayton ran his finger over Tony's facial scratched. "What happened?"

"Self inflicted," Big Tony lied again. The image of Yurgi Svoboccen fighting him for the life ring entered his foggy mind. Big Tony reached the ring first and used one of his hands to stiff-arm Yurgi's head to keep him away.

"Why did ya do it, Yurgi?!"

"Stupid bitch-slut-whore- is shaking me down with her lawyer." He sucked in and coughed out salt water. "I had no choice, I tell you!" His eyes begged for mercy as his arms flailed about to keep himself afloat.

"You know what, Yurg?"

"*Da?*"

"Fuck you." Big Tony drowned the man. The task had been quite easy. Yurgi was a poor swimmer and his Tiger Woods golf-suit weighed him down.

Clayton's renewed questioning snapped him out of his memory.

"Why did you hurt yourself?"

Big Tony pretended not to hear the question. He wanted to forget. The feeling of being adrift at sea with no one in sight terrified him. He'd been in the ocean for hours. The thought of a Tiger shark rushing up from the murky depths and biting his legs off, kept repeating in his mind. The feel of the boats deck beneath his feet was heaven.

Tonya brought Big Tony some water. "Drink only a little at a time or your kidneys might shut down."

He downed the coffee mug of water in seconds.

"Why would someone hit you in the head with a golf club?" Tonya asked as she took the cup from him.

"I don't know." He looked at her out of the corner of his eye. "Where are y'all headed?"

She proudly put her arm around Clayton's shoulder and kissed him. "Hawaii. We're getting married. Then scuba diving, fishing, and no responsibility."

Clayton felt like he'd won the lottery when she had proposed to him.

"So what are y'all gonna do about me?"

"We'll drop you at the next port on our way." Clayton went to refill the mug with more drinking water.

"In Italy?" Big Tony pressed.

Tonya felt sick at the name of the country of her old prison. Clayton and her had figured out that they were still wanted fugitives there. Especially if Renauld survived the fall from the window.

"I don't think that we'll be stopping anywhere there," she said. "We're anxious to get hitched, so why go out of the way? We're already in international waters so we might as well keep going."

Big Tony sat back against the yacht's comfortable seat for a moment. The boat was rolling pleasantly form side to side. He wondered how much of it was the sea and how much of it was the concussion. He made a decision. He would screw Yurgi's brother in Odessa.

He took a second mug of water from Clayton and took a sip. "Do you have a satellite phone or chip-to-shore radio that works?"

Clayton hesitated. "Sometimes it works, sometimes it doesn't."

"I need to reach the Vatican."

"I guess you were hit in the head," Tonya interjected.

"Seriously lady. I've got to give them the name of a ship. They're promising a fat reward."

"You won't tell them the name of our ship or position?"

"No. Why?"

"Make your call." Clayton handed Big Tony a radio receiver and began setting dials. "No ship name. No location. If they demand on, then lie. I'll try and get you the Italian coast guard and they'll have to relay your message."

The radio call took over an hour to make. Finding the right channel with the Vatican's property. He gave them name and told them that he would contact them concerning the reward.

"I owe you my life," Big Tony said to Tonya and Clayton after the transmission. "I'll probably be dead in a year or so 'cause I've got cancer. Whatever the reward money is, I'd like ta leave it to you when I kick." He laughed for the first time in a long while. "As a weddin' present."

Clayton heard the whole radio transmission. It was a small world after all. "You wouldn't care to share your story with us would you?"

"Sure. Why not." Big Tony relaxed. "We've got time. But first I want ta know about you all. Where are ya goin' after Hawaii?"

"Boston." Tonya winked. "To meet my in-laws."

Clayton gulped and stared wildly at his fiancée.

"Don't worry sweetie." She grinned. "They'll come around."

Chapter 41

The Vatican.

Three weeks had passed since the stabbing-poisoning brawl that led to Cardinal D'Anglese going to the Ospedale del Celio, in Rome. His secret self-inflicted stab wounds were healing nicely.

News of *Il Redentore's* assassination comforted him. The hospital gave the bad news to the patients the morning after the shooting occurred but D'Anglese already heard the news from the Swiss Guardsman who was assigned to watch over him. D'Anglese acted mortified at the news while secretly rejoicing. The investigation would most likely die with the man, for Commander Occhibelli would surely resign.

He lay awake at nights wondering how successful Ferroli's hit men had been in killing the double-dealing Frenchman, gypsy-girl, and American. A piece of the puzzle didn't quite fit and it really bothered him. Plus there was mention of Ferroli and some recordings. Surely the old man didn't record their conversations or he would have been charged already.

Daily issues of Rome's *Il Messaggero* newspaper made it into his lap every morning. The paper announced that *Il Redentore's* killer had been arrested fleeing the Holy City. The assassin's photograph was on the front page.

D'Anglese recognized him as being the man in the park who had tried to blackmail him for gold. He was a gypsy but the paper said he was an Arab. Some crazed Muslim fundamentalist who hated Christendom.

D'Anglese didn't think that the gypsy man was the type who could pull off such expert paramilitary moves or the type who could have squeezed into the small stone coffin. The whole thing didn't make sense and that too unnerved him.

Commander Occhibelli showed up at the end of the week with four Swiss Guardsmen. They were there to transfer D'Anglese back to the Holy city in a white security van.

"Hello Cardinal," Occhibelli said as D'Anglese climbed into a whicker wheelchair. "I hope you've mended well."

There was something in the man's greeting that frightened him. "Yes, Commander. Thank you for your concern. I figure that someone else would be picking me up today, for surely you've resigned by now."

"Not before I conclude me duties, *dear Cardinal*." He wheeled D'Anglese out of the room and to the security van which was parked nearby. He didn't say anther word to the man and the Swiss Guard followed suit.

The journey back to the Holy City became long to him. The van was stone silent.

After the drive D'Anglese was wheeled straight into Saint Peter's Basilica which had been closed to the public until further notice. They lifted him in his wheelchair and into the restricted corridor which led to the Secret vaults entrance.

D'Anglese sweated. "Why are we going down her, Commander? It is very dusty down here and counter productive to my full recovery."

No one answered him.

The vault entrance appeared familiar to him except for the door.

Instead of a sliding stone slab there was a large steel door with hinges that faced him. In the center of the door was a small shoebox sized hole with a hinged door that was open and leaned out to them.

The reinforced steel portal opened to reveal Cardinal Bitono standing behind it. "Hello Francis, I wish that I could say I'm happy to see you but it is just not so."

"Pardon me?!" D'Anglese tried to get up out of the wheelchair. Occhibelli punched him back into the seat and shoved his chair into the main vault past the new door.

The place had been cleaned up and emptied of all its remaining contents. The Leonardo electronics room had been resealed and filled with concrete and rebar. The glass doors and climate controllers had all been removed.

A shower, bed, and exercise bike were installed in the main chamber.

A creeping realization began to haunt the obese cardinal.

Cardinal Bitono stepped out of the vaults to join Occhibelli. He slammed the metal door shut and locked it. They could still address D'Anglese through the food pass thru opening in the door.

"We were going to offer you the chance of suicide," Occhibelli said bitterly. "But those concerned agreed that your punishment must be harder then that."

"We saw the videotape, Francis," Bitono added. "Plus we listened to the audio tapes of you and Cardinal Ferroli. After reviewing both everything fell into place for us."

D'Anglese leaned forward in his chair and stared at the ground. "I'm sorry."

"You're a sick bastard, D'Anglese," Occhibelli admonished him. "I hope you rot sown here." He turned around and left. He had to post his resignation.

Cardinal Bitono checked to make sure no one was around to hear his final conversation with D'Anglese before he left him to begin serving his life sentence. "'You killed the leader of the lodge, Francis. Certain punishments await you. Some day." He hit the door with his fist. "You've betrayed yourself, the brotherhood, and all of the men who have made lifetime sacrifices to advance out stratagem. There's a dead child, mother, father, Bishop, and Pope. This didn't have to be, Francis."

"Please..."

"Please what? Please help?!" Bitono shouted. His face was bright red. "I'm afraid the time for help has passed!"

"Hah...How long do I have to stay down here... brother?"

Bitoino began to walk away. "Forever."

D'Anglese stared sobbing. The last remnants of lights disappeared after Bitono turned off the chamber light. The vaults were so cold.

He grabbed a hold of his ears and clamped down with his fingernails. He screamed, "Nooooooo!"

No one was left to hear him. Not even his sanity.

Epilogue

Commander Occhibelli resigned and left the Holy City without saying farewell to his men. He felt that he had failed them and his presence only disgraced them. He returned to Switzerland where he found employment working at his younger brother's vineyard. Eventually he moved to France. He was tired of the old Swiss locals who always remained him that he was responsible for the death of the Pope.

Cardinal Ciatti was elected as the next Pope. He names himself, Pope John Paul III, and called for a return of the Church's duty to act as the people's moral and religious authority. The IOR (Vatican Bank) was left untouched as the price for obtaining the P2 vote. The brother hood realized that Ciatti wasn't the brightest of men and his reign could be undermined quickly with the proper manipulation. The Church's status quo would have to last a little bit longer.

Tonya's Uncle was found dead in his Italian prison cell before he could stand trail for the murder of *Il Redentore*. Sash's death was ruled a suicide despite the fact that he was hung in the same way that Roberto Salvi had been. No one claimed the body although Pope John Paul III offered him public forgiveness.

Renauld Fouchet was arrested by the Italian police for murder, fraud, and Value Added Tax evasion on the money that they had found. He was sentenced to fifteen years on the fraud and tax evasion charges. Shannon had given the prosecutors evidence against him. However, he managed to cut a deal with the State to waive the murder charges of the Italian hit men in return for his testimony against his old mulatto associate, Jean-Phillipe.

Jean-Phillipe didn't appreciate his rise from subordinate to "ring leader" based on Renauld's fabrications. He was sent to the same prison in which Renauld was. He exacted total revenge. The uneducated prisoners discovered what the term Eunich meant.

Talli and Sal Goldberg's bodies were discovered in a new shopping center construction excavation near Malibu. They went missing six months after *Il Redentore* was murdered. Their fingers had been chopped off while they were kept alive and were force fed to them.

An FBI profiler mentioned that this mutilation was a standard method of operation by Russian crime families to signal that the victims suffered from too much greed. The agent suggested an audit of their finances. It was later discovered that Goldenberg had a long standing relationship with Yurgi Svoboccen's brother. Goldenberg sent the man bi-monthly payments which turned out to be half the amount of Yurgi's daily alimony payments.

Clayton and Tonya were married beneath a long waterfall in Hawaii. The couple had their first baby, a girl, and a year later. They named her Kathreen.

Clayton went back to work at the family newspaper in Boston. He commutes to his and Tonya's four-bedroom home in the suburbs. They recently purchased a golden retriever. His name is Buster.

Svetlana helped the Swiss Guard recover the cargo containers which held the Vatican's property. Her tip that the Colonel was in the second container with orders to kill whoever opened the door without the secret knock, saved the Swiss Guard's lives. She was rewarded with ten thousand U.S. dollars and relocated to Argentina. She abandoned prostitution and runs her own café.

Cardinal Bitono furthered *Il Redentore's* dream of forcing the church to change by covertly stealing the secret vault's hard rive from one of the Russian cargo containers. The computer had scanned text and records files of everything that had been stored in the vaults. Bitono ailed the computer to the American Association of Atheists.

He knew they'd make sure all of the information would omen out into the public domain. They would assume that the proof of Jesus being a myth would dispel the idea of God once and for all but they would be wrong. One doesn't need to have Jesus to have God.

The information would cause a stir and the Church would be forced to come up with practical was of helping people learn a new way of communing with God. That's where the brother hood came in.

Big Tony Bassano reneged on his wedding cash promise to Clayton and Tonya. The Vatican paid him two hundred fifty thousand dollars for his tip that led to recovery. He used the money to travel across the United States and ride three rollercoaster's of every shape and size. Eventually he wound up in Las Vegas where he blew the rest of the money on cocaine and bookers. He figured that this wouldn't be a bad way to go out. After six months of partying and not death he began to wonder.

He saw a new doctor. His cancer had entered into full remission which with lung cancer was almost impossible. The doctor told him, "Basically Tony, its a miracle."

THE END

Author's Note

The Vatican Job does not represent the opinions or views of the Roman Catholic Church. This novel is a work of fiction and was written with the intent to entertain; nothing more. I'm sure that many Catholics will take offense to some of the revelations contained in this work. I expect to be accused of "smearing" the Church's good name.

The inquisition is fact. The Roman Catholic Church *killed* and tortured hundreds of thousands of innocent human beings in the name of God. The Church launched numerous crusades against fellow Christians who didn't share all of their views. Please keep in mind that before the invention of the printing press, the majority of Europe and Eurasia's population were illiterate. One had to proclaim to believe in whatever the Roman Catholic Church said for them to believe in or else suffer the consequences. Thus, in the beginning of Catholicism; the Gnostics, Cathars, and Pegans were forcibly "converted," or in most cases they were simply killed. It is no coincidence that Catholicism raised into being in Rome and not in the supposed "Holy" land of Israel. *Why?*

When the average American Christian is asked, "Where did the Holy Bible come from?" Their answer is almost always, "God." If you ask them to trace the book's origins back to the beginning they give you a blank stare. The thought of researching a book which they claim dictates the majority of their actions in life never occurred to them. It is as if they quietly believe that the book appeared out of thin air in a glowing light. This is a dangerous assumption.

The Roman Catholic Church was *the sole custodian of the Holy Bible.* Supposedly, Saint Peter was the first to carry the chronicles of the New Testament (the Jesus story) and that there has been an unbroken succession since. That isn't necessarily true as my fictional character, *Il Redentore* explains in this fictional story. The suppressed "evidence" kept in the Vatican's secret vaults was taken from reality in little read public documents which are authenticated by the Church itself.

The New Testament is a construct made by the Roman Catholic Church to establish a centralized religious authority that all followers must be subservient to. Historical facts show that The Holy Bible was edited and "revised" over the centuries by various Roman Catholic councils. Interesting considering the Holy Bible is considered the word of God. I guess He lacked a good editor.

The revisions and editing became necessary for the Church as more people became literate and the inconsistencies of gospels were exposed. At one point *the Church openly banned the Holy Bible* as a "forbidden" book in its forbidden books index. They were hoping that they could force the faithful to go back to blindly accepting the Roman Catholic Church's edicts and the new interpretation of the scripture (which just happened to favor the local regional politics at the time).

In 1517, a German monk by the name of Martin Luther protested the Church's widespread abuses (a recurring theme throughout Church's history). He contested the Church's sale of pardons to sinners in return for money, among other questionable practices. Forty-years later, Luther's *Protestant* (One who protests) *movement* was established over half of Europe. This period was known as the Reformation.

The Catholic Church "believed" that the way to salvation was through good works and acts of grace; while Martin Luther preached that the only way to salvation was through faith and belief in Jesus Christ alone. This schism has led to the creation of a host of separate Christian religions which all differ on their individual New Testament beliefs.

Martin Luther was branded a heretic by Pope Leo X and the Emperor of Rome issued the Edict of Worms (which was an open contract to end Martin Luther's life without reprisal to his assassin).

All Christian religions originate from the Roman Catholic one. Countless wars have been fought in the name of Jesus, yet so many of the religion's followers have no idea about where and who recorded their master's teachings. Given the Catholic Church's admission of forged (outright fake) gospels being incorporated into the Bible which is still read today as religious fact and a blueprint for peoples' "righteous" actions, shouldn't there be cause for concern?

The majority of my characters revelations about the Catholic Church, the "historical" Jesus, and the Holy Bible come from the non-fiction book, "*The Christ Conspiracy*" by Acharya S, ISBN 0-932813-74-7; Published by Adventures Unlimited Press, One Adventure Place, Kempton, Illinois, 60946; auphq@frontrier.net. This is an excellent and thought provoking book. I highly recommend reading it if some of the religious things *Il Redentore* says in my novel interest you.

As for the other events that transpire in The Vatican Job concerning the Institute of Religious Affais (IOR), or Vatican Bank; this arm of the Church was implicated in real life in nefarious activities with an outside bank that is still in operation. The P2 Freemason Lodge was also publicly linked to this scandal and a large number of Roman Catholic Clergy are still active P2 members (despite a long standing Papal ban.)

In my novel I assign certain goals to the P2 Brotherhood. These "goals" are pure fictional creations of my own. The P2 is a secret society and thus their real-life motives, goals, and activities are kept secret. Only the P2's members can speak on the group's objectives and they aren't talking.

The Italian culture and people are absolutely remarkable. Their contributions to food, art, and architecture can't be overemphasized. Like all cultures, there are always a few undesirables who don't represent the majority of the people. Obviously this book is a crime novel and there are some Italian mafia characters in it. These people are not characteristic of the majority of the Italian people and should be viewed as so.

Some of my critics might accuse me of "Catholic Bashing," but I would refer them to the history books. *Does my book create any new scandal which the Church hasn't already been involved in?* No. The Catholic Church has done some good for the poor in the third world but their overall record is pretty appalling. Just read, *"The Dark Side of Christianity,"* by Helen Ellerbe, ISBN 0-9644873-4-9.

The religious views of my fictional characters don't necessarily reflect my own personal views. I do believe in God, just not all of the dogma and special interests created to go with Him. There are long standing questions concerning the Bible and Christianity which need to be asked and answered *truthfully*. I wrote this novel to be fun, entertaining, and informative. I decided to be bold and float something out in the market that isn't "safe" in the traditional fiction sense. If you find some of this work's revelations offensive, I apologize. But if the Christian religion is totally pure as a custodian of the Master's teachings (as many of its fundamentalist followers claim), there shouldn't be anything to worry about, right?

Legal Disclaimer: The books I listed in this author's note were books that I used as a part of my research. The authors of the above listed publications and their publishers have not read this novel nor endorse or have the same opinions as this author. I have only listed them for readers who are interested in such material.

Thank You.

Please recommend this book to a friend and purchase at:

www.VaticanJob.com

Check out further info on the controversy, post your comments, and chat with other readers on your views presented in this novel.